The Strange and Deadly Portraits of Bryony Gray

E. Latimer

tundra

Text copyright © 2018 by E. Latimer
Cover image copyright © 2018 by Janet Hill

Tundra Books, an imprint of Penguin Random House Canada Young Readers,
a Penguin Random House Company

Library and Archives Canada Cataloguing in Publication

Latimer, E., 1987-, author
The strange and deadly portraits of Bryony Gray / E. Latimer.

Issued in print and electronic formats. ISBN 978-1-101-91928-6 (hardcover).
—ISBN 978-1-101-91929-3 (EPUB)

I. Title.

PS8623.A783S77 2018   jC813'.6   C2017-902358-6
                                     C2017-902359-4

Published simultaneously in the United States of America by
Tundra Books of Northern New York,
an imprint of Penguin Random House Canada Young Readers,
a Penguin Random House Company

Library of Congress Control Number: 2017938004

Edited by Lynne Missen
Text and jacket design by Five Seventeen
All frames from "Mouldings, mirrors, pictures and frames" (1884)
by Geo. N. Lee & Co. (Chicago, Ill.)/Internet Archive
The text was set in Plantin

Printed and bound in the United States of America

www.penguinrandomhouse.ca

1   2   3   4   5   22   21   20   19   18

This book is dedicated to Shaun, who has supported me through every up and down of the writing journey

Prologue

ady Priscilla Dashworth liked to collect beautiful things. She had, lining the corridors of her grand old mansion in the countryside, exactly fifty-two bottles of cut glass, twenty-one chunks of crystal cut into the shapes of various farm animals and nineteen Persian rugs that set off the wallpaper just right.

But the pride and joy of her collection of collections was what she found the most beautiful of all: herself. That is to say, Priscilla Dashworth collected portraits of herself. Large portraits that took up entire walls; miniature portraits with exquisite details that could only be seen under a microscope; black-and-white charcoal masterpieces; and careful oil paintings with delicate strokes. She even had a series of paintings that portrayed her as various mystical creatures—mermaids and dryads and things of a scandalous nature.

These portraits covered the walls of every room, until there was hardly an inch of space left. If it had been anyone else collecting portraits of herself, people would have said she was quite mad, but Lady Dashworth was exceedingly wealthy. So it was decided in the surrounding villages that she was merely eccentric.

It was on a particularly rainy and miserable Tuesday that Lady Dashworth's newest portrait was delivered to her. She met the deliveryman on the doorstep.

"Your painting, Miss," he said eagerly.

"Yes." Lady Dashworth motioned him inside. "Bring it into the library. Gerard will handle payment. Do hurry, I want to see it."

The deliveryman bustled in, making his way around teetering stacks of books, carrying the paper-wrapped portrait before him.

"Here." She hurried down the hall, almost feverish now in her excitement. Hands trembling, she snatched back the curtains by the window seat. The only bare space left to hang a painting was one lonely patch of white wall beside the window. The painting would just fit. "Here, let me see it."

The deliveryman gave a startled grunt when she nudged him to one side with her hip and set about tearing at the wrapping on the painting. The sound of rending paper filled the air, and when the last shred of brown wrap drifted to settle on the floor, Lady Dashworth had already hung the painting in place. She stepped back with a gasp, hands clasped to her bosom.

"Oh," she breathed, and rapture shivered over every inch of her skin. "Look how magnificent I am."

"My lady is truly magnificent." The butler, Gerard, had appeared soundlessly at her side. He placed one white-gloved hand on the deliveryman's elbow. "If you will follow me, sir, we will discuss the matter of payment."

Lady Dashworth was vaguely aware that the delivery-man was putting up a half-hearted protest, insisting he stay and make sure she was satisfied. But then Gerard was escorting him out and she couldn't tear her eyes away from the portrait. Everything else faded into the background.

She'd been skeptical when she'd first sat for the painting. How was a thirteen-year-old girl supposed to compare with the master artists she'd commissioned up until then? Not to mention, the girl wasn't quite all there, if the rumors were to be believed. And the fact that the studio had been in a dusty old attic with makeshift lighting hadn't eased any of her doubts. But the child was supposed to be some sort of prodigy, and now here was the evidence. Her own face—shapely, pale, dark eyes sparkling with a thousand secrets—stared back at her.

A thrill went through her.

The Priscilla in the painting was perched on the edge of a red fainting couch. She was bent forward slightly, hands on her waist. The smile on her lips was devilishly playful. Her eyes glittering. Knowing. *Alive.* So very alive. In fact, it was almost as if the painting was watching her.

Something rose up in Priscilla's breast, freezing her lungs. She took a faltering step back.

The painted Priscilla's smile stretched, just the small-est bit. She seemed to lean forward an inch.

Impossible.

Lady Dashworth took another step back.

The painted Priscilla winked.

Lady Dashworth raised a shaking hand to her mouth. Surely she was hallucinating.

The painting shook, rattling in its frame. The painted woman *moved*.

Heart thundering in her ears, Lady Dashworth opened her mouth to scream. Nothing came out, only a raspy little wheeze. All the air had been sucked out of the room, it seemed, making it impossible to draw breath. The bell-pull: if she could just reach it, she could call for Gerard. Good, loyal Gerard, who had never let her down. But her feet were rooted to the carpet. She couldn't move. Why couldn't she move?

There was a horrible tearing sound as the canvas bulged outward, and then a hand emerged, and the painted lady reached out, fingers wrapping around the inside of the frame. This time Lady Dashworth did manage a scream. The arm shot out, speckled and whorled with spots of skin-colored paint, textured with brush strokes. Clawlike fingers seized Lady Dashworth's throat, and her scream died in a wheezing gasp. Still, she couldn't look away, couldn't break her gaze as she struggled. Even when spots of light had begun to burst, blending with the cold lights in the painting. Even as the canvas yawned and gaped and sucked her last years away. Even then, she couldn't look away from those dark, dancing eyes.

The painted lady smiled.

ryony Gray's reflection was misbehaving. She stared, quite mystified, into the looking glass above the fireplace. It was an ugly mirror, with a blocky black frame filled with grotesque gargoyle heads. She had protested when Uncle Bernard moved it there last month, but he'd claimed it would brighten the attic.

Her reflection seemed to be facing *away* from her. Everything else was all right; her long blonde hair was braided in a single plait down her back, and she was still wearing the ridiculous lacy dress Aunt Gertrude had forced her into that morning. The dress itched, and Bryony wiggled her left shoulder. In the mirror, the reflection didn't budge.

She blinked, and everything was normal again. Her reflection faced forward. It scratched its elbow when she scratched hers.

Her imagination. Or a trick of the light, perhaps. She was always telling Aunt Gertrude the attic was too dim. How was she supposed to paint if she ended up going blind?

There was a faint, disapproving sniff from the corner, and she turned back to the woman on the red fainting couch under the window. Aunt Gertrude sat ramrod straight. She wore a severe black dress, the collar of which went up so high that it looked as if it were attempting to swallow her entire head. The dress was nearly as starched and stiff as Aunt Gertrude was, and since the woman didn't hold with things like lace or decorative buttons, it was entirely plain, save for a bone-colored cameo pin at her collar. Thank goodness she wasn't painting Aunt Gertrude; that would have been an exceedingly dull portrait indeed.

"Stop lollygagging, child. Did you finish the portrait yet?" Aunt Gertrude's voice, as thin and reedy as the woman herself, always grated on Bryony.

"No." She huffed a breath out through her nose. She had been working on the background of the painting, which was already fairly tedious. She didn't need to hear Aunt Gertrude's whining on top of it. "If it gets any more depressingly dim, I won't be able to finish the portrait at all. Painting downstairs—"

"Is out of the question. Not with your temper tantrums," Aunt Gertrude snapped.

Bryony glared at her. They both knew it had nothing to do with her temper. Aunt Gertrude had shut her away in the attic at seven years old, the second she'd begun to paint. The message had been clear: painting was all that was allowed. No playing outdoors. No speaking to other children.

No hope of ever being anything but a child prodigy.

"I won't have this argument again. Stop changing the subject." Aunt Gertrude frowned, her thin face full of disapproval. Then she looked up, fixing dark eyes on Bryony. "What would your patron think if I told him you were slacking?"

Bryony's eyes flew open wide. "Don't you bring him into—"

"You know this portrait is very important. As your Uncle Bernard said, this one is commissioned for the museum." Aunt Gertrude smiled thinly, and Bryony shot her a look of pure irritation. Her aunt was ridiculous. Bryony hadn't forgotten what a fuss the woman had made over her tenth portrait, when she'd painted that rotund little woman, what was her name? Madam Williams? Aunt Gertrude had lectured Bryony on taking it seriously, had insisted that her art was going to redeem the family name.

As if art could make her aunt a part of high society. The woman's temper was every bit as bad as Bryony's.

Even now, Aunt Gertrude's cheeks flushed bright red and her nostrils flared as she drew a deep breath and smoothed her hands over her starched black dress, patting the cameo at her throat. "We need that portrait in the museum so everyone can forget this latest nonsense." She looked down at the folded newspaper Uncle Bernard had brought in yesterday. It was a tiny piece, no longer than two hundred words, but it had been enough to send her aunt over the edge.

Rumors Abound in Case of
Mysterious Portrait Disappearances

Bryony had skimmed the article several times already. There was one quote in particular that had caught her eye:

> The family of Lord Remington, missing five days now, has contacted the authorities to inform them of the connection with Bryony Gray, the young artist who painted Remington's portrait the day before his disappearance.

She remembered Lord Remington clearly: a gray-haired old man with steely blue eyes. He'd been an unnerving subject to paint, staring at her sternly from across the room all the while. She could hardly say she was sorry he'd disappeared.

Then again, said disappearance was what had triggered this ridiculous article, and Aunt Gertrude's resulting fit of temper. As if it was *her* fault that the newspaper had spun some story about the people she painted disappearing. After all, she'd have a hard time making people vanish when her aunt and uncle kept her locked in the attic, wouldn't she?

"That's three people missing now. *Three.*" Aunt Gertrude scowled, stomping over to stand behind her, peering over her shoulder at the mess of papers on the desk.

Having Aunt Gertrude so close sent a shiver of distaste through Bryony. The smell of mothballs permeated the air. She gave the woman a sidelong look.

Aunt Gertrude kept the key to the attic door on a long silver chain around her neck, and now, as she leaned forward, it swung back and forth, glittering in the lamplight.

Bryony pressed her lips together tightly, repressing the urge to reach out and snatch it. Not yet; it wasn't time. She'd been planning her escape for weeks. She would do it properly this time, and she wasn't about to mess it up by making some kind of insane grab for the key.

She glanced over at the portrait by the window, a pair of blond-haired twins in red frock dresses. They each held the string of a pull toy—a yellow, wooden bird with beady black eyes—and both stared sullenly out of the frame. The girls had been Bryony's age, but nothing about the sitting had been enjoyable. They'd been terrible brats the entire time. Neither of them had wanted to hold the wooden toys, in spite of their mother insisting they were "utterly darling." They had performed a sort of terrible duet, each one stomping and screaming in turn until their mother had bribed them with the promise of ice cream.

Now the portrait sat there in the single, dusty beam of sunlight sliding through the drapes, the twins glowering from the canvas. She'd captured them a little *too* well.

As she stared, the picture seemed to shimmer the slightest bit, and Bryony glanced away quickly, telling herself it was a trick of the light.

"Stop staring into space," Aunt Gertrude snapped, and before Bryony could get the newspaper she was looking at up between them, her aunt reached out and snatched at the tip of her ear, pinching it sharply between finger and thumb. "Sit."

Bryony glared at her stubbornly, eyes watering, and Aunt Gertrude's thin lips went even thinner. The pain in the top of Bryony's ear increased, until she finally collapsed into her chair with an unhappy growl.

Aunt Gertrude released her ear. "Try not to act so strange. You're always in a daze, or staring out the window or at your own reflection. Little wonder people are whispering about you!" Aunt Gertrude picked up the newspaper and brandished it at her. "This family doesn't need any more scandal."

Bryony rubbed her stinging ear. "A scandal like my father, you mean?"

As soon as she said it, she wished she could snatch the words back. They hung in the air between them, and in the shocked silence that followed, Aunt Gertrude's face slowly began to turn red. Bryony winced, bracing herself, half expecting her to erupt like a volcano.

Aunt Gertrude leaned in until they were eyeball to eyeball.

At last she took a deep breath, nostrils flaring. She tapped one bony finger on the desk, and said, in a low, angry voice, "Finish the portrait of the twins. Have it done by the end of the week."

Bryony spluttered. "What? But . . . that only gives me three days."

"I suppose you should have thought about that before slacking. Clearly, you need to be taught the importance of completing projects on time." Aunt Gertrude turned abruptly, tossing the newspaper at the desk. It slid off and flopped to the floor with a sad little thump. "I'll be in to check on your progress. If you're not working fast enough, you can go without dinner every night until it's done. That should motivate you, don't you think?"

No dinner and a ridiculous deadline for the portrait. Bryony could feel her temper rising.

She shot up as her aunt marched for the door, her face burning. "I hate you! I wish you weren't my aunt! I wish my father would come and take me away from here!"

Aunt Gertrude whirled around. For a moment her mouth worked and nothing came out. Then she said angrily, "You're just like your father. Bernard's brother always did have a rash temper." She had one hand on the doorknob now, glaring over her shoulder. "And we're your only family. You should be grateful we didn't give you to the workhouse after your foolish mother left you on our doorstep. Imagine, dumping a three-year-old on someone like that. Leaving someone else with your responsibility. Rude, terrible woman."

Bryony glowered at her. She'd heard this rant before.

"Get back to work on that portrait. I'll be in to check on you tomorrow. And you can put any thoughts of leaving out of your head right now. Your father isn't coming for you. He's *dead*!"

The door slammed, rattling stacks of faded china on a few rickety shelves, making the curtains at the window stir, and sending up a puff of dust.

Bryony's voice was small in the silence. "I don't believe you."

Chapter Two

The next morning, she was back at work on the portrait. All she had left were tedious background details now, and Bryony found herself glassy-eyed after a few hours. All the while she tried to ignore the fact that the twins' eyes seemed to follow her wherever she moved.

Her hands shook slightly, and she pressed them inside the crooks of her elbows, trying to ignore how much her wrists were aching. As a distraction, she thought about the letter from the patron, safely hidden under the floorboards. The key to escape, to finding her father.

She thought again about her aunt's words the day before; she was so adamant that Bryony's father was dead. It couldn't be true. Not with the way her aunt and uncle acted whenever she mentioned him. She kept thinking about who he could be, what he might look like now. She had nothing to go on. Once, she'd found a family album in the back of Aunt Gertrude's sock drawer, and she'd discovered an old photograph of her mother. Not pasted into the book with the rest of the photos but shoved behind the back flap and out of sight. She was a pale, waifish young woman. She did not have Bryony's golden hair or her sharp nose; she just looked rather . . . faded. It could have been the age of the photo, but somehow Bryony didn't think so. Her mother looked as though someone had stolen a part of her away and never returned it.

It was no mystery what had happened to her ten years ago. She'd had no family of her own to claim her, and so she was buried in the Gray family plot, a dismal stretch of space behind the church Aunt Gertrude attended every Sunday.

The real mystery was her father, the one who had given her her golden hair and the dimple that only seemed to show on her left cheek. And her last name, the one her uncle and aunt couldn't seem to erase no matter how hard they tried. Gray.

There was a muffled thud from outside, the familiar sound of a carriage door closing. Bryony's feet seemed to carry her across the room before she even made up her mind to walk. She knew she should continue painting, but she was so tired; she could use a breath of fresh air and a distraction from the terrible twins.

Aunt Gertrude's "always staring out the window" comment came back to her then, and she ground her teeth and gave the battered drapes a hard tug. Of *course* she was always staring out the window, much the same way creatures in zoos stared out from behind the bars of their cages. It was her only glimpse of the world outside.

In any case, the sound of the carriage was what really drew her, because she knew what it meant. The neighbors were home.

The Griffin Funeral Parlor next door was a huge, Tudor-style mansion with a fenced-in backyard for outdoor funerals. It wasn't actually *meant* to be a funeral parlor; the neighbors had renovated it when they'd moved in six months ago, and Aunt Gertrude hated it. She said it wasn't a proper place for a funeral home, that it was too macabre for the neighborhood. She'd started several petitions to have it knocked down, but it never seemed to work.

But it wasn't the funeral home that fascinated Bryony so much as the people who lived there.

She pressed one hand against the glass, ignoring the smudgy prints she was leaving. It was her—the neighbor girl and her brother. They were dismounting the long black funeral carriage in their driveway. Bryony watched as the boy, tall and weedy, stepped down first. He looked all around before he stepped away from the carriage, as if he expected traffic in his own driveway. Next came the girl, with her pale, heart-shaped face and chin-length wavy black hair. She had on a gray riding dress, which was slightly rumpled and clashed with her long beige jacket. She seemed to spill out of the carriage rather than dismount, ignoring her brother's offered hand, skipping over the last step so hastily that she stumbled a little before catching herself. She appeared to be talking animatedly the entire time, gesturing with both hands as they made their way up the driveway followed by the hulking, top-hatted form of their father, who was escorting his wife on one arm.

Bryony leaned forward and tugged the window upward with a grunt. Uncle Bernard had nailed it shut months ago, perhaps thinking she'd make some mad escape onto the roof, but she'd managed to pry the nails halfway out with a rusty spade she'd discovered in one of the trunks. Now the window opened half an inch, just enough to let the neighbors' voices drift in.

She leaned forward, pressing her ear to the crack in the window.

" . . . said her reflection smiled at her?" It was the deep voice of the father.

"You know how she is. She's getting more and more cracked in her old age."

This was followed by an unpleasant laugh from the wife, and Bryony frowned, pressing her ear harder to the window. *Reflection*, had she said?

She could hear their footsteps echoing between the houses, beginning to fade as they walked away.

"Honestly, Doris, be nice. She's your mother. And she's just lonely," the father said gruffly. This was followed by the muffled sound of a door slamming, which cut off the conversation completely.

Bryony straightened up, disappointed the family had disappeared inside so quickly. She was burning to know more. Was Doris's mother really senile, or had the woman seen the same sort of thing Bryony had? And if so, how was that possible?

For a few minutes she watched the front door of the house, half hoping someone, anyone, would come back outside.

A few times now the neighbor girl had gone out onto the widow's walk, on the very tip-top of the roof. Since her house was just a bit taller, Bryony had been able to peer over the windowsill and watch her pacing back and forth. Often, she would imagine they were friends. That the girl had come to visit, and they were laughing and talking. Talking about everything and anything. About books and paintings and . . . whatever it was friends talked about. She knew from listening at the window that the neighbor girl had a smooth, high voice and a lovely laugh, and sometimes, when Bryony sat there in the dark and thought about it hard enough, she could almost imagine she could hear the other girl. But when she opened her eyes, the picture always dissolved, leaving her sitting alone in the single dusty bar of light falling from the attic window.

And so, for the most part, she simply watched.

The neighbor girl would be splendid to paint, somehow she knew this instinctively, even though she was too far away to pick out every feature.

Sometimes she thought about painting both of them, the boy and the girl. She would have them stand together, paint them side by side, against a plain backdrop. Or perhaps the girl would stand a little ahead of her brother. Both of them were dark-haired, dark-eyed, but the contrast of the girl's petite frame and the boy's tall, lanky one would make such an interesting picture.

But if she had to choose only one of them to paint, it would be the girl, without question; she was simply more captivating. There was something a little wild about her, some unique and mysterious quality that Bryony was sure she could untangle if only she had the chance to work it out on the canvas.

The attic door creaked, and Bryony whirled around, dropping the drapes as if they were on fire. Aunt Gertrude's thin silhouette in the doorway made her heart plunge into her stomach. What terrible timing!

"I . . . I was just finishing up on the background—"

"Well, you clearly have enough time to gaze out the window, so of course you must be nearly finished." Aunt Gertrude's boots made sharp cracking sounds as she strode across the room. She held a silver tea tray out before her, with a china cup and saucer and a sandwich on a plate. When she reached the easel, she set the tray down on the desk beside it with a thump and bent to examine the portrait.

A moment later, Aunt Gertrude snapped upright, her face stern, and Bryony stifled a groan. "You've barely finished half of the background! What did I say about turning this in on time?"

Bryony glared at her, already feeling her stomach rumble. She pressed her lips together tightly. If she blew up now, her aunt was liable to take the sandwich back downstairs. Of course, she had a stash of food collected for her escape, but she'd rather not dip into her supplies.

Taking a deep breath, Bryony did what she always did in order to clear her head. She thought about all the interesting facts she'd learned about art in her lessons:

Baroque style, encouraged by the Catholic Church, is a use of exaggerated motion to depict religious themes. Realism: began in France in the 1850s—

Perhaps she would try it someday.

Another deep breath and she could finally trust her voice to be steady. "I'm making good time."

"Not good enough, obviously." Aunt Gertrude strode toward her, and Bryony had a sudden, horrible realization: she hadn't remembered to push the window back down. It was still open a crack. She opened her mouth, about to say something, anything, to distract her aunt.

"Get back to the painting." Aunt Gertrude grabbed the drapes and began to tug them over the window. "I don't want to see these curtains drawn next—"

She froze, the curtain in her hand swinging gently back and forth.

Dread clenched Bryony's chest. Aunt Gertrude was staring down at the nails in the window. Her lips flattened into a thin line, and she dropped the curtain and turned on Bryony.

"Why is that window open? Bryony Gray, did you pull up the nails?" No sooner were the words out of her mouth than Aunt Gertrude blinked, looking even more put out. She had slipped and called Bryony by her last name.

Usually she did everything she could to deny Bryony's father had ever existed.

Bryony sputtered. "I just wanted fresh air. I didn't— you can't—"

"I can't *what* exactly?" Aunt Gertrude's voice was climbing, a sign that she was about to boil over like a hot kettle. "*Do* enlighten me. What is it I can't do in my own house?"

"I just wanted some air." Bryony tried to keep her voice from shaking. "It gets so stuffy in here."

"Spying on the neighbors, more likely."

Her mouth dropped open, and Aunt Gertrude jabbed a finger at her. "That's what I thought. You've been nothing but

distracted since those people moved in. Watching their horrible backyard funerals, are you? We're putting an end to *that*.
I'm going to have your uncle nail this window down again."

Bryony glared at her. "As if you can stop me looking
outside. You—you're beastly!"

Aunt Gertrude's brows jumped, and then came down
again in fury. "Well," she said, her voice taut and trembling, "I suppose that's true. Nails won't be enough to
keep you from distraction. I'm afraid he'll have to paint
the window black. It will look ugly, but—"

"What?" Bryony's shriek was enough to startle Aunt
Gertrude, who flinched and then recovered herself an
instant later, eyes narrowing in outrage.

"That's right! Clearly this is nothing but a distraction,
so that's what we're going to do!" She yanked the curtains
in front of the window so firmly that one of them tore at
the edge, and then she whirled around and stomped
toward the door.

"You can't do this!" Bryony ran after her. They couldn't
paint over the window, her one portal to the outside world.
She wouldn't let them. "Please, you can't—"

"Get back to work." Aunt Gertrude didn't bother to
look at Bryony while she tugged the key from around her
neck. "And I'm moving your deadline, since you clearly
need the motivation. You're to have the painting finished
the next time I come up here."

She swung the door shut and left Bryony standing
in stunned silence, waiting for the familiar metallic click.
Hearing it, Bryony snatched the teacup off the tray with
trembling hands and pitched it at the door with all her

might. It shattered against the frame, splashing the doorway with hot tea and sending shards of porcelain skittering across the floor.

She froze, gasping for breath, sure that Aunt Gertrude would come charging back in. But there was only silence from the other side of the door.

———

It took one last day to finish the portrait. Bryony painted for most of it, until the sun started to slide behind the buildings in a smoggy orange glow and shadows began to stretch across the attic floor. Her wrist throbbed, and she had completely abandoned any hope of completing the mathematics paper, or starting the English and Latin lessons her last teacher had left behind, but at exactly four in the afternoon, she finished filling in the last bit of background and placed her paintbrush carefully in the tray before collapsing on her bed.

A moment later a sharp knock on the door sent her scrambling upright.

To her relief, it was the round face of Uncle Bernard that appeared in the doorway, red with exertion. With no escape attempts from Bryony in the last three weeks, Uncle Bernard had been in a much better mood. Usually she despised his oily manner, and the way he seemed so insufferably pleased with himself at all times, but at the moment anything was better than Aunt Gertrude.

"My stars," he panted. "These stairs will be the death of me." He mopped his forehead with his sleeve. "Bryony dear, is the painting all ready?"

Bryony folded her arms over her chest, eyes narrow. "Yes, she made clear the vital importance of having it ready immediately. I had no supper last night."

"Ah, yes." Uncle Bernard shut the door and tucked the key into his breast pocket, a gesture that wasn't lost on Bryony. Good behavior or not, he wasn't about to set the key down in front of her.

"She does get in a temper from time to time, doesn't she? Myself, I get promptly out of the way when she gets into one of her moods." He gave a mock shudder and then laughed at his own joke.

How like her uncle to pretend he was just as helpless as she was against the woman's temper. Bryony had seen him placate Aunt Gertrude with his oily tones on more than one occasion, but he would never do it on Bryony's behalf unless there was something in it for him.

"Ah, excellent, here it is." Uncle Bernard strode across the room and stopped in front of the portrait, hands on his knees as he pretended to examine it, though she knew he was still catching his breath. "Hmm . . . well, well. Excellent job, my dear." He straightened up slightly and took what must have been his first proper look. He flinched. "Oh my . . . er . . . very solemn, these two. Don't look as if they've got a sense of humor, do they?"

"The only tolerable ones were the wooden birds, and I dare say they had more personality than either of those girls." Bryony watched as her uncle picked up the portrait carefully and tucked it under his arm. "She threatened . . . the window . . . " She could hardly form the words.

It shouldn't matter to her. After all, she wasn't staying. But still . . . her plans weren't ready yet. She'd be here a while longer, and she couldn't bear to think about sitting in complete darkness for even one day.

He paused in front of the door. "Ah, yes, she told me about that." Uncle Bernard shook his head. "You two, always needling one another. I'll talk to her, but you've got to promise to be on your best behavior tomorrow."

Bryony straightened up. "What's tomorrow?"

"You've got another commission. A Lady Abney, or some such." He chortled, thick brows wiggling as if they were sharing a delicious joke. "I know your aunt is in knots over that newspaper article, but I do believe it's made you more popular, my dear. You'll be all the rage soon. Did I tell you this piece is going to the museum? Isn't that exciting?"

"Yes, you did mention that."

The museum down the street. She'd been once, last year, and it had been wonderful. But now—now she knew Aunt Gertrude wouldn't be taking her to see the museum again. Not with the way they'd been quarreling.

When she said nothing else, Uncle Bernard's grin faded slightly. "Well, it's good news, my dear. No need to look so glum."

She nodded at the newspaper on the desk. "What's the matter with these people? Why are they still coming if they think the disappearances are connected to me?"

Uncle Bernard snorted. "People love a scandal. They know very well that none of the disappearances mean anything. Likely, Lord Remington has gone off hunting without telling anyone, and Madam Williams is rumored to have run off with the cook." He patted his round stomach and chortled to himself again. "Hardly blame her— the man made the best dinner rolls I've ever tasted." He shook his head. "You see, people will insist on making a story of everything. And rumors make you popular. It's working in our favor, isn't it?"

When his remarks were met with nothing but silence, he shrugged and bustled out, the portrait tucked under one arm. His cheerful whistling faded, as the door slammed shut.

Bryony stared after him, listening yet again to the click of the key in the lock.

Chapter Three

The woman who perched on the old bar stool in front of Bryony's easel looked a little bit like a birthday cake. The tiered layers of her lacy pink dress reminded Bryony of the horrible cream-and-custard cake Uncle Bernard had picked out the week before for her thirteenth birthday. As if that towering pink monstrosity somehow made up for everything.

"Why have you stopped painting, girl?"

Bryony didn't turn around, examining the woman's reflection in the big mirror over the fireplace. She was, in fact, waiting for Aunt Gertrude to bring her more black paint, though there was little need to explain it to the woman if she was going to be so rude.

She continued to stare at her new client's reflection. Lady Abney shook coils of silky blonde hair out of her face, ruby lips pouting in what appeared to be a practiced expression, possibly one she believed to be fetching. In truth it made her look rather like a fish. Over her shoulder her friend, Lady Plumberton, hovered, hands clasped in front of her. Occasionally she would lean sideways to peer out the window—which Aunt Gertrude had finally agreed not to paint black, after a promise of good behavior—taking in the busy streets of London.

It didn't seem possible, but Bryony thought she might be even lacier than Lady Abney herself. Lady Plumberton was much more attractive, though, with a round, pale face and wide, sparkling eyes. Why hadn't she been allowed to paint *her*?

Shuffling over to the easel, she smoothed one finger over the scrap of paper Aunt Gertrude had deposited on her paint tray that morning. It read, in black, spidery scrawl,

Lady Abney (sitting) and Lady Plumberton

Both of them rich, spoiled snobs, by all appearances. The type that would be insufferably nitpicky about how they were painted, which always made for a tense sitting. And if that wasn't bad enough, every so often they would bend their heads together and whisper to one another, all the while darting sharp looks at Bryony. Were they even here to be painted? Or were they just here to stare at her and speculate about all the gossip going around? Would Bryony be accosted by a long line of people asking for portraits who only wanted to come gawk at her like some bizarre creature in a petting zoo?

She was starting to hate that newspaper article as much as Aunt Gertrude did.

With a long-suffering sigh that she didn't bother to muffle, she turned back to the women and picked up her paintbrush, studying Lady Abney as she sat. She was a pudgy, pale sort of woman. Not beautiful, but trimmed with so much lace and layered with so much face powder that she gave the *illusion* of beauty. At least, until you got a little closer.

There was a subtleness to true beauty that Lady Abney did not possess. A certain curve of the face or shoulders. Something you couldn't replicate by pulling faces in the mirror. Lady Plumberton had it.

Bryony thought about refusing to paint until they switched positions. It was a bit like choosing to paint a picture of an old boot when a bouquet of roses was sitting next to it.

She'd only started painting for clients three months ago, and there had been very few who were *naturally* beautiful. Uncle Bernard had laughed when she'd dared to voice that opinion. Money is beautiful, he'd said. When she was famous she'd be able to paint anyone she wished, he told her. If that was truly the case, then Bryony couldn't wait to be famous.

Lady Abney shifted, and the hideous pink dress rustled. "Why isn't she painting me, Lottie?"

"I've no idea, dear. Girl, start painting. And take a few years off, would you?" Lady Plumberton gestured at her friend. "Leave out the crow's feet; they're terribly out of fashion."

Bryony sighed. Clearly, the women had been so caught up in fluffing their skirts and gossiping that they'd missed the fact that her aunt had left to get more supplies. "I've run out of black paint. My aunt has gone down to get more," Bryony said, matter-of-factly.

Lady Abney blinked, evidently expecting further explanations, or an apology. When neither was forthcoming she looked rather put out.

"Well, paint my dress, then," she demanded. "You haven't run out of pink paint, have you?"

Bryony had to bite her lip to keep from being rude. That was not how this worked. As if she could simply fill in random bits like a child with a coloring book. There were proportions to think about; one didn't start from the bottom and travel up, like some sort of anarchist. There was an *order* to portrait painting.

Besides, pink wasn't the problem here. No amount of pink could make Lady Abney a worthy portrait subject. Bryony set the brush to the canvas and began on the neckline of the woman's foolish dress. They might complain to Uncle Bernard if she didn't at least *look* like she was painting. She had behaved herself beautifully all morning, and she had to keep up the illusion if she wanted her relatives to let their guards down.

From the doorway came the dry rustle of satin and Aunt Gertrude's voice. "Bryony dear, I've got more paint for you. You're lucky your patron sent another letter along this week. We just stocked up."

Another letter from the patron she'd never be allowed to see. The latest in a long string of missives kept from her ever since the first had arrived. Aunt Gertrude blamed that letter for everything, all her escape attempts and backtalk, all her "rebellion," she called it, as if Bryony were William Wallace, the famous rebel knight, storming castles and throwing kings off their thrones. Twice last month, her aunt had come up and emptied all the boxes and chests, leaving clothing and linen strewn across the dusty floorboards. She'd ripped all of Bryony's precious books off the shelves and thrown them on the ground; even her favorite books on famous painters of England—Uncle Bernard had bought them for her birthday, a new one each year—hadn't been spared.

Her aunt and uncle had given her that first letter thinking it would inspire her to work hard—and behave. And it *had* inspired her. She was determined to get out of the house and find this patron. Her first escape attempt a month ago had been an ill-planned, impulsive thing, a matter of dashing out the door when her aunt had her back turned. It had only resulted in Aunt Gertrude dragging her back upstairs and bolting the door, demanding that Bryony give the letter back. Bryony had refused, and from that day on she hadn't been allowed to see any of the patron's other letters. Aunt Gertrude seemed to think that if she found that first letter, it would put a stop to all of Bryony's bad behavior.

Of course, if Aunt Gertrude knew what was really in that first letter, if she knew what Bryony planned to do about it, she'd rip her painting books to shreds in a rage.

So Bryony kept the letter hidden, and the spot under the floorboards burned hot and bright in her vision and sent prickles of panic over her skin each time Aunt Gertrude clacked over the hollowed spot with her spiky-heeled shoes. But Aunt Gertrude was nearly always talking far too loudly to notice any difference.

Fighting off a rush of hot anger, Bryony replied with only a grunt, tongue poking out between her teeth as she concentrated on getting the ruffles just right. Honestly, there was never any point arguing with her aunt. There was a faint clank as Aunt Gertrude placed the glass bottles of paint on the end table near her elbow, tut-tutting her disapproval into her left ear. "Ladylike answers, Bry dear."

As she leaned forward the key swung gently back and forth, glittering under the gas lamps, practically asking Bryony to reach out and snatch it up. Apparently, she was to be tempted again and again.

She had to resist the impulse. That wasn't the plan.

The Society of Orientalist Painters was founded in 1893. The—

"Don't let your mind wander, sweetheart." Aunt Gertrude's voice was honey sweet, but she moved closer, leaning over her shoulder, so near that Bryony could smell her cloying perfume.

"Then don't crowd me like that!" It came out before she could stop it, and her aunt snapped upright.

"Now, Bryony love, a civil tongue for our guests, if you please."

She did *not* please, but she bit her tongue to keep from saying so.

"I should say." Lady Abney shifted on her stool, setting her hands primly in her lap. "This girl has been nothing but impertinent, Mrs. Gray." Bryony, while annoyed at the insult, was rather amused to catch sight of Aunt Gertrude's face. The corner of her thin mouth twitched downward ever so slightly, and her fingers smoothed over the bone-colored cameo at her throat. The truth was, Aunt Gertrude had been introducing herself as "Lady Gray" for weeks now.

Bryony's last two paintings had put her aunt and uncle in high demand in some art circles, socially speaking. But there were still the rumors to contend with, and the fact that the Grays had long since fallen out of favor. It didn't matter how much money you had. You could dress a hog in frilly petticoats, but, in the end, it would still wallow in the mud.

She immediately pictured Aunt Gertrude up to her neck in mud.

"Why is she smiling like that?" Lady Abney demanded.

Bryony narrowed her eyes at the woman, clutching the paintbrush so hard it creaked.

"Darling." Aunt Gertrude's voice was low and tense.

"She sassed me." Lady Abney touched her hair, primping, as if she feared Bryony's sass had frizzed her curls. "You should be stricter with her. I don't care if she *is* unstable, or the source of all this delicious gossip. It's no excuse for bad manners."

Unstable? Bryony straightened up slowly and set her paintbrush down, fingers trembling. She turned to Aunt Gertrude, who was already squaring her thin shoulders and drawing herself up taller, as if to brace for a storm.

"Now Bry—"

"Is *that* what you've been telling people about me?" She slammed her fist down on the table beside the easel, making the paint jars jump and clatter. Deep in the pit of her stomach the rage began to swell again, filling her insides with a prickly, unpleasant warmth.

Aunt Gertrude shrieked, snatching up the vials of paint. "Those are expensive! Your patron—"

"Have you told *him* I'm unstable too? Is that why he's never met me?" Horror flooded through her, dampening the anger as quickly as it had come. Bryony's face grew hot, the tips of her ears burning. "Is that why you keep him away from me?"

And to think she'd dreamed of living with her patron. Imagined them in a pretty little cottage by the water. She would paint on the beach, in the bright open air, while he looked on and told her how very talented she was, just like in the letter. How ludicrous all of that was now. Her uncle and aunt were never going to let that happen. They were doing everything in their power to be sure he never met her. And perhaps he never *wanted* to meet her.

Her entire plan, so carefully laid out to the last detail, the only thing that had kept her going the last few weeks, shattered. She'd interpreted the letter wrong. Her patron didn't want her to run away and find him; he thought she was some type of lunatic.

Her throat burned, and tears began to prickle.

"I'm so sorry, ladies. She has these fits, you see." Aunt Gertrude leaned in again, eyes darting from Bryony to the ladies—who were sitting in shocked silence—and back again. She hissed like an angry goose. "Behave yourself or you won't be allowed out ever again."

Bryony's heart beat impossibly loudly in her ears. Aunt Gertrude could hiss all she liked, but she couldn't slap her or lose her temper in front of the two women. "I don't care."

It didn't matter if her patron thought she was unstable. She would disabuse him of the notion. She was nearly ready now. For the last week she'd been saving pastries and wrapped chocolates. Uncle Bernard had given her a steady stream of them ever since she'd completed the portrait of that Dashworth woman. He'd been so pleased with it. She'd also been skimming bits of her meals, squirreling away sandwich halves and sweet cakes under the floorboards.

This time, she would be more careful not to get caught. She'd carefully observed and written down her aunt and uncle's schedule, and discovered a Tuesday at noon was best. From what she'd gathered by listening at the door of the attic, Aunt Gertrude would be out for tea with her bridge ladies, and Uncle Bernard at his gentlemen's club.

"Don't be difficult." Aunt Gertrude switched from angry hissing to soft pleading, wide eyes darting back to Lady Abney, who had folded her arms over her frilly bosom and was glaring her displeasure at both of them. "Just finish the painting."

The painting. That was all her uncle and aunt cared about. They'd probably spread the rumors about Bryony themselves in order to make her seem more interesting. Maybe people would buy more portraits that way.

And apparently Aunt Gertrude was telling everyone.

"No." Bryony frowned at her, furious. How many people thought she was disturbed now? What about when Aunt Gertrude had taken her to the opening of the museum down the street last year? All she could think about was the gentle smiles people had given her, the women who patted her fondly on the shoulder, like . . . like a puppy or something. Had they all been expecting her to have a fit at any moment?

She rounded on Aunt Gertrude, who was looking very nervous and a little ill, her trembling fingers smoothing frantically over her cameo again. But before all of her feelings could come pouring out, Lady Abney's shrill voice sounded from the corner. "It's my birthday, and we paid for this child to paint me! Now start painting!"

Bryony stared hard at Lady Abney. The frilly woman flinched.

"Fine. You want me to paint? I'll paint."

The sound of the glass vial shattering on the floor was incredibly satisfying. Black paint sprayed upward, splattering her shoes and the bottom of Aunt Gertrude's gray dress. She ignored her aunt's horrified shriek, grinding her shoe into the glass and paint, grinning over the top of her canvas at the shocked faces of the ladies.

There would be a price to pay later, of course, and not just a few simple bruises. Likely she wouldn't eat for days.

She was too angry to care.

They wanted unstable? They would get it. Let them talk about this for weeks to come. Let them print another stupid newspaper article about it.

"Here, I'll paint you. Just watch." Bryony picked up a brush, reaching down to drag it through the paint on the floor. Slowly and deliberately, she jabbed at the canvas twice, giant black spots for Lady Abney's eyes, and then once more, a gaping maw where her red lips should have been. The paint was dripping down Lady Abney's face, as if the painted woman were crying black tears. "I like you better this way."

Aunt Gertrude seemed to have recovered slightly. She bumped Bryony out of the way with her hip, leaning forward to inspect the portrait. "You've ruined it!"

Lady Abney scrambled off her stool, nearly tripping on her own skirts in her haste to get a look. Her friend put a hand out to steady her, but Lady Abney shrugged her off, rushing toward the canvas. Aunt Gertrude put her arms out in an attempt to block her. "No, my lady, you mustn't—"

"Let me see!"

Bryony stood back as the woman barreled forward, pushing Aunt Gertrude aside so hard that she nearly dropped the remaining paint vials. Her friend followed her, and both women rounded the corner at the same time. When Lady Abney caught sight of the portrait, she stopped dead, eyes bulging. Her mouth formed a beautifully round O and her cheeks drained of all color. A strangled whine began to emanate from her throat, a noise so high-pitched that Bryony thought it would probably irritate neighborhood dogs within a few miles' radius of the house. Mercifully, the sound stopped after a few seconds, but the woman's mouth began to open and shut, as if she wanted to say something but wasn't capable.

Definitely a fish, Bryony decided, a trout, perhaps. She flinched as Lady Abney rounded on her, skirts rustling angrily. "You wicked, nasty child!"

For a moment it seemed that the woman might strike her, and Bryony braced herself. But Lady Plumberton grasped her friend's arm and the woman took a shaky breath, nostrils flaring. Lady Plumberton turned back to Aunt Gertrude.

"She's completely ruined my friend's birthday gift. The newspaper was right. Wait until the reporters hear about her nasty temper. You can rest assured that brat will never work again." She picked up her skirts and, turning to give Bryony one last furious look, stormed out, towing her friend behind her. Her footsteps clattered halfway down the stairs and then paused before continuing.

"And burn that picture," she shouted behind her. "It's an abomination!"

Chapter Four

Nearly an hour later, Bryony sat in the middle of the attic floor, still surrounded by glass shards and drying paint. Her hands shook as she clutched the first letter her patron had ever sent, and she tried to concentrate on the swooping handwriting, to ignore the raised voices from downstairs.

To the caretakers of Bryony Gray,

After seeing one of Ms. Gray's portraits in the household of a family friend, I find myself fascinated with the skill and vibrancy she displays, and I would formally request a meeting with her and her guardians. As both a benefactor and lover of art, I hope to father the modern-day artistic movement in London.

When you told me about her during the show I had little idea how wonderful her work would turn out to be. She is clearly a great talent. Such a gift, and at her age!

I hope she will paint for me someday at my residence in the countryside. I would be pleased if she would find

my estate a place of inspiration for her creative spirit.
She will find the grass is green, and the house is large
and grand, a Tudor-style manor with white-on-gray trim.
It is my fondest wish that Ms. Gray will someday
regard me as family.

Most sincerely,
Your friend from the art show

All clues. They had to be. And the line about his house
was an invitation, she was sure. Her entire plan revolved
around it. The description of the house in the country.
How he would like her to come visit there. The description
was so specific. Bryony traced the tips of her fingers over
the middle line. The one she had read a thousand times.

. . . father the modern-day artistic movement.

Not just a turn of phrase, and not a misinterpretation
on her part, she was certain of that now. For some reason,
he wasn't able to come fetch her, so he'd laid the clues out
for her to find. He was terribly, terribly clever. He was
sending her a message. And every time Uncle Bernard
went pale at the mention of his brother, or Aunt Gertrude
told her in that shrill, panicky voice *never* to speak of it
again, it only confirmed what she suspected. Her father
was the patron, but he was smart enough to keep it hidden
from her uncle and aunt. He knew they'd never let him
near her if he revealed his identity. It was obviously a hint,
the way he talked about family in the letter.

He must have met them at an art show in disguise. It was tremendously daring of him.

He wanted her to find the letter and come to him, to his house in the countryside—but this wasn't nearly enough to go on. Bryony nearly crumpled the letter in her frustration, but instead she pressed it carefully between the pages of a book before laying it gently in the dark space under the floorboards, sliding the wooden plank back into place and pushing it down with the heel of her boot.

Downstairs, the yelling continued. Uncle Bernard was having a turn at the moment.

"It isn't going to hurt her reputation. People love eccentricity—I don't care what that silly woman said." A sharp click punctuated the last word. Uncle Bernard flicked his pocket watch open and closed whenever he was thinking. Bryony knew it drove Aunt Gertrude batty.

"It's happening all over again." Her voice went high-pitched, almost hysterical. "It's been years. The rumors about *him* have just started to die down. People are inviting us to parties, Bernard. *Parties.* And now that woman is going to go straight to the reporters. Lord only knows what's next! Perhaps the *police* will show up on our doorstep!"

"Don't be ridiculous, darling." His voice was soothing. "You know it's a bunch of drivel. It's what the newspapers thrive on. Besides, we can't think about that right now. We have far more pressing concerns. The patron keeps insisting I bring her over. I don't know how much longer I can put it off."

Aunt Gertrude's yelp of "*What?*" could have shattered glass, and Bryony winced. Her chest swelled with excitement, though. She *knew* it. Her uncle had been keeping her patron from her.

But now it sounded as though he was insisting on meeting her. They hadn't driven him away after all. Perhaps Uncle Bernard would keep putting him off, and then the patron would have enough of it and kick the attic door down and carry her away from here.

Perhaps on the day she'd picked for her escape— Tuesday, exactly a week from now—she'd go through Uncle Bernard's study again. Last month, before they'd begun locking her attic door, she'd hit the ultimate jackpot, a book he'd hidden away from her. Something the patron had given him as a gift. He'd taken it up to show Bryony when he'd first received it, gloating as he showed her the leather cover. It was a book of the occult—about curses, particularly, if she was interpreting the pictures correctly. The cover was plain leather, with a simple, five-point star on the front. Just inside a tiny "1900" had been stamped, meaning the book had been published just the year before. The text was all in Latin, accompanied by smudgy charcoal illustrations that looked as though they'd been done rather hastily. Phases of the moon and astrological events, it seemed.

Silly nonsense, she'd always thought, but it had belonged to *him*. Her patron. Her mysterious father. She had been secretly sure that he had meant it for *her* because Uncle Bernard had refused to show her the note it came with. He had bragged about how expensive it was, but when Bryony went looking for it, she'd found it stacked carelessly on one of the end tables, dangerously near a cup of coffee.

She'd rescued it and stashed it away under the floorboards, where it could keep the letter from being lonely in its dark hiding spot. Uncle Bernard never even noticed it was gone, and Bryony alternated between being relieved and furious about this. He didn't deserve any sort of gift, least of all a book as beautiful as this one.

Downstairs the voices continued. "The attic is in shambles right now. And she just threw a massive temper tantrum. She isn't ready."

"Don't fret, love. She can be reasoned with. You know that. We'll dress her up and get her ready to dazzle. It will be fine. We've put it off long enough, and we can't risk offending the patron. We need the money for all the paint supplies."

That was laughable, since the patron was the one supplying the money for the paint. Very likely "paint supplies" was code for tailored clothing and a brand-new wing on the mansion. She grimaced and leaned over to pick up her favorite paintbrush, stroking her fingers over the smooth wood. The grip was worn down and polished from years of use.

Neoclassicism: a reflection of the Enlightenment of Europe. Romanticism: work based on emotion. Impressionism: radical free-form and quick, imprecise brushstrokes.

Facts helped her focus. Facts were just . . . facts. They weren't emotional; they were nothing to get angry at. They stayed solid and the same no matter what you did. And the very best facts, to her mind, were about people like her.

She fixed her eyes on the canvas.

There was something very odd about the painting. Not just the black splotches where the eyes should have been, or the gaping, circular mouth. It was something stranger still.

The painting was still *wet*.

The black paint glistened in the flickering gaslight, the painted lady's hollow eyes leaking rivulets down her cheeks.

"What if those women slander my good name?" Aunt Gertrude's muffled voice demanded. She sounded scandalized at the very idea. "I've only just connected with Lady Gilderoy. What if she doesn't invite us to her next extravaganza?"

Bryony could hear heavy footsteps and knew that Aunt Gertrude was pacing, shoes clack-clacking noisily on the floor. She was upset but distracted, judging by the long pauses in her stomping. Probably straightening pillows and plucking at the lace doilies on the couches. It was ridiculous that Bryony knew that. Sad, really. But she spent so much time up here, sometimes lying on her bed staring at the ceiling, or looking out the window, that she was quite used to hearing her aunt stomp around downstairs.

She could predict what mood Aunt Gertrude would be in on any given day by how loud her footsteps were as she moved about the house. In the mornings, if she could hear her taking tea in the kitchen and slamming the pot down, clack-clacking to the parlor to snap at one of the maids, she knew not to start anything.

Bryony flinched as the sharp clacking resumed.

She could even picture the shoes: ankle boots with ivory buttons. The same ones her aunt had worn the night of the museum opening last year.

She remembered everything about that night.

Aunt Gertrude dangled it over her head constantly, telling her that if she would only be good, if she would only behave, she could go out again. It worked, at least partially. Even just hearing the clack of her aunt's boots was enough to send a wave of longing through her. All the lovely bright paintings she'd seen!

And all the people, dressed in silk and lace and poring over art as if it were the most important thing on earth. Of course, now she knew the reason people had stared at her. How they'd talked *about* her instead of *to* her.

Bryony shifted her attention back to the portrait, to the blobs of black paint that refused to dry. She was glad she'd spoiled her stupid aunt's stupid social life. Hopefully the woman would become a social pariah, just as Bryony's mother had been. She'd heard bits and pieces of the story the few times she'd been downstairs. The servants hissed behind their hands and darted wide-eyed looks at her, but never spoke out loud. And never to her. Still, she knew there had been some type of family disgrace that centered around her mother and her father. And that her father had once been investigated by the police. That her uncle and aunt had fallen out of favor simply for being associated with him.

She didn't want to believe he could have done anything wrong. Sometimes she would sit by the window and daydream about him. Maybe he was a spy for the government, or a commander in a war in one of England's many "civilizing missions" or quests for domination. Perhaps he'd had to go into hiding, so nobody knew where he was. His secret identity was the patron, and he was desperate to come back and see his daughter. Only it wasn't safe.

Whatever the truth was, it was apparent that his very name was taboo. When Bryony was very small, she'd asked about him for the first time. She'd been surprised to see Aunt Gertrude's face go parchment-paper-white, her eyes round like saucers, her lips forming a straight, tight line. Thinking about it gave Bryony a kind of nasty satisfaction. It would serve her aunt right if she was never accepted into high society, if she had to stay home and only dream of invitations to fancy parties. Let her learn how it felt to be trapped in one place all the time.

Of course, if the family name was disgraced again, the rumors would say it was because of the deranged niece. And then nobody would want to be painted anymore. And Uncle Bernard certainly wouldn't spend any money on paints if the patron chose to stop supplying them. Her smile faded.

Bryony chewed on her thumbnail, staring at the portrait again. The painted version of Lady Abney was unspeakably hideous. It wasn't even finished properly: the pink frills around the neckline were blurred, and the blonde curls were absent. There was only the beginning of hair, which looked a bit sad. Plus, one arm was still missing.

Lady Plumberton was right about one thing: the painting should probably be burned. But how well would it burn if the paint was still wet? And *how* was it still wet? It had been a full hour.

Tentatively, she reached out and poked at one of the blotches on the canvas. Her fingers came away dry, not a spot of paint marred her skin. Bryony frowned.

The painted woman was still crying black streams. She looked at her more closely. The paint was *moving*, running down Lady Abney's face. Impossible.

She leaned in even closer. On the canvas, the painted woman's right hand twitched.

Bryony backed up quickly, and her elbow brushed one of the paint vials on the table. It crashed to the floor with a sharp crack, sending a splatter of white across the floor to mix with the black paint from earlier.

No. She sucked in a long breath and leaned away, pulse quickening, tongue sticking to the roof of her mouth.

The voices downstairs stopped, and then started up again, louder. "You spoil her, Bernard. You indulge her silly whims too much."

She forced herself to step forward, squinting at the painting. It had to be a trick of the light, like the mirror the other day. Or perhaps her eyes were tired from concentrating for hours in the flickering light. Bryony ground her teeth, irritated at the thought. Her aunt was going to ruin her eyesight because she was too cheap to put in more lamps. On top of that, she couldn't properly run away if she couldn't see. She needed to be able to identify the house in the country with the white-on-gray trim.

On the canvas, the image of Lady Abney flickered, as if Bryony had blinked once or twice very rapidly. Only, she hadn't. She recoiled, breath catching in her throat, sure she wasn't imagining it now.

It was important she stay calm. Focus. *Georges Braque was the first artist to have something displayed in the Louvre.*

44

Leonardo da Vinci didn't eat meat. Richard Dadd believed his father was the devil.

Admittedly, facts about artists going insane weren't helping.

Bryony glanced around, catching sight of the mirror over the fireplace.

It was empty.

She blinked once, hard, and looked again. Still empty. And she wasn't out of frame at all. Evidently, her reflection had had enough of all this and wandered off.

Bryony squeezed her eyes shut and stubbornly went on with her facts. *Michelangelo died in Rome at the age of eighty-eight. Francisco Goya was court painter to the Spanish Crown.* She opened her eyes.

The painted woman was larger than she'd been just moments ago. Closer to the frame. Bryony stared, alarm slowly seeping into the cracks between her bones and muscles, paralyzing her completely. Somehow she found her voice. "You stop that," she said, trying to sound as stern as possible. "You're not even finished yet . . ."

The lady in the portrait twitched again, much more visibly this time, jerky movements that brought her closer and closer to the frame.

Bryony jumped back, feet slipping on a smear of white paint. She had time for one sharp squeak of dismay and then she was falling, arms pinwheeling, hands grasping for something, anything. She went down hard.

Something cracked when she hit the floor, and there was a sharp pain in her elbow, but there was no time to check for broken appendages. The horribly disfigured

Lady Abney was leering at her from the canvas, and as Bryony looked on in terror, the woman—monster, really—lifted her one good arm and snaked it forward. The canvas bulged in the middle.

Bryony squeaked and scuttled backward, crablike on her elbows, dragging herself through glass shards and paint. Pain blazed in the palm of her left hand, but she ignored it, too fixated on the scene unfolding before her. There was a sharp rending sound as the canvas tore, and then a spiderlike hand crawled out, followed by a long, white arm. The canvas ripped open wider and wider as the creature came through.

Bryony was completely frozen.

A shoulder pushed its way out—awkwardly, slowly— and then the canvas tore wider still, revealing hollow black eyes, still weeping paint that ran in tracks down a pale, powdered face. It was impossible that they should focus on anything; there were no pupils, no irises. But still, they seemed to fix on Bryony as the monstrous woman tore herself bit by bit from the canvas. The easel finally gave way, collapsing under the weight, tipping forward and crashing to the floor with a sound so thunderous that the voices from downstairs went silent.

In the seconds that followed, there was only the dull scrape and bump of the creature grasping at the floorboards, pulling her body the rest of the way out of the painting.

From her position on the floor, Bryony tilted her head back to look up at her, at this *thing* that her painting had birthed, and wished feverishly that she'd stuck to painting bowls of fruit and bunches of roses.

The creature pulled herself off the floor, brushing her voluminous skirts down in an eerily prim gesture, exactly as the real Lady Abney had done. She turned to face Bryony, revealing the blank spot where her left arm should have been. The painted woman seemed to consider Bryony, tilting her head to one side. Her face remained as still as a marble mask—there was no expression at all—and yet Bryony could have sworn she was being studied.

It was all over. No more attic, no more Aunt Gertrude and Uncle Bernard, no more painting. That last part was a shame, really. She would have liked to try painting what s*he* wanted, for once. Not the frilly ladies her relatives picked out for her. Something truly beautiful.

That was neither here nor there, though, and the very last thing she should be thinking about, considering the terrible creature she'd just created. The painted woman continued staring, and the silence stretched out, taut as a bowstring.

Bryony managed a shaky smile. "I'm . . . um, I'm really very sorry about your arm. I didn't get to finish."

The monstrous woman didn't blink. Perhaps she couldn't.

Bryony flinched as the painted woman moved abruptly, stepping closer, thrusting her face into Bryony's, her head tilting from side to side. As if considering something.

Her breath caught in her throat, but a moment later the woman seemed to lose interest, turning away to pick delicately through the maze of wooden chests and old furniture, heading toward the window.

Horror rose up in Bryony's throat. The painting was going to escape. What would happen if people saw it?

Uncle Bernard would never let her out of the attic after this. She'd be locked up until she was as old as he was.

She tried to scramble to her feet, but the room tilted around her. When the attic finally stopped spinning and she looked up, it was to see a flash of pink disappearing from the corner of the windowsill.

Chapter Five

It was gone.

She blinked, crossed and uncrossed her arms, and shivered. The window, wide open from where the monstrous woman had wrenched the nails out, was letting in quite a draft. She should probably shut it, but Bryony didn't seem to be able to move. Instead, she stared at her books lined up neatly on their shelves. There were fifty-two of them; she'd counted. They were reliable and constant and sturdy. Exactly like the statistics and facts their yellowed pages held.

Next to their solid, unchanging presence, what she'd just witnessed seemed altogether impossible. A nightmare she was yet to wake up from.

Bryony squinted harder at the textbooks, as if they might give her courage. Clenching trembling hands into fists at her sides, she considered what she'd just seen.

She didn't have much to go on, having been locked in the attic for the last six years, but mirrors and paintings had behaved consistently up until now. They generally didn't move on their own, as a rule.

She shook her head, trying to convince herself to wake up. Weren't you supposed to pinch yourself if you were dreaming? She dug her fingernails into the back of her hand.

Nothing happened. The attic stayed the same.

Bryony sat there, frozen.

At last, a strange, dull kind of thumping jerked her back to the present. It started downstairs, was cut off with a crash, and was followed by complete silence. Bryony continued to sit there for a moment, uncertain.

Something wasn't right.

When she pushed herself to her feet and started for the door—muttering a string of unladylike words that would have caused Aunt Gertrude to break out in hives—the room tilted wildly around her.

Bryony glanced down at the floorboards and realized the source of her dizzy spells. She was losing a great deal of blood. She jerked her hand up and cringed at the shooting pain. There was a wide gash in the center of her palm, and a piece of glass jutted out of the wound like a tiny, glittering shark fin. Bryony sucked in a breath, nostrils flaring, and carefully pinched the shard between her finger and thumb before yanking it out. She grimaced, dropping the glass onto the floor at her feet.

There was a sizable puddle of black and white paint mixed with smears of pink from Lady Abney and blood from her hand, and the whole mess was dripping steadily down into a crack in the floorboards. Bryony chewed on her bottom lip, feeling ill. She needed to stop the bleeding and clean up this mess before Aunt Gertrude got up here. And there was still the matter of the runaway painting.

One of the nearby trunks provided a handkerchief, which Bryony used as a makeshift bandage, binding the wound as securely as she could. That would have to do until the bleeding stopped.

Another crash from downstairs—it sounded as if something had broken. She turned, hesitating. What if the painted lady was downstairs?

Making her way deeper into the stacks of chests and boxes, Bryony yanked on the middle drawer of an old desk that sat under a layer of dust in the corner. It opened with a shriek and rattle, and there it was, the long metal wire she kept hidden there, bent exactly in the right place to fit the attic lock.

It was the work of a few seconds—she'd practiced picking the lock repeatedly over the last few weeks. Then the tumblers clicked in just the right way, sending a thrill through her, and the door drifted open. Just outside, the stairs descended in a sharp, rickety slope. Beyond that, the house was eerily silent.

She descended the steps, which creaked and groaned beneath her, announcing her presence. The living room was empty when she entered, though all the lights were blazing. Aunt Gertrude's parlor, normally spotless, was in shambles. The elegant teak coffee table was lying upside down in the center of the room, looking rather like an upended turtle. The silk-paned room divider had collapsed, and one side was torn. A good deal of broken china, glistening shards of fine white teacups and saucers, lay scattered about, and crooked tracks of black paint had leaked through a thin crack in the ceiling, streaking inky black fingers down the flowery wallpaper.

"What on earth happened?" she breathed into the silence. A terrible thought occurred to her then, a vision of the deranged Lady Abney crawling, spiderlike, down the wall of the house, entering the parlor window and spiriting her relatives away.

But when she walked over to the window, carefully picking her way through the mess, she found it locked. Perhaps the painted woman had dragged them out the front door. Bryony hurried down the hallway, which was dim and silent and filled with the faint scent of Aunt Gertrude's potpourri. In the entranceway she discovered there was nothing out of place. The ivory umbrella stand was still upright in the corner, the closet doors were neatly shut, and the doormat hadn't moved an inch. No one had been in or out. She even checked the closet, finding her uncle's and aunt's coats still there. They hadn't gone out.

Back through the hallway again, into the parlor.

As she turned away, a flash of movement caught her eye, making her jump. But it was only the mirror on the door of the armoire.

Her reflection was in the very center, arms at her sides, head tilted down. Bryony glanced down at her hands, which had flown up to her mouth during her moment of surprise, and were still hovering in the general vicinity. That reflection was most certainly not right. The Bryony in the mirror was looking straight at her now, and she was *smiling*, a horrible, sneering expression that wasn't at all like her real smile. What's more, the face in the mirror was subtly different, longer and thinner, older-looking, with smooth, sparkling skin. The reflection was most certainly *wrong*.

The room seemed to blur at the corners, and Bryony took a deep, shaky breath to steady herself. Grasping about for facts, she found none. Fear had paralyzed her, wiped her mind blank. She shook her head. It would do no good to give in to the terror.

"Did you do something to my relatives?" Her voice trembled.

The reflection didn't move an inch; she just stood there and smiled that horrible smile. But from down the hall came a tremulous whimper, a sound so slight she might have missed it, if her nerves hadn't been so on edge.

She hurried down the hallway, wiping sweaty palms on her dress, pausing at the entrance to the parlor.

"Hello?" Bryony called. "Who's there? Aunt Gertrude?"

The faint whimper came again, and in the corner, just beside the big bay window, the red velvet curtain shivered violently. Bryony crept closer, footsteps whisper-soft. The curtain seemed to anticipate her approach, for it fluttered and trembled as she drew nearer.

She reached out, ever so slowly, and grasped the velvet between her finger and thumb. Someone was breathing— sharp, shallow breaths, just short of hyperventilating. She was fairly certain it wasn't her.

"Aunt Gertrude?"

She drew the curtain to one side, revealing a very small person curled up in the corner, wearing a black dress and a white apron.

"Hello," Bryony said. Confronted with someone so tiny and afraid, she felt a little bit braver. She kept her voice very quiet and calm. "Can you tell me what happened here?"

The small person turned out to be one of the maids. Bryony didn't recognize her, though, so perhaps she was new.

Upon seeing who it was, the maid uncurled slightly and stared at Bryony with wide, doelike eyes. "You're the niece," she said. "The disturbed one."

When Bryony narrowed her eyes, the girl flinched, tucking her head back down again and pulling her floppy white cap over her eyes, much like a snail retreating into its shell. Bryony said the unladylike words again, softly and under her breath. At least with Aunt Gertrude gone she was free to use whatever language she liked. But growling and grumbling wasn't going to get her anywhere with the terrified maid, so she used the most soothing voice she could muster.

"You have to tell me what happened here. Where are my uncle and aunt?"

Trembling, and without emerging from her floppy white cap, the maid lifted one long, pale arm and pointed. Bryony frowned, trying to follow the line of the girl's finger. "The tea set ate them?"

The white cap moved from side to side. *No.*

Bryony looked over at the only other object in the vicinity. Another mirror. Her skin began to crawl, and her voice, when she spoke, was only a trembling gasp. "It's the mirror, isn't it?"

The white cap moved up and down. *Yes.*

Bryony drew another deep breath in through her nose and took a step toward the mirror, her reflection's dark eyes meeting her own. Somewhere in the distance a siren wailed. She took one step forward, then another. Her palms were damp with sweat.

"Mirror," she said, forcing her voice into firmness. "Did you do something to my uncle?"

The reflection moved her head back and forth once. *No.*

The back of her neck prickled. "Mirror," she said softly. "Did you do something to my aunt?"

The reflection smiled wider, nodding once. *Yes.*

An iron band squeezed the breath from her lungs. Lights blurred and danced in the corners of her eyes, and she reached out to clutch the arm of the couch. Impossible, she wanted to say. Instead, she asked a question: "What did you do?"

The reflection moved an arm, ever so slowly, lifting one hand to point at Bryony's feet. As she looked down, slowly, a tight knot began to form in her chest. There on the carpet was a very small pile of ashes, as if someone had been sweeping up the fireplace and left it there.

"What?" She backed up a step, head spinning. When she looked at the mirror again it was beckoning to her. Crooking one finger. *Come here.*

"No!" Bryony turned, rushing toward the curtain, pushing past to grab a fistful of the maid's white apron. "What did it do?"

The maid shrieked, struggling, and Bryony, seized by a fit of frustration and panic, shook her so hard her teeth clacked together. "Tell me what happened! Why is it pointing at the ashes like that?" She experienced a terrible sinking feeling whenever she looked over at the little pile on the carpet.

The maid was barely coherent, but she gasped out words between hiccupping sobs. "Mirror . . . reflection . . . she just . . . crumbled."

Bryony's fingers went numb, and she released the poor maid's apron. "No. You're lying."

But the girl had already curled in on herself again, yanking her hat down over her eyes. Clearly, she was done talking.

This couldn't be happening. Mirrors couldn't turn people into piles of dust. And paintings didn't crawl out of their canvases and walk away either. And where was Uncle Bernard? He had to know what was going on.

Bryony straightened up and let the curtain drop back in front of the girl. Now that she wasn't busy trying to shake information out of someone, her surroundings came back into sharp focus. The ruined parlor, and the deep, eerie silence of the house. In contrast, the siren outside had risen in volume and been joined by several others. There was also the faint sound of something breaking, and what sounded like a faraway scream.

What on earth was going on out there?

Bryony left the parlor, forcing herself not to look at the mirror as she went past. In the front entrance the sirens were louder, and she placed one hand on the cool doorknob, staring at her bitten-down nails as she took a deep breath and opened the door.

Chapter Six

ut on the doorstep she breathed in the cool evening air. Though the cityscape looked the same as it did from the attic window, with its jagged smokestacks and spires rising against the sunset sky, there were several great spirals of black smoke rising in the distance. The road in front of the house, which was usually filled with hackney cabs and shoppers rushing back and forth on both sidewalks, was completely silent.

The streetlamps were a shade brighter than she was used to, having seen them only through the window for so long, and Bryony shut her eyes for a moment, breathing deeply and feeling the cool air brush past her cheeks and stir her hair. The smell of London was something she would have to get used to, the mixture of coal smoke and the faint, putrid scent of the Thames. It wasn't good, exactly, but it wasn't bad either. It was just . . . outside.

She opened her eyes.

There were still cabs and carriages in the streets, but they'd been abandoned, doors flung open, motors left running. Bryony watched in astonishment as a pony trotted by on the sidewalk, the driver's seat of its carriage empty.

What on earth had happened here? Had the painted woman done this? If that was the case, it was certainly her responsibility to stop the creature. She would have to find an adult first, though. A single girl couldn't stop a rampaging, one-armed monster.

Bryony took a deep breath and looked around. She needed to find Uncle Bernard . . .

And what? Warn him about the painted woman? That secret was clearly already out. And so was Bryony, finally out of the attic, like she'd been planning for weeks and weeks. In fact, she was frustrated to have caught herself thinking about finding Uncle Bernard. Had she grown so dependent on her jailor that she would run straight back to him?

She was free to find her patron now. He would know what to do, wouldn't he? Either way, if she was going to find an adult to help her deal with all this, she would rather it be him than her uncle.

To start, she needed to make her way into the country and begin looking for the house with the white-on-gray trim, and the first step was finding a ride. Bryony looked up and down the street, biting at her thumbnail. Not a single driver remained in the cabs and cars, and she certainly didn't know how to drive either one. Tilting her head back, she took in the buildings for the first time since stepping outside.

The windows of the houses were empty and dark, but she spotted movement in a few, curtains fluttering. People may have been watching her, but nobody came outside to ask if she needed help. She was in the middle of the city all on her own.

Suddenly, the enormity of it hit her. She'd read all about London in her textbooks, memorizing everything she could in preparation for her escape, but nothing had prepared her for how *big* the city was. The buildings seemed impossibly tall. Gray cement blocks loomed over her, the eyes of a hundred windows leering down, cold and uncaring.

London was endless, each massive, castlelike building glued to the next, like a towering fence. The distance was punctuated by them—spires and church steeples and taller buildings still. The city somehow sprawled before her for eternity and hedged her in at the same time.

Her breath caught, and then continued, wheezing in and out of her lungs. She couldn't seem to get enough oxygen. The city was sucking it away, replacing it with soot and smoke and the stench of garbage.

Bryony's chin trembled, and she clenched her teeth, hands flying to her chest, trying to pull in air. A picture of the attic flashed in her mind, her quiet, dim attic with the soft orange light of the lantern, the rows of books, the dusty furniture. For one guilty, desperate moment, she wished herself back there.

No. Just breathe. Edvard Munch can't bear to be separated from his paintings. He paints in pastels. His painting The Scream *was a study of himself.*

She probably looked like that right now, hands on her face, mouth hanging open.

There, aways down the street . . .

The Museum of Art was still open, light shining through every window. It was the only building that didn't loom dark and abandoned, the only windows through which orange light glowed like a welcoming beacon.

She stumbled down the street, weaving through abandoned cabs whose engines were still rattling loudly, dodging another carriage as the horse towed it past. Several minutes later, she paused at the door of the museum, tilting her head back to take in the wrought-iron sconces and the ivy that carpeted the rust-red bricks. The building was familiar, her memories of it tinged by joy.

Something in her chest loosened, and she was able to breathe deeply at last. Relieved, she pushed her way through the door.

The insides of the museum were brightly lit, the lamps along the brick walls blazing. The first room she walked into was the lounge area. When Aunt Gertrude had brought her here, it had been wall to wall with ladies in elegant dresses and gentlemen in tuxedos, all laughing and chattering gaily over delicate flutes of champagne. Now, standing in the center of the empty room, with its high, white ceiling and elegant urns positioned along the walls, she could almost hear the faint sound of gaiety. The ghost of a celebration long past.

It was exciting to see it again. In spite of the trembling in her limbs and the twisting of her stomach, she longed to take in the rows of achingly beautiful paintings and imagine who had created them. The souls that burned behind each image. People like her.

Well, perhaps not exactly like her. Somehow it seemed

unlikely that Monet or Rembrandt's masterpieces had ever peeled themselves off the canvas and run off to terrorize the countryside.

"Hello?" Her voice echoed back a thousand times, and she shivered and rubbed her arms. If the museum was closed for the night, why hadn't the doors been locked? Why were all the lights still on? Slowly, she made her way to the door on the far side of the lounge, trying to step softly so her footsteps wouldn't echo so much.

The room beyond was in complete disarray.

Someone had knocked over a heavy vase in the corner, and the porcelain shards were scattered across the floorboards. Most of the paintings hung crookedly, as if they'd been knocked askew by a great earthquake. One had even fallen, revealing the brown paper on the back, the floor scratched around the golden frame.

There was a crooked trail of pink sludge smeared across the walls, and over and between each picture, and Bryony inched forward, squinting at it. She lifted one shaking hand. Her fingers were only inches away from the sticky trail before she dropped her hand and backed away.

Probably best not to touch it.

Most of the paintings had been punctured, some torn right through—and all of them were empty. The result resembled a hallway of strange windows, some displaying empty pastoral scenes and blank backgrounds while others featured chairs and stools without occupants. It was as if the painted people within the frames had all fled, punching through the canvases and spilling out into the real world just as Lady Abney had.

Bryony swallowed hard and kept walking, curling her fingers into fists.

The room narrowed into a hallway next, taking her down another row of ruined paintings and torn canvases. She walked more quickly now, feeling a little out of breath. From down the corridor, where it branched off in two directions, came a rustling noise and a small groan. Bryony froze, shoes skidding on the floor. She was irritated to find that her arms and legs were trembling again. Now wasn't the time to fall apart. "Hullo?"

The groan came again, fainter this time. Perhaps someone was in trouble. Rounding the corner as quickly as she could, Bryony nearly stumbled. There was a man— or was it a mummy?—on the floor in the middle of the gallery. The skin on his face was so shriveled it was nearly gone, brown and leathery and gaunt. His eyes bulged in their sockets as he dragged one hand over the floor, fingers squeaking on the polished wood. The rustling sound continued as he tried to pull himself forward.

Bryony shrieked and threw herself backward, nearly upending the porcelain urn that stood in the corner. It wobbled loudly and she grabbed hold of it and hung on, fingers biting into the lip of the urn. She had read about Egyptian mummies, but certainly hadn't come across anything about them moving.

The man gave a final wheeze and then flopped forward. One arm twitched, and then, at last, he lay still. On the wall behind him one of the portraits moved. Just a flash, a flicker of green and blue paint.

Bryony stuffed a fist in her mouth and pressed her back

to the wall, trying to stay as still as possible. Her eyes darted from the mummy to the canvas in front of her. The portrait was of a tall, pale-faced man in a green jacket. A duke of some kind, judging by his gold buttons and the lace at his cuffs and collar.

It was the only painting that still had someone in it, but somehow that wasn't any sort of comfort. The man in the painting . . . she was sure he'd moved. And the way he looked now, with his beady, black eyes and the smirk on his cold, white face, he seemed almost alive. Did his eyes glitter, or was it her imagination?

Bryony slid along the wall, trying to put space between herself and the painting. Nothing else stirred. The mummy— or was it a man?—didn't move. Slowly she unpeeled herself from the wall and crept forward, fingers still pressed hard to her mouth. If she made noise, it might wake something up again. The mummy must have come from one of the paintings. Though he looked different than Lady Abney had. More lifelike.

He was also currently sprawled in front of the door she'd just walked through, so though she very much wanted to turn tail and run out of the museum, she had to force herself to keep going. There had to be a way out on the other side.

David Roberts: traveled to Egypt in 1838, produced a series of Orientalist paintings in oil.

Feeling braver, she was about to plunge forward when a terrible dragging sound came from behind—a rattling, scraping noise that made the hairs on the back of her neck go up.

When she whirled around, her heart flew into her throat and stuck there.

A woman was limping through the doorway, into the room and toward her. No, not a woman, she realized, another painting. Like Lady Abney.

This new painting was dressed in gold-and-blue robes, and she carried a crooked staff in one hand. This she let trail behind her as she came, and it bounced and clattered and skittered over the floor with a sound like rattling bones. The shepherdess—for that's what she was; Bryony was quite sure she'd seen this painting before—staggered forward, as if she were still mastering the ability to walk. Her face was flushed, almost lifelike, and perhaps from a distance people would be fooled. But the closer she got, the more obvious it became that her face was unnaturally stiff. Her expression painted on, eyes glossy and dead.

When those dead eyes fixed on Bryony, the shepherdess opened her red lips and shrieked, a high, shrill noise that echoed through the museum. Bryony gasped, stumbling backward, shoes sliding on the floor. Another scream and Bryony turned, flinging herself through the doorway and around the corner, arms pumping, breath ragged in her throat. That terrible scraping sound increased, loud and insistent on her heels. *The painting was chasing her.*

The next room and the next were a blur, and she caught a glimpse of more empty canvases, more bright pink trails of paint, and then she skidded around another corner and something snatched her arm, yanking her hard to the left.

Bryony bit back a cry as she crashed to the ground, smacking her knee hard on the tile floor. Her elbow, by

64

contrast, hit something soft and springy that went "oof!" upon impact. She whirled around, bracing herself to fight off whatever it was, a mummy, another murderous painting . . . and found herself staring straight into a pair of wide blue eyes.

It wasn't a mummy this time. It was a girl.

She was slightly taller than Bryony, and her dark hair was cut unfashionably short and a little crooked on one side, as if the girl had done it herself in front of the mirror with scissors.

The strangest thing of all was her outfit. The girl's dress was long, with silver hemming at the bottom, and it was perfectly fashionable, but perched on her head, slightly too big and most definitely crooked, was a white pith helmet topped by goggles, the type explorers wore. A pair of sturdy black boots peeked out from beneath the hem of her silky dress, and she wore a belt slung low over her hips with a number of strange brass objects attached to it.

For a moment they only stared at one another, and then the dragging sound was suddenly very loud and very close, and the girl's eyes flew open even wider. She snatched at Bryony's sleeve and yanked her down, ducking behind a set of ornate jade vases tall enough to obscure both of them. The girl pressed her finger to her lips.

The shepherdess rounded the corner, head swiveling this way and that in darting, birdlike movements. Then she reared back, stretched her mouth wide and screamed again, a high-pitched tea-kettle noise filled with rage and frustration. The sound made both girls jump and clutch one another in fright, but neither made a sound.

The painted monster stopped, going quiet so abruptly that Bryony's stomach dropped. Had she spotted them behind the vases?

But the monster didn't turn. She stalked forward, lifting her shepherd's crook, trailing the curved staff over the wall. It left a smear of brown paint and then bumped over a first painting, and then another and another as the shepherdess dragged it forward.

Just like the pink trail, Bryony realized with a start. Only there was no pink trail in this room. All the paintings were full. The portraits along the walls still had their subjects in them. There were snooty dukes and ladies, and serene-looking ministers and cardinals. At the very end, a pair of twins were painted arm in arm, identical expressions of sullen resentment on their faces. Bryony felt a jolt of recognition. It was strange to see something she'd painted hung in the gallery, like *real* art.

For a moment it was perfectly silent. Not one of the paintings moved.

At least, not until the shepherdess dragged the staff across the portraits.

Bryony could have sworn there was a flicker of something in one of the cardinal's eyes. The barest hint of a wicked gleam.

Then the room was empty. The shepherdess had doubled back, still searching for her, no doubt. It was silent, save for the sound of the two girls breathing heavily. Bryony's heart thumped loudly in her ears.

For a moment the two of them sat perfectly still, listening to the shuffle and thump of the shepherdess's staff grow quieter and quieter. It was only when it had finally faded away to nothing that the girls turned to face one another. Neither of them had stood up yet, so it was a strange sort of meeting. Face to face, sitting on the cold tile floor.

Finally, the other girl cleared her throat. "To be perfectly honest, I'm still not sure if this is a dream or not."

For once Bryony couldn't think of anything to say. Her tongue felt clumsy. Too big for her mouth. She knew if she tried to speak she'd make a terrible mess of it. She knew this girl. She'd seen her from the window, pacing the widow's walk.

It was the girl next door. How ridiculous that the first time they should ever meet would be in a museum full of murderous portraits, in the middle of a crisis that Bryony herself seemed to have created.

"I'm Mira," the girl said, and she folded her hands carefully and placed them in her lap, as if she wasn't sure what else to do with them.

Up close Mira was even more fascinating. Her neck was long, pale and graceful, and a little bit swanlike. Her face had been perfectly sculptured, all marble panes and angles.

Wouldn't she just be the most wonderful subject to paint? The brush would move softly over those perfect features, those delicate sloping shoulders, those long pale arms. Bryony was already planning exactly how she would mix the paint to match the shade of Mira's dark hair.

She felt a little thrill go through her, all the way down to the tips of her toes. Perhaps she and the girl were, in fact, meant to be great friends. The best of friends.

Perhaps her dreaming hadn't been so outrageous.

"What are you doing here? I didn't see you before." Mira glanced around the room, giving the paintings a long, suspicious look. "My brother and I were on their evening art tour. He kept saying nothing good ever comes of an art tour. It does look like he was right, though I thought it was lovely before that one-armed lunatic came through." Mira shuddered. "Duke Williams was here to see his portrait when it . . . it just touched him and he shriveled up. I thought I was dreaming."

"I think I saw him in the lobby." There was a second of horrified silence in which Bryony opened her mouth, and then closed it again, her face flushing bright red. She tried not to think about the pile of ash on the carpet, or picture Aunt Gertrude shriveling to dust. She squinched her eyes shut tight and forced the thought away.

It wouldn't do any good to start panicking now.

When she opened her eyes, Mira was staring at her expectantly.

She faltered, not sure how to explain everything. That *she* had let that one-armed lunatic loose on the unsuspecting city of London. Perhaps if she admitted it, Mira would decide they couldn't be friends.

It was suddenly very important she say just the right thing. It was vital that the other girl like her. *Like* her, not pity her or think she was an interesting bit of gossip. She wanted Mira to find her interesting and charming and rakishly careless, like the heroes of the adventure stories she'd found on the attic shelves.

"I've come to find a ride into the countryside," Bryony

said, and she put her hands on her hips and tilted her head just so. Did that look rakish?

It was hard to look rakish sitting down.

Mira only stared, unaffected. "You couldn't find one?"

Bryony gave up on the pose and let her hands drop to her sides, feeling more than a little silly. She wasn't rakish; she wasn't even brave. As soon as she got free of the attic all she'd wanted to do was find Uncle Bernard. To walk straight back into the hands of her jailor. The thought made her face burn.

"Not so far." *Unless*—a thought popped into her mind—*unless she knows how to drive?* No, that was ridiculous. Mira didn't look much older than her.

Before she could say anything else, a terrific rending sound came from the other side of the room, the familiar sound of canvas ripping, and Bryony shot upright, snatching at Mira's sleeve. "Come on. We've got to go!"

They both scrambled up, Bryony leading the way, holding tight to Mira's hand. They ran past the jade vases, pelting through the center of the room toward the door. On the walls around them some of the paintings had begun to move. The tearing sound was coming from the portrait of the twins. The girl on the left was still frozen, her frown still in place, her eyes still glassy. The other was scowling even deeper, dark brows drawn down, red mouth twisted in rage. One hand stuck out through the center of the canvas, long white fingers clawing the air.

She was really beginning to hate that painting.

"Go! Go!" Mira cried behind her, and Bryony put on a tremendous burst of speed, chest heaving, fear firing electric jolts up through the soles of her feet and into her legs, sending her hurtling across the room.

"Wait! My notebook."

Mira's cry made Bryony stumble, and she looked around to see the other girl dart back into the doorway, snatching a blue book up off the tiles. As she did, the first twin dropped from the painting, sprawling to the floor with a heavy thud and a scream of triumph.

Bryony yelled over the noise. "Are you mad? *Run!*"

They ran.

Past more portraits, nothing but a blur of faces on either side. Bryony felt sweat spring up on her forehead and the palms of her hands as the hallway kept unfolding before them. An army for the shepherdess to bring to life.

Down another hallway and another, until they could no longer hear the shrieking of the twin.

With any luck, the paintings would get lost in the endless corridors and rooms of the museum.

"We've got to find my brother," Mira panted, and then she raised her voice over the clatter their boots made on the tiles. "Thompson! Thompson, where are you?"

"No, don't—" Bryony began, but stopped abruptly as they rounded a corner. A stone giant loomed in their pathway.

Bryony shrieked and skittered to a stop, shoes sliding on the slick tiles, and Mira slammed into the back of her, catching Bryony's arms just in time to keep them both from going over.

The stone giant was massive, at least a head taller than the average man. It was a statue of the Queen, dressed in a billowing ball gown, her scepter in one hand and the crown jewels in the other. It was all done in marble, the Queen's features frozen in regal disapproval.

The girls stood still, barely breathing, clutching at one another. Bryony's heart seemed to have lodged itself permanently in her throat and refused to come back down.

"It's not moving," Mira breathed.

It wasn't. The statue was content to remain a statue, it seemed, and Bryony let out a relieved breath. "Oh, thank goodness."

If the statue had come to life, the consequences would have been too terrible to think about. A rampaging woman made of stone simply had to be more destructive than the painted monsters.

"We have to find my brother," Mira repeated, giving Bryony's sleeve a tug. "Please, help me find Thompson?"

Bryony wanted to tell Mira that it wasn't safe to stay in the middle of the museum. But Mira had saved her earlier, so she only shrugged helplessly and nodded. "Where did you last see him?" The question seemed silly, like Mira's brother was a pocket watch or a pair of gloves she'd left lying about.

"On the tour back in the main hall." Mira glanced over her shoulder, shifting from foot to foot, fidgeting with the belt at her waist. "Right before the one-armed woman came in."

"All right," Bryony said. "Maybe we should—"

Noise from behind the statue made them both stiffen, and she whirled around, ready to run if the Queen came to life after all. But the statue didn't move, and when the noise came again it sounded more like a pathetic whimper than the scream of rage the shepherdess had made.

"Thompson!" Mira flung herself forward, around the side of the statue, and Bryony followed.

There was someone huddled behind the stone skirts of the Queen, curled up into a ball of skinny arms and legs. When Mira had said "her brother," Bryony had pictured the distant, lanky figure in the driveway. But now, as he unfolded himself from his hiding place, it became apparent that he was only slightly older than Bryony herself. His eyes were wide with panic, and his face was completely white.

"Mira!" he said. "You're in my delusion too. How splendid!" His voice went high-pitched with hysteria, with a whinnying kind of laugh at the end, and Bryony felt her chest begin to squeeze again, an echo of his panic. She pulled in a sharp breath and fixed her eyes on Mira, who looked a trifle annoyed, and not at all frightened anymore.

Mira tilted her head back, as if to ask for patience from the heavens, and she gave a heavy sigh before reaching down to poke her brother's arm. "Shhhh, Thompson. This isn't a delusion. At least, if it is, I'm having it too. Anyways, hush up. You're going to attract their attention if you start crying."

Immediately he was all scowls, very stern and unafraid. "I'm not crying, thank you very much. I simply don't wish to be strangled by a madwoman. And a *fictional* madwoman, at that. If I'm going to be murdered, I insist it be by someone who actually exists!"

"Picky, aren't you?" Mira reached out and snatched at her brother's sleeve, hauling him to his feet. "Come on. This place is full to the brim with paintings. It isn't a good idea to hide in here."

"I wasn't hiding," he said, indignant. "It was a tactical retreat."

"Mother isn't here." Mira wrinkled her nose at him. "You don't have to pretend to be brave."

"Let's go." Bryony was starting to get jumpy again. In the distance something was stirring, and there was a dull thump and shuffle from down the hall, growing louder and joined by other noises that carried through the museum.

They needed to leave—now.

Chapter Seven

nce they were through the doors Bryony slammed both shut behind them and slumped against the wooden surface, wishing there was a way to lock the building from the outside. It was fully dark now, and the roads were still empty. The lamps bathed the silent street in an eerie orange glow.

They made their way back toward the houses, not slowing down until they were around the corner and out of sight of the museum. Then Thompson stopped, bending over with his hands on his knees, his face pale in the dim light of the streetlamps. "What on earth is going on?"

"Perhaps it was a spell. Like a type of voodoo or something. Some cultures accept that as fact, you know." Mira looked positively delighted by the idea.

"No," Thompson shook his head. "Don't be silly. There's no such thing."

"And paintings don't kill people either, right?"

Bryony fixed her eyes straight ahead as the siblings bickered. She needed to figure out what to do next, and this wasn't helping.

"Mass hysteria spreading person to person. An epidemic of the mind. Perhaps there's mercury in the water supply. Hatters used to go mad from it all the time, you know." Thompson's hands fluttered like pale birds, brushing at his jacket, picking at his buttons. His face was white and pinched.

Mira rolled her eyes. "Of course you think it's a plague. You refused to take your mask off for an entire month after the last scare. How do you expect to be a doctor if you're too busy dying all the time?"

"Surgeon," he said primly. He straightened up and began walking again. "Not a doctor."

"Anyways, I think it's all rather exciting. It's just like what happened to Isabella Bird when a mob attacked her in China. Or when those cannibals in—"

"Must you relate everything back to that insufferable woman! And take that hat off; Mother would have apoplexy."

Bryony ignored them, keeping her head down as she walked. Her mind was fixed on the events of the last few hours, trying to puzzle out exactly what had started this. First, the strange rumors about her portrait subjects disappearing. Then her mirror acting strangely. And now this. And all of this had happened after she'd started painting real people.

Plus, the patron—her father—had wanted to meet her. Apparently he'd been so firm on the matter that Uncle Bernard hadn't been able to put him off any longer. Perhaps he'd needed to warn her about something. Had he somehow known this was going to happen?

"I think it was me." It just sort of came out.

"What?" Thompson stopped, and so did Mira.

Mira blinked, wide blue eyes fixed on Bryony's face, as if she were waiting for an explanation. The other girl had been paging through the book she'd dropped earlier, a small blue-and-white notebook with the words *Travel Notes* scrawled across the front. Now she stared, pen hovering over the page.

She wasn't about to write Bryony's confession down, was she?

"I think I must have triggered this somehow." Her stomach was full of sour milk; her lungs were filled with glass. "I think I started all of this, with my paintings."

The siblings both stared at her, and there was a long moment of silence, in which Thompson's brow creased, his eyes darting back and forth over her face, as if he were thinking very hard. Then his eyes went wide, and his hand shot out, his finger wavering in the air. "Paintings! You're—you—" he spluttered. "The newspaper. You were in the newspaper. You're Bryony Gray."

Bryony's heart sank. Thompson was very pale, and he was staring at her incredulously. Mira, on the other hand, seemed thrilled.

"You were in the newspaper? Capital! Wait until Mother hears we met a famous person."

Thompson was still spluttering. "But that's ridiculous. That article was preposterous. It can't possibly . . ." His words trailed off, and Bryony shrugged helplessly.

"It seems that it *can* possibly. Just look what's happening."

"But you didn't paint all of those." Mira gestured at the gallery behind them with her pen.

"No, but all of this started happening as soon as I started painting people. The last three people I painted seem to have vanished. And even I could see that the paintings were . . . strange." She shivered, thinking of the way the twins' painting had seemed so watchful, how their eyes had followed her every move.

"Highly unlikely that a single person caused this phenomenon." Thompson kept running his shaking hands down the fabric of his jacket, patting himself down as if to check that all of him was there. "Mass hysteria," he said, gesturing at their surroundings, "is the only explanation."

"I feel quite sure I'm not hysterical." Mira folded her arms over her chest and shook her head.

"You wouldn't know if you were," Thompson said patiently, as if he were explaining this to a very small child, "because you'd be too hysterical."

"Poppycock."

"Yes, well . . ." Thompson began fiddling with the buttons on his jacket, his fingers trembling. He darted small, quick glances about himself, as if he were afraid to look for too long in any one place. "Let's get out of here." He began walking and then stopped when nobody followed, his expression irritated. "Come along, Mira."

"Bryony, are you all right?"

She looked up to find Mira watching her. Even as distracted as she was, the intense way Mira studied her was enough to make her stomach flutter. It was as if the other girl could see past her flesh and bones to her thoughts inside. Perhaps she would see the longing Bryony felt when she thought of painting Mira. She glanced away, feeling foolish. "I've had a number of realizations."

She stood up straight. She should get back home, retrieve the book and the letter and pack some food before setting out. Do things properly.

"What sort of realizations?" Mira asked.

Bryony didn't answer, staring out at the jumble of cabs and carriages on the road, not one of them manned by a driver. "We must get to the countryside. Do either of you know how to drive?"

They didn't, and Thompson seemed rather put off by the question, demanding to know what sort of madcap plan she was contemplating.

Bryony ignored him. She began to march back down the street to the house. Some small part of her wanted to stay, to linger before she parted ways with Mira. But she couldn't pull other people into this mess, not when she had caused it. Besides, she wouldn't be alone. Once she found a way into the countryside, she would finally have her father. They'd figure this out together.

Her boots were so loud on the cobblestones that she didn't hear anything behind her until Thompson's voice cried out, "Mira, slow down. Where are you going?"

Bryony halted, turning around to find Mira hurrying after her. Her skirts were rucked up to her knees, her too-large boots clunking on the cobblestones. It was a wonder this girl, all arms and legs, hadn't fallen on her face yet.

"Are you coming with me then?" Surprise and hope mingled, and Bryony tried to suppress her look of delight when the other girl nodded. "Why? Aren't you afraid? I just said I probably caused all of this."

Mira clutched the blue notebook to her chest, her face thoughtful. "That depends. Are you going to paint me?"

What a question. She couldn't answer it the way she wanted to, couldn't admit that she had thought about painting Mira. Because that would be almost as good as a threat, wouldn't it?

"No, I won't paint you."

"Then I've nothing to worry about."

Thompson caught up to them at last, stopping just short of running into his sister. He leaned forward, hands on his knees, panting. His features were the color of ripe tomatoes. "I say, Mira, that's not on."

"Someone's got to document this." Mira flapped the notebook at him, her face glowing. "This could be some kind of important discovery! History in the making, Thompson. This is just like when Mary Kingsley discovered those exotic fish in—"

"It's *nothing* like any of your ridiculous books!" Thompson threw his hands up. "Can you imagine what Mother would say about us taking off with a complete stranger?"

Mira grinned at him. "I'm sure she'll write us lovely obituaries if this girl murders us."

"That's not the slightest bit funny!" He lowered his voice to a shaky whisper, eyes darting to Bryony's face before looking away. "She's probably a bit mad, it isn't—"

"I'm not mad," Bryony said crossly, "or deaf, for that matter. I can hear you."

Thompson ignored her entirely, turning to Mira with a pleading look, palms in the air. "We have to go home and stay there, lock all the doors, board up the windows."

Bryony scowled at him. He was going to drag Mira away from her. He wanted to lock Mira up and throw away the key, and all the while he would tell her it was for her own good. He and Aunt Gertrude would get along splendidly.

"They're in Hertfordshire for two more days still. Mother will never know." She turned to Bryony and added, "Coroners' conference. I'm rather hoping it's enough to bore them to death."

"Absolutely not! I'm putting my foot down." Thompson actually looked like he was about to stomp his foot, but instead he straightened his shoulders and jutted his chin out. "We can't be out here. I'm older, so you've got to listen to me. Mother said."

Mira reached out and poked him in the shoulder, eyes sparkling. "Don't be such a stick in the mud. Mother isn't here, and this is our chance for a real-life exploration. And besides, you're only a year older than me. Come off it, Thompy."

"But *why?*" Thompson's shoulders slumped, and he ran his hands through his hair, worrying it until it stuck up wildly. "Why can't we just go home? And don't call me that, you know it irks me."

"I need to record all of this for my book." Mira patted her pockets with one hand, forehead creased. "Hold on, where did I put that pen?"

"For God's sake, Mira! Life isn't one of your adventure

stories. It's actually dangerous out there." He hesitated, then reached out and made a half-hearted attempt to snatch the blue notebook. When Mira danced back and scowled at him, he folded his arms over his chest. "Do behave! Do you want me to tell Mother about those ridiculous explorer books you've got hidden about your room?"

Mira's mouth dropped open, and Thompson looked instantly guilty. "You know I didn't mean that, not really. But you're *pushing* her lately. Sneaking around all the time and eating your food with the wrong utensils just to make her angry. Honestly, when you hacked all your hair off before Sir Albert's dinner party, I thought it was the academy for *sure*. I was certain it was all over."

"But it wasn't." Mira tried to give him another cheerful smile, but it wobbled a little bit at one side.

"My point is, we don't need another disaster waiting for her when she gets home. This is too dangerous."

Bryony snorted. "So now you've decided it's not safe. A little while ago this was all a hallucination."

Thompson glared at her. "I'm not about to let her run off with *you*." He put a protective hand on Mira's shoulder, which she promptly shrugged off. "Your family is trouble. The newspaper got one thing right: you lot are strange. I've heard about your uncle and aunt. How they keep you locked in the attic because you're unsta—"

"I am not *unstable*." Bryony's shout rang out so loudly in the silence that a flock of pigeons was startled from the roof of the museum, rising up into the air all at once with a thunderous flapping of wings.

They all jumped, and no one said anything for a few seconds. Bryony's breath hitched, and she couldn't look at Mira. What if she believed Thompson?

She shook her head, as if she could dislodge the thought. This was ridiculous; she couldn't get involved in other families' problems. There was no time. She had no idea if this thing had spread to other museums, or all of the nearby houses. It could be that every mirror and painting within a hundred yards of her was bent on murder. She couldn't be sure. All she knew was that it had to be stopped. That she'd be the one to stop it seemed only reasonable, given that she'd started it. She had to find her father. But first things first. As much as she disliked the idea of going back to the attic, she had to be sensible about this. She needed to pack a bag to take with her.

Bryony whirled on Thompson, who took a step back, eyes wide. "Oh, do relax," she said peevishly. "Look, there's no telling how far this thing has spread. Just remember to get rid of all your paintings." She started to hurry away, up the short drive that led to the great dark mansion, and the letter and book under the floorboards.

One last thought occurred to her as she took the steps two at a time, and she turned to call over her shoulder at the siblings, who were still standing in the middle of the street staring dumbly after her. "Oh, and be careful around mirrors, will you? Maybe cover them when you get home? They seem to have a mind of their own lately. I'm not sure what they're after, but I expect it isn't anything pleasant."

And with that, Bryony slammed the door shut.

Chapter Eight

The house was completely silent. She walked through, turning lights on to chase away the eerie dimness of the night. She'd been hoping against hope that Uncle Bernard might be there, that he had simply gone out to get more of the blackberry wine he loved so much. But the back door to the kitchen was wide open. The last remaining servant had plucked up the courage to flee.

After establishing that nobody was home, she covered all the mirrors, yanking bedsheets off all the beds in the house and liberating the dining room table of its lacy white cloth. She ran from room to room making sure each mirror was draped with something, careful to keep her eyes averted from every reflection, even covering the kettle in the kitchen. By the time everything was done, she was panting, and she mopped at her brow with one of the remaining pillowcases. Aunt Gertrude would have had a conniption.

She dropped the pillowcase and proceeded up to the attic, going as quietly as she could. There was probably no cause for the tension she was feeling; the whole house seemed empty. The monstrous Lady Abney wouldn't have come back, would she?

Bryony paused at the top of the stairs, leaning forward to peer around the doorway. The attic was silent and dim, and when her eyes finally adjusted, a pang of shock went through her. The attic was even messier than before—like it had when Aunt Gertrude ripped it apart looking for the letter. All the drawers of the furniture had been opened, the contents dumped on the floor. The shelf near her bed had been tipped over, and her textbooks—her precious art books!—were strewn across the floorboards, their pages crumpled.

There was a crunch as she stepped forward, and she looked down to see a dusty copy of *Hamlet*. The book had landed open, and she stooped down and picked it up, feeling a jolt of anger when she saw the torn pages. It hadn't been her favorite book, but she'd liked the poetic sound of the words when she read them aloud, and the bits about the ghost.

Hand over her mouth, she stared around the rest of the attic. All of her books had been emptied off the shelves and dumped here and there, and pages trailed across the dusty floorboards like crumpled autumn leaves.

Next, her gaze fell on the big empty fireplace, and then on the space above it. A patch of wall that seemed strangely empty. What had been in that spot?

The answer hit her in the next second, along with a flash of panic.

There it was, propped up beside the fireplace, the big

glass mirror with the scrolling iron frame. And her reflection, square in the middle.

Blast! She hurried forward, panicked, nearly tripping over her own feet. Yanking open the linen trunk, she snatched up the first piece of fabric she saw. It unfurled into a long white tablecloth with a *snap*, sending up a cloud of dust. Fighting back a sneeze, she turned back to the mirror.

Her reflection stared back, holding the same sheet, smiling at her in a very unpleasant fashion.

"Oh no you *don't*." She launched herself forward, sheet thrust out before her. It flapped in her face as she ran. With her vision partly obscured, she could only glimpse a bit of her reflection, but enough to see that it was running toward her with the upraised sheet, mouth open in a silent scream of triumph.

"No!" She leapt the last few feet, thrusting the sheet out, smashing her knees on the fireplace. Pain shot up both legs. Just before the white sheet fell, she caught a final glimpse of her reflection, face contorted with fury, hands stretched out toward her. Then it was over. The sheet settled over the mirror and stayed there.

Bryony shivered and turned away, glancing around the room to make sure there were no other reflective surfaces. It would be just like her to get sucked dry by a mirrored jewelry box or something. There didn't seem to be any more murderous reflections in the near vicinity, so she took the chance to look around more thoroughly.

Someone had definitely been here, and they'd been looking for something, carelessly rooting through her things and tossing them aside. But why would anyone do that when she'd already escaped the attic? Her aunt and uncle would have no reason to—and besides, they were nowhere to be seen.

One thing was certain: whoever had done it was long gone. But before they went, they'd trashed the place, even rifling through the things on her easel. She spotted her favorite paintbrush—the one with the perfectly smooth dark-wood handle—lying on the floorboards, half under an upturned side table. She took a deep breath and crouched down to pick it up, tucking it carefully behind her ear.

Anger had been building up, prickling over her skin like hundreds of tiny needles at the thought of a stranger going through her things, but now a thought came along that changed the anger to panic. What if they'd discovered the hiding place beneath the floorboards and spirited away the book and the letter inside?

One, two, three giant steps from the fireplace to the loose floorboards. She sat down and worked her fingers into the tiny notch, slowly pulling up the board. It seemed to take forever, and shudders of dread kept running down her spine. She half expected to find it empty, nothing but a dusty space beneath the floor.

At last her trembling fingers succeeded in prying up the board.

The contents of the shallow nook were in shadow, but she knew exactly where everything was. There was a tin of chocolate pastries, leftovers from Uncle Bernard's fit of generosity. Right next to that was a bag of hard candy she'd been saving. And nestled safely between the two was the book.

A rush of relief surged through her as she reached out and seized it. She balanced it across both knees, handling it reverently. Bryony took a deep breath and clutched the book to her chest before standing up to survey the room once more. Out the window, she could see the warm glow of yellow light shining through the windows of the neighboring house. Mira and Thompson must be inside, probably talking about the events of the day together. Perhaps they were scared, but at least they had one another.

A pang of loneliness stole her breath away. If only Mira *had* come with her, she wouldn't be in this great big house all alone, struggling to figure out what to do next. It was too much, and she found herself overcome for a moment, blinking back tears, clutching the book so tightly she could feel her nails biting into the leather cover.

She eased her grip but did not let go. It was no use falling to pieces; it wouldn't help anyone. It was late. She was tired and confused and today had been exhausting. She wouldn't figure anything out in this state.

Bryony shuffled over to her little cot in the corner of the attic and slid between the sheets, not bothering to undress. She kept hold of the book, letting the solid weight and the warmth of the leather cover comfort her. The book was a promise. A promise that someone out there cared. That her patron would know what to do. In fact, he was probably looking for her now. The more she thought about it, the more it made sense. He would come calling in the morning, probably, now that her uncle and aunt were out of the way.

At this, a wave of relief went through her and she relaxed into the mattress, finally shutting her eyes. Still clutching the old book to her chest, she slid into a deep, dreamless sleep.

Chapter Nine

It was the light that woke her. It filtered in through the dusty attic window, a shaft of sunlight that seemed to split the foggy morning with the specific purpose of landing in her left eye. Bryony blinked awake. Groaning, she draped an arm over her face.

Then the events of yesterday flooded back in one great wave, and she sat up with a gasp. Her arms were empty. Where was the book?

There. It was on the mattress where she'd been lying, wedged halfway under her flat pillow. Horrified to find she'd been sleeping on it, Bryony snatched it up and balanced it on one knee.

Now that it was morning, her thoughts about the patron finding her seemed a little silly. Who knew how far away his house in the country was. He might have no idea her uncle and aunt were gone.

Carefully, she flipped the front cover open, searching the inside flap for any hint of where the book came from. During her previous inspections of it, she hadn't so much been searching for who her patron was but what he was like. This time, instead of poring over the contents, she inspected the inside covers. If only there was a name written somewhere, perhaps even an address for a "return to owner."

But of course, there was nothing; she knew that already. She sighed and pulled the letter out, unfolding it carefully, studying the words written in curling, sloping handwriting. They were still the same, of course. She wouldn't get any more out of the letter from just sitting here: she had to go to the country and find her patron.

First, she hurried over to the desk, shuffling through her papers until she found what she was looking for, a map of London, which she slipped into an old shoulder bag she'd found for her escape. Next, she walked to the window and peered out again, but there were only the still, dark forms of empty carriages and buggies. No one in sight. Dejected, she made her way to the spot beside the floorboards.

As if to echo her frustration, her stomach began to growl. It was breakfast time, and she'd missed dinner last night in all the chaos. She leaned forward, prying the lid off the tin, grabbing one of the sweet cakes. The frosting was sweet on her tongue. It was slightly stale from its week in the attic, and it was certainly strange to eat cake for breakfast, but still, it was delicious.

Perhaps it was because of how utterly engrossing the sweet cake was, but for whatever reason, she didn't hear anything until someone exclaimed, "Are you eating *cake* at a time like this?"

She jerked upright. Thompson was standing in the attic

doorway, dark brows drawn together, his red mouth curling down. The very picture of disapproval.

She meant to say, "What are you doing here?" but it came out slightly garbled, and punctuated by a spray of chocolate crumbs.

Thompson gave her a despairing look, and then a heart-shaped face appeared over his shoulder, blue eyes blinking quizzically around at the attic. She was wearing the same white pith helmet and belt today, but her dress was a deep-purple silk, which set off her dark hair.

Mira. Bryony smiled at her.

"You have chocolate in your teeth," Mira said.

She snapped her mouth shut and looked very hard at the book in her lap, cheeks burning. "Why did you two come back?" she mumbled. Thompson began to stammer something, and when she glanced up at him he was every bit as red-faced as she was.

"Well, I-I've decided not to . . . that is—"

"You were right about the mirrors. We missed covering one in the parlor last night and it nearly got Thompson this morning. He was walking right toward it." Mira walked farther into the attic, eyes still fixed on Bryony's face, and Bryony touched her lips self-consciously. Was she covered in chocolate icing? How humiliating.

"Lucky I had the dust cover from the couch at hand. But we thought we should come see you." Mira was looking around the attic now, which wasn't much better. The little cot in the corner was unmade, the sheets in a twisted clump in the middle, books spread out over the pillow. It was embarrassingly obvious that Bryony lived up here. What must Mira be thinking right now?

"Horrifying." Thompson's voice wavered, distress evident on his face. "Someone's been through our house. Things were knocked over and there was paint on the walls." He glared at Mira. "*Someone* left the door unlocked."

"I'd rather be burgled than attacked by my own reflection," Mira said, as if this was somehow a positive spin on things.

"Yes, well. Reflections acting of their own accord are just as bad. Hideously irregular." Thompson shuddered.

"His reflection wanted him to come over to the mirror," Mira added.

"Yes, they all seem to want that." Bryony drummed her fingers on the leather book. Best to return to the business at hand. This was no time to be blushing over what some stranger thought of her. "I don't suggest it."

"Well," Thompson smoothed one hand down his jacket and cleared his throat. "I, um, decided that you seem to know more about this sort of thing. So, ah—"

"So he shrieked like a schoolgirl and ran all the way here." One corner of Mira's mouth twitched, and she pressed her lips together.

"I did not *shriek*," Thompson sputtered. "I—it was merely a noise of . . . of warning." He brightened. "Like a battle cry."

Mira rolled her eyes and sank down onto the floor beside Bryony, so close their knees were nearly touching. Their skirts pooled out around them, fabric overlapping in blue and purple. The objects attached to Mira's belt made clunking sounds on the floor as she settled in.

Bryony stared at a brass telescope near the girl's left hip.

"What have you got there, something to break the spell?" Mira asked.

Bryony tightened her grip on the book. "It's not a spell."

Mira only shrugged, staring pointedly at the book.

"My patron left me the book. It's my map, of sorts. I mean, this is." She held the letter up between two fingers, but when Mira looked at it expectantly she felt such an intense urge to show it to her that she put it carefully into her pocket instead, tucking it away. She liked Mira very much, and it would be so nice to have someone else to talk to about the letter, but it was possible the other girl would laugh at her, or tell her she was being foolish.

"You said earlier that you needed a ride into the countryside." Mira leaned back and tilted her head to one side. "What's in the countryside?"

Probably there was no harm in explaining. "I have to find my patron. I believe he may have tried to warn me about this. I'm hoping he knows something." She couldn't bring herself to say what she truly hoped: that her patron was secretly her father. Saying it out loud seemed far too daring.

Thompson paced back and forth, picking his way over jumbles of boxes and bags of clothing, still raking his fingers through his hair. "The sooner you resolve this madness the better. Where does this chap live?"

"I . . . in a house in the countryside. I expect I'll know it once I see it." Her hand started to drift up to her pocket and the letter, almost of its own accord, and she forced it down.

Thompson paused in his pacing to stare. "But . . . you've been there before, right?" When she hesitated, he threw up his hands. "The countryside is massive! There are thousands of houses. You've never been there! You clearly don't have the address! Do you know anything useful at all?"

Bryony tightened her grip on the book. Tears prickled the backs of her eyes and anger burned through her. It would have been easy enough to convince herself that it was all directed at Thompson, but she wasn't entirely sure if that was true. Some of it, perhaps, was pointed inward. Because he was right. She'd behaved like a foolish little girl, dreaming she'd find the house based on three lines of description. "I'll wager I know more than you know about things, you big stupid—"

"I didn't even mean it that way. You're behaving like a child."

Mira snapped upright, her blue eyes glittering as she scowled at her brother. "You be quiet, Thompson. She isn't me. You can't speak to her that way."

To Bryony's surprise, Thompson actually went quiet, but his mouth worked for several seconds afterward, as if he wanted to say something but then thought better of it. Then he muttered something in the direction of his shoes and stalked off, making his way over to the window.

That was it. She absolutely didn't like Thompson. It wasn't charitable to wish the painting of the shepherdess had got him, and she was trying hard not to. But she and Mira should be going to find the patron together. Maybe they'd discover it was her father after all, and together they'd stop the chaos and live happily ever after.

"He tries to hold you back all the time, doesn't he?" She darted a look at Thompson, who was now leaning his elbows on the windowsill.

Mira's eyes were on the book again, and she reached out and smoothed her fingertips over the cover. Then, sliding her fingers underneath, she took it gently, and Bryony had to resist the urge to jerk it back out of her hands. For a moment Mira only blinked down at the book, as if she were thinking very hard. Then she said, "He's frightfully nervous, that's all. He's that way about everything, all the time."

"You're not." Bryony gave Mira a sidelong glance. The other girl's face was smooth and calm, though her mouth turned down slightly at the corners. "You're brave."

Some emotion flashed across Mira's face, there and gone so fast that Bryony couldn't be sure what it was. "I'm not that brave." Her voice was tight.

Bryony shifted, not sure what to think. "What I mean is, doesn't it make you mad to have family try to . . . I don't know . . . contain you?"

Mira began to leaf through the book, and Bryony's fingers twitched a little bit. She'd grown so used to keeping it hidden.

It seemed as if Mira wouldn't answer, but then she exhaled and said, "Father hasn't said a full sentence to me since my thirteenth birthday." She looked up, blue eyes on Bryony's face and added, "That was four months ago, by the way. I sneak down to spy on him while he works. Do you know, I sometimes find him muttering away to the bodies? He'll talk to them but not me. Apparently, they have better conversations, he and these dead people."

Bryony stared at her, not entirely sure what to say.

"Mother is far worse. That's why I have to hide my explorer books from her. She took away the first one I ever bought. Said it wasn't fitting reading material for a lady." Mira's face flushed slightly, two red spots appearing high on her cheekbones. "She's desperate to marry me off to Sir Albert Hawtrey." She darted a sideways look at Bryony. "If you're not sure what to think of Sir Albert, just picture a breakfast sausage in a silk waistcoat and top hat. He's horrible, but he's some distant relation to royalty, so Mother's got the wedding all planned out."

"That sounds awful." It was really the only appropriate thing to say.

Mira nodded solemnly. "So you can see why Thompson is the only member of my family I tolerate."

A thought occurred to Bryony, and she glanced over her shoulder to make sure Thompson was still by the window. "What's the academy? He mentioned it before."

Mira's face went dark. "Oh, he means *Flappy*. Florence Le Angle's Preparatory of Proper Etiquette. Mother keeps threatening to send me off each time I do something outrageous."

Bryony's eyes went wide. "It sounds ghastly."

"It is. I've heard rumors." Mira pursed her lips, reaching up to touch her hair. "She nearly sent me after the hair incident. It was worth it, though, just for the look on sausage-boy's face. He was utterly disgusted. Anyway, Thompson managed to talk Mother out of it."

Footsteps made them both jump, and then Thompson was standing over them, as if he'd been summoned by his name. Bryony flushed guiltily. Hopefully he hadn't heard any of that.

"Do you know his name?"

Bryony stared for a second before she realized he was talking about her patron. "My uncle and aunt wouldn't tell me." She dropped her chin in her hands, miserable, refusing to look up at Thompson as he stood there. Of course he thought she was a child, maybe even addled. She had acted like it. What kind of plan had "going into the countryside" been? A terrible one, no plan at all, was the answer.

" Maybe the book has a clue." Mira laid it out in her lap. "It is handmade, isn't it?"

"I . . . think so?" She chewed her lower lip. What was Mira up to?

"Now may not be the best time to discuss book collections," Thompson said witheringly.

Mira ignored him. She opened the back cover of the book and slid one thumb along the leather flap. Then she dug her nail into the edge and pushed, and Bryony gasped as the leather came up with the sticky sound of dried glue ripping. "What did you do that for?"

Mira handed her the book, placing it carefully in her lap. "Pull it back and look."

Bryony's hands shook slightly as she lifted the leather flap. There, on the inside of the board, was a name written in black ink.

Constantine.

"Sometimes the bookbinder will leave his signature." Mira sat back, smiling. "Luckily, this one did."

For a moment, Bryony could only stare at the black ink in surprise. All the times she'd flipped through the book, searching for some sort of clue, and here it was. Pulling that flap up never would have occurred to her. If only her precious textbooks had facts about book binding in them!

"Brilliant! Good thinking on that one." Thompson's voice was right next to Bryony's ear, and she jumped, shooting him an irritated look.

"Don't *crowd* so."

He looked affronted, but he backed away a step, muttering to himself. "Blimey, you're an odd duck."

She ignored that. "Mira, you know about old books?"

"A little."

"She spends half her time hunting through used bookstores. She practically lives at Old Man Fiddick's shop down the street," Thompson said.

"Mostly because Mother refuses to go in there to haul me out. She hates Mr. Fiddick." Mira's amused expression went sour as she stared down at the book. "She thinks women don't need to read."

Thompson pressed his lips together, shooting a sideways look at his sister. "Yes, well, regardless of her opinion on the matter, I'd say it came in handy just now."

Bryony traced her thumb over the edge of the leather flap, careful not to touch the ink, though that was probably silly; it was long dry. "Could you find out who this man is?"

"Likely Mr. Fiddick will know him, if he's a bookbinder." Mira got to her feet, dusting off her skirts. Then she offered Bryony a hand.

Carefully, Bryony closed the book and tucked it under her arm. She was sure her face was red as she clasped Mira's outstretched hand. "Can you tell me how to get there?"

"I'll show you." Mira's eyes sparkled. "I'm coming with you."

"I beg your pardon?" Thompson sat up straight. "We have no idea what's out there right now. The streets may not be safe."

Not *this* again. Bryony glared at him. She badly wanted Mira to come with her, and her brother was going to ruin everything. "Your house is more dangerous than the streets are right now. The streets don't have mirrors and paintings."

"She's right, we can't go home," Mira added. "You know she's right, Thompson."

"You're a bad influence." Thompson scowled at Bryony, crossing his arms over his chest.

"And you're a chicken." She gave him what she hoped was an equally scathing look.

There was a moment of silence in which Thompson frowned, glancing over at Mira. What followed was some sort of strange, silent argument. The siblings seemed to be disagreeing on the matter, but they managed to do it without saying anything at all, simply tilting their heads and frowning. Thompson shaking his head. Mira shrugging and gesturing at him. It was a little baffling to watch, and she pressed her fingernails into her palms and clamped her mouth shut to avoid interrupting them. Why couldn't *she* have this secret language with someone? Perhaps she could make one up and share it with Mira.

That way they could communicate without speaking.

Finally Thompson turned to Bryony, his expression cross. "Yes, all right," he said. "So we go to Mr. Fiddick's shop, track down this bookbinder fellow, who tells us where this patron is, who solves the problem of the killer paintings, and we all get home in time for mid-afternoon tea. Is that the general idea?"

Bryony was sensing a hint of sarcasm. "Unless you have a better suggestion."

A muscle in Thompson's jaw twitched, and he stared hard at Mira for a few seconds before nodding slowly. "I . . . suppose the plan is logical enough."

Mira looked startled, and then she smiled hugely and gave Thompson a good-natured punch in the shoulder. "Smashing! I knew you'd come around, darling."

Thompson just winced and rubbed the assaulted limb, but his mouth lifted slightly at one corner. "Well, shall we go then?"

Bryony dusted off her skirts. "Is the shop within walking distance?"

When Mira nodded, Bryony turned and led the way down the attic stairs. This time, before walking out the door, she retrieved her coat and fished the spare house key out from under the stone planter on the front stoop. She might be off to save London from being overrun by murderous paintings, but she wasn't in such a hurry as to forget all sense of propriety.

"All right." She straightened her shoulders and tucked the key into her bag before looping the strap over her shoulder and turning to Mira. "Lead the way."

They'd walked several blocks before they began to see people again. But the farther they got from the museum, the more people were out and about. When they turned the corner onto Oxford Street, Mira, who'd been marching forward with confidence up until that point, slowed to a halt.

"Oh, my. This is rather unexpected."

Bryony could only stare, having never seen so many people in one place before.

People crowded the street in groups—there had to be at least a hundred of them!—and conversation buzzed in the air around them like swarms of angry bees. Everyone was speaking in low voices and gesturing over their shoulders in the direction from which the children had just come. Occasionally, an annoyed shout would rise above the buzz—cries of "That's ridiculous" and "Just rumors!"— but mostly people seemed to be looking about fearfully, faces white, eyes darting this way and that.

"So, the paintings haven't been this way yet." Thompson kept looking up and down the road, his brow furrowed. "They must be in another part of the city. They could be anywhere."

Mira bit at her thumbnail. "You're right. I should have brought my net." When Thompson and Bryony both stared at her, she shrugged. "You know, to catch one."

"Where did you get a net from?" Thompson sputtered.

"Last week at the flea market, when Mother was busy looking at hats." Mira winked at him and patted her leather belt. "For wild game. You know, safaris and such."

"Blimey. Mother might as well give up on finding you a husband. Unless she wants to send you after one with a bloody *net*." Thompson rubbed his eyebrow with a gusty sigh, and Mira laughed.

"No thank you. If I caught a husband, I should only put it back right away."

"Right, you two. Concentrate." Bryony nudged Mira, and they both turned back to stare at the obstacle in front of them.

The crowd stretched all the way down the street with no end in sight. Bryony stood on her tiptoes and squinted, trying to see over people's heads. Oxford Street was incredibly long and narrow, zigzagging this way and that until the jagged edges of shops and public houses ahead disappeared into the fog.

Thompson's eyes were wide. "We'll never make it through all this."

"Yes, we will. They'll move for us. Watch." Mira plunged forward, wiggling her way between people, effectively clearing a path with loud *excuse me*'s and, *pardon me*'s as she elbowed her way through. Bryony was surprised to find that she was right: people looked down at them, startled, and then moved out of the way as they pushed past.

They went by the window of a tea shop, the hanging sign swinging gently on its chains as if it, too, were disturbed by all the commotion. Inside the shop a group of lacy women and men dressed in neat black overcoats and bowler hats were arguing with the owner. The argument seemed to be over the fact that they were *not leaving*, as far as Bryony could hear. The shops were closing early, perhaps due to the rumors.

There were several carriages parked in the road, and one of the drivers was arguing with the crowd.

"I *have* to go that way, I've got deliveries!"

Bryony and the others passed a single police officer, his face slightly flushed, his helmet crooked on his head. He was surrounded by a growing crowd, all of whom were trying to tell him what they'd seen. One fellow, red-faced with excitement, waved his arms as he spoke. "Just got back from your station. They didn't believe me!"

"I saw it too," another man interjected. "I had to flee the house! Portrait of me late wife knocked me flat on me rump! She was a real pill when she was alive, but I didn't expect that."

Thompson stopped so suddenly that Bryony nearly ran into him. "Should we tell him about the museum? The police should know where this all started." He blinked rapidly, and a muscle in his jaw twitched.

Bryony chewed the inside of her cheek, her mind working furiously. The officer would ask questions, and she would be forced to give her name. Someone would recognize it and put two and two together: all the strange rumors about her and her paintings. The events happening right now.

"We can't," she said finally. "He'll ask questions. Do you know how long that will take? We have to find my patron and stop this madness now, before more people end up like that duke fellow at the museum. Besides, they probably already know *something* is going on." She waved one hand at the crowd.

Thompson gaped at her. "But shouldn't we warn them about the museum in particular? That place is a death trap. It's probably still crawling with paintings."

Guilt began eating away at her stomach. She hadn't so much as thought about what might happen if anyone walked into that place. They would scarcely know what to make of the situation. But she couldn't go back there, not with all these people standing around looking for someone to point fingers at. Thankfully, there hadn't been any picture of her in the newspaper, but it wouldn't be long before someone remembered the article or mentioned something about "that strange Gray girl" and the witch hunt would start.

"Look, the shop is just there." Mira indicated a tiny shop a few feet away, a small brick building wedged between two larger ones. Sure enough, there was a hanging sign in the shape of an open book above the window. "Thompson, you tell the police officer what we saw while we pop in. We'll meet on the front steps after, all right?" She hooked an arm through Bryony's and began to steer them toward the bookstore.

"Well . . . but what do I say?" Thompson turned after them, hand wavering in the air. "Hold on, what do I tell them—"

"Just tell them about the museum, how it's spreading," Bryony called over her shoulder. Then Mira was tugging her around, and the two of them hurried toward the bookstore.

Chapter Ten

Mr. Fiddick's bookshop was wedged between a women's hat shop and a "purveyor of fine antiques."

The latter, Bryony observed, just looked like an assortment of old junk.

Thankfully the crowd had thinned out in front of the shops—apparently no one had any use for books in the current crisis—so it didn't seem likely they'd have any problem getting in to see the owner.

"He's usually in on Wednesdays, unless it's lunchtime. There," Mira said, and her face lit up. "The open sign is up, so he must be in."

"Good." Bryony pushed on the door, which creaked inward with a ponderous groan of rusty hinges. Instantly she was surrounded by the musty but not unpleasant smell of very old books, and the faint scent of pipe smoke. The store did not appear to be laid out in any organized fashion. It seemed shelves had been dragged in and left wherever they ended up. There were shelves in the center of the room, impeding foot traffic, and even a pair that had been pushed so close together that customers would have to wedge themselves in between if they wanted one of the books. To add to the chaos, there was such a great quantity of books that some appeared to be escaping the shelves. There were stacks in the corners of the store and on all the windowsills. Even piled up in front of the desk, as if Mr. Fiddick had built himself a fortress of literature.

The man himself was nowhere in sight, so Bryony walked into the stacks, mouth open wide as she looked around. There'd been a shelf full of books in her attic, but nothing even close to this. Mira followed her until they'd reached the center of the shop. The girl's eyes were wide, her expression dreamy. "Isn't this place wonderful? How many adventures do you think there are in this one room?"

Bryony would have loved to stay here, just the two of them, and browse the shelves, but she forced herself to turn away. "We should find Mr. Fiddick."

"He's probably back here somewhere."

Bryony followed Mira deeper into the stacks until they reached a second desk all the way in the back corner. This desk was much neater than the one at the front, with only a few dusty books stacked up in the middle. Above it was an enormous, rectangular painting in a gilt frame. It showed a fleet of sailing ships on calm blue waters, clouds of cannon smoke billowing up between the wooden hulls. In the right-hand corner a tiny rowboat was in peril, the passengers throwing up their hands as the boat slowly went under. The colors were heart-stoppingly beautiful: white clouds of smoke against a mass of periwinkle-blue water, cunningly painted to reflect the ships between the frothy whitecaps of the waves.

"Alexey Bogolyubov," she breathed. "Eighteen fifty-three."

"It's beautiful." Mira tilted her head to look up at it. "Also, not alive and trying to murder us, which makes it particularly nice."

Bryony frowned, taking a step closer. Mira was right. She half expected to see the waves ripple, or the ship rock back and forth, but nothing moved. A memory of the pink trail smeared over the portraits in the museum came back to her, and the way the shepherdess had dragged her crook across them. She had a hunch about that, and this practically confirmed it. "They didn't get to this one. They didn't spread it here yet."

"I'm glad," Mira said.

"It's called *The Battle of Athos*." Bryony couldn't tear her eyes from the canvas. "It's a masterpiece."

"Indeed it is," a deep voice said from behind them. "Few good things come of such unstable times, but great artwork is one of them."

Bryony whirled around. There was a very old, grizzled man in a faded tweed jacket leaning over the desk. Mira cleared her throat politely.

"Hello, Mr. Fiddick. I hope you don't mind, but we've come with a favor to ask you." Mira pushed the brim of her helmet up and gave him a wide smile.

"What's this, another of your madcap adventures? Does it have anything to do with the crowd outside my store?" Mr. Fiddick shoved his little round spectacles farther up his nose. He peered nearsightedly at Bryony. "Ah, you've brought a friend, my dear. Is she an explorer too?"

His tone was patronizing, and Bryony glanced over at Mira, startled.

Mira's smile stayed in place, though Bryony thought it looked a little strained. "Yes, this is Bryony Gray. She's part of the favor, actually. And yes, it does have something to do with the crowds. Bryony would like to find the man who made her book."

"I would ask what exactly a book has to do with a great load of people running about in front of my store, but . . ."

Bryony suddenly found herself under the dark-eyed scrutiny of Mr. Fiddick, who seemed to be examining the very depths of her soul. Or at least he was very focused. "I believe," he said softly, "I can hazard a guess."

She had to repress the urge to squirm. "Uh, nice to make your acquaintance . . . sir."

"Bryony Gray," Mr. Fiddick said, and his face was stern. "Yes, I've met your uncle. Came in here to buy textbooks a time or two. I heard all about you."

Her stomach sank, but all that Mr. Fiddick said next was, "Well, come on then, let's see the book."

She undid the clasp on the front of her bag and carefully drew the book out.

Mr. Fiddick's eyes lit up when he saw the leather cover, glittering with a light that made her want to shove the book straight back into the bag. But it was too late. The old man was already holding out his hand for it, and Mira was watching expectantly.

There was no way to find out who this Constantine was without his help.

Reluctantly she held out the book, and Mr. Fiddick took it. As he did, his hands shook slightly.

"What is it?" Bryony said. "Is it famous?"

Mr. Fiddick grunted, nodding sharply. He ran one hand over the front cover. "It's a Constantine original. No two are alike, and as a general rule the man doesn't make them anymore." He set the book down on the table, gently turning the pages, face full of reverence. "Ah, I had one once. You wouldn't believe what it sold for."

Bryony's fingers twitched. The urge to snatch the book back was nearly overwhelming. But at least she knew one thing now: if this Constantine chap had custom-made the book for her patron, then he would definitely remember his name. It was a start.

"Where can we find Constantine?" she said eagerly.

"Find him?" Mr. Fiddick stared at her, eyes round and owlish behind his glasses. Then he let out a bark of laughter and shut the book with a snap. "My dear girl, one does not *find* Charlie Constantine."

Bryony narrowed her eyes at the man. She didn't find this nearly as amusing as he seemed to. "Why on earth not?"

Mr. Fiddick's expression went sober. "Because nine times out of ten the man doesn't wish to be found. A few years ago he retreated from society, just as his bindings were becoming popular. His books were selling like hotcakes."

"What is it, anyway?" Mira reached out to touch the leather cover, tracing the symbol on the front with her fingertip. Her eyes sparkled. "Does it contain the ancient secrets of a lost civilization?"

"It's a grimoire." Mr. Fiddick smiled, which was rather unpleasant, since it revealed crooked teeth stained yellow with tobacco. "They're fake spell books. Very popular a while back. Books about magic and curses and potions. People loved them. They'd get together and have these ridiculous séances. Chanting nonsense from a book made it seem more realistic."

"A spell book." Bryony stared down at the book. It was a little like seeing it through new eyes. She'd thought her father had collected rare books, but . . . was it possible he had fancied himself some sort of seer? Perhaps that was why no one in the family ever talked about him. "But, none of it's real . . . ?"

"Of course not." Mr. Fiddick gave her another penetrating look, one that made Bryony feel as though she'd swallowed a brick. "There are no supernatural events, no black magic, no such thing as witches. People just love a frightening story. Isn't that right, Ms. Gray?"

Bryony stared at him. Her face began to heat up. "Yes, I suppose you're right." She snatched the book from the counter and returned it to her shoulder bag. As soon as its reassuring weight was back in place, she felt relief wash through her.

She hadn't believed in magic before, but if it wasn't magic that had made her paintings come alive, then what was it?

When she looked up, Mr. Fiddick was still staring, which was enough to convince her it was time to leave. "Thank you for your time, Mr. Fiddick." Bryony turned and started for the door. "That was very informative."

Mira hesitated for a moment, and then followed Bryony. "Yes, thank you very much."

Mr. Fiddick took off his spectacles and began cleaning them with a faded blue cloth. He didn't answer, or even look up, but just as Bryony was about to round the corner he said, "You're still going to look for him, aren't you?"

She turned around. The old man was still intent on his glasses.

"You don't know this yet, Mr. Fiddick, but something very nasty is headed this way. I have to at least try to stop it."

He sighed. "I was worried it might be something like that." Replacing his glasses on the bridge of his nose, he finally looked at them again. "I've been told that he frequents the tearoom at Mivart's Hotel over on Brook Street these days. If you're foolish enough to waste your time looking for him, that would be a good place to start."

Mira's face lit up. "Thank you, that's very helpful."

The old man frowned. "Yes, well, I'd warn you about getting tangled up with the Gray family"—he gave Bryony such a severe look over the top of his spectacles that she backed up a step—"and fraternizing with certain types of people, but I expect it's entirely too late."

Mira's face clouded over and she seized Bryony's hand. "I shall fraternize with whomever I please," she said firmly. "And besides that, Bryony Gray is the very best sort of person. And you'd think that too, if you spent more than five minutes with her. I should think you of all people would know not to judge books by their covers."

The old man ran a hand over his chin and raised one steel-gray brow at Mira. "You may be right, Ms. Griffin. But all the same, be careful."

ack outside the shop, Bryony breathed deeply, trying not to think about the things Mr. Fiddick had said. She and Mira sat side by side on the doorstep, waiting for Thompson.

A soft touch at her elbow and she looked back into Mira's blue eyes, which were wide with concern. "Are you all right? You seem quite out of breath. I'm sorry about him. He's frightfully grumpy. I mostly tolerate him because he drives Mother away."

"I'm fine, it was just . . . the smell of smoke became rather overwhelming," Bryony lied. She had to swallow past the lump in her throat when Mira nodded sympathetically, and she glanced away quickly. An odd mix of exhilaration and dread filled her stomach, and it was causing quite the turmoil, as if a tempest were brewing inside of her.

Mira had looked so fierce defending her that it was almost worth being insulted. And besides that, she'd found exactly what she wanted: the next step in her plan. Still, the old man's comment about the Gray family bothered her. Even if her father was a bit cracked—thinking he was some sort of wizard—it pained her to hear a stranger saying the same things her uncle and aunt had said. How many people knew the rumors? And why hadn't she demanded to know what Mr. Fiddick had heard about her family?

Perhaps she should barge back inside and—

"Have you thought about what you'll do next?"

Bryony looked up, startled, to find Mira staring at her. "What? I thought we should wait here for Thompson."

Mira grinned. "No, I mean, what you're going to do after you find your patron and we solve this?" She leaned forward, eyes shining. "You could do anything. You could go explore new countries, sail across the ocean. You could go around the world in eighty days, just like in my books." She paused, her smile fading. "It's lucky you haven't got any family to stop you."

Bryony sat up straight, blinking at the other girl in disbelief. "Wh-what do you mean it's *lucky*? It-it's not lucky to have no one . . ." she sputtered, badly wanting to say what was on the tip of her tongue. That all she'd been doing was searching for her family. Hoping that her mysterious patron was actually her father. It was ludicrous to think being orphaned and locked away in an attic somehow made her *lucky*.

Mira winced. "I didn't mean to say—"

A relieved-sounding, "There you are!" interrupted the argument. Thompson strode across the street to meet them, and the closer he got, the more evident it became how flustered he was. His shirt had come untucked, and his hair stood up wildly, looking a little as if he'd been struck by lightning or caught in a gale.

"What took you so long?" Mira said.

Thompson swallowed, looking back over his shoulder. "He wouldn't let me leave until I told them all about the museum and all the paintings . . ." His words trailed off and he shoved his hands into his pockets. "Anyways, no matter. What did you two find out?"

"Why are you so red in the face?" Bryony took a step closer. It was odd that he hadn't finished his story; up until now he'd taken every opportunity to whine and complain. Suspicion churned in her gut. "What else did you tell the police officer?"

Thompson licked his lips and continued to stare at the ground.

"You didn't tell him about Bryony?" Mira cried. "Oh, Thompson, you didn't!"

"He wouldn't let up." Thompson shuffled his feet, kicking at one of the raised bricks of the doorstep. "He knew I knew something. And I couldn't lie to the police! All I did was mention your name and he sort of latched on to it. That article—"

"Thompson, you—you terrible coward!" Mira spat the words at him, and he flinched as if he'd been slapped. "You're going to ruin everything."

"I had no choice!"

"Who knows what they're going to do now! This could be a real problem," Mira said.

"I'm sorry, all right? Honestly I am. You needn't yell."

Mira ignored him, turning to give Bryony an apologetic grimace. "He's always been like this. He told everyone about Father's extra toe last year at the family reunion, just because he thought Aunt Nora looked at him funny over the dinner table. Turns out she was only choking on a bit of roast beef. Mother was furious, said he'd humiliated the good Griffin name."

Thompson's face turned even brighter red, and he pressed his lips together tightly and shook his head.

Bryony folded her arms over her chest and glared at both of them. "As fascinating as your father's extra toe is, we've a serious problem here! Now that this numpty has told everyone who's responsible for this, they'll be out looking for me. You didn't tell them what I looked like, did you?"

"Of course not!" Thompson looked affronted. "I gave them the wrong description, actually."

The knot in Bryony's chest loosened a little. "Well, at least you're not a total idiot."

Thompson sputtered and then fell silent, his face pinched and pale.

She'd already been frustrated about Mira's "lucky" remark, and now this. And the worst thing was, neither sibling seemed to realize how dangerous this might be. What with Mira making jokes about toes . . .

Perhaps Mira didn't care about her at all. What had Mr. Fiddick said in the shop? *Another madcap adventure?* Had there been a string of Bryonys in Mira's past, all people the girl had followed around in hope of excitement?

"For all I know, they're forming a party to hunt me down as we speak," Bryony snapped, and then immediately wished she hadn't said it. A shiver crawled down her spine, and she glanced around at the busy street. Nobody was taking any notice of her at all; they were far too busy shouting at one another, demanding to know what was going on or telling everyone within earshot what they knew. The crowd around the police officer was getting even bigger, with everyone shouting at him to explain what was happening. No one was even glancing her way. Still, she felt they had better leave now just in case the officer decided to tell people what Thompson had said. She took a deep breath and turned back to the others. "All right. Let's go ask after this Charlie Constantine fellow then, since he's our only lead."

Both siblings had gone sober and quiet in the face of her admonishment, but now Thompson's dark brows drew down low. "Wait, Charlie Constantine? What do you want with that scoundrel? Surely Mr. Fiddick is mistaken."

Mira whirled on her brother almost in unison with Bryony, and they both shrieked at the same time. "You *know* him?" Thompson staggered backward, his expression alarmed.

"You didn't say it was *Charlie* Constantine. There's more than one person in London with that surname, you know."

"More than one bookbinder?" Mira stared at her brother incredulously.

"Total numpty," Bryony growled at him. "Completely useless."

"No need to be rude about it." Thompson glared back at her. "And you won't find him. Father looked for him; he went on and on about his cursed books. Collectibles, he called them." He dropped his voice, and his eyes darted this way and that over the street. "I shouldn't think Father would have wanted Mira to ever meet him. The man holds . . . *held* disreputable company."

"How do you mean?" Mira tilted her head to one side. "Does the man gamble?"

Thompson looked uncomfortable. "No. Well, maybe. I don't know."

"Honestly, I don't care if the man dresses in women's bonnets and waltzes with chimney sweeps on Tuesdays and Thursdays," Bryony snapped at him. "I just need to find him. Mr. Fiddick said he's at Mivart's Hotel."

Thompson opened his mouth and then shut it again, expression scandalized. He was probably about to say something about women's bonnets, but before he could get anything out, Mira grabbed his arm.

"Hold on. Thompson, look. What is that?" She was staring over Bryony's shoulder, blue eyes round with fright. Her face had gone pale, freckles standing out in stark contrast.

Bryony whirled around. The first thing she saw was the church steeple rising up out of the rooftops, gray stone with a cluster of black spikes on top, like some kind of dark crown. She knew the church; she'd seen it from her attic window whenever the fog wasn't too thick.

A black cloud spiraled up from the steeple, trailing into the gray sky.

"Something's on fire." Thompson's voice was tremulous. "I suspect it's nothing. They'll put it out."

Bryony bit the inside of her cheek, not convinced. "I wonder if it's the paintings causing trouble, if they've spread all the way—"

"No, look up *there*." Mira had been peering through her brass telescope, and now she handed it to Bryony.

It took a moment or two to get used to looking through the tiny hole, but when she did, the church steeple came into focus, and Bryony drew in a sharp breath.

There was something clinging to the side of the steeple, a human-shaped figure. Bryony reached up with a trembling hand and twisted the telescope, like she'd seen Mira do, and the figure grew larger.

It was a woman in a bright pink party dress, blonde hair shorn and hacked away. A woman with dark pits for eyes, hanging on to the steeple with one arm. The painted woman's head swiveled this way and that. She was searching the crowds below.

Bryony fumbled the telescope, nearly dropping it. "We have to go. *Now*."

"What? What are you on about?" Thompson snatched the telescope away from her, pressing it to his eye. "What are you—*Oh*. Oh my good Lord."

"We have to find a carriage and get out of the main streets. There's going to be a stampede as soon as people see that."

The three of them hurried down the road to the next street, and the next, until the crowd was thinner than it had been on Oxford Street.

"How far away is Mivart's?" Bryony looked around at the people walking by—quite a few of them seemed to be headed for Oxford Street, but nobody here seemed to be panicking yet—then back over her shoulder at the street, searching for an available hackney cab or trolley.

"Far enough to get us out of this general area." Thompson leaned into the street, waving wildly at a passing cab, and then sighed with relief when it started to turn toward them, pulling up to the curb.

The driver dismounted and held the door for them, smiling widely and greeting Thompson with a brisk nod and a doff of his cap. After they'd settled in, Thompson drew the curtains back from the window and the three of them peered out, keeping an eye on the crowd and the church steeple in the distance.

It seemed they were just in time, since a ripple of disquiet had begun spreading down the road. Arms were raised, pointing at the cloud of smoke rising up beside the church steeple, and Bryony stiffened as a shrill scream sounded from somewhere in the distance.

Thompson knocked on the wall at the front of the coach, signaling the driver to go faster. When he leaned back he began plucking at his jacket again, shifting in his seat, darting wide-eyed looks out the window.

The way he acted, like he was permanently on the edge of a panic-fueled meltdown, reminded her of Aunt Gertrude. The thought sent a pang of sadness through her, which she found a trifle surprising. After all, her aunt had been nothing but nagging and bossy, and she was always grasping and pinching at things with those bony fingers of hers. Not to mention the fact that she had been an active participant in keeping her only niece locked in an attic for six years.

Really, I should be glad she's gone.

And perhaps she would have been, if Aunt Gertrude

had died of influenza or expired from a bad case of the mumps, but it hadn't been anything natural that struck her down. As horrible as she'd been, she didn't deserve to be turned into a pile of ashes by her own reflection.

Mercifully, these dismal thoughts were interrupted by the sudden lurch and bump of the carriage, and Thompson's gusty sigh of relief. "Rougher roads, but at least we're well away from the crowd now."

It was true. When Bryony tugged her side of the curtain back, she could see the streets were far narrower here, the buildings tall and crooked and crammed together. A more middle-class sort of neighborhood without any shops, and, in turn, much quieter. The cabbie must have sensed the buzz of alarm coming from the main streets and taken an alternative route.

"Thank heavens." Thompson slumped in his seat. "I was sure the crowd would spot her on the steeple and go into a frenzy and crush us to death."

"How grim you are." Mira laughed, eyes crinkling at the corners. Now that they were out of danger she was perfectly cheerful again. "Stop worrying. I expect we'll find Constantine right away, and he'll tell us exactly how to stop all the murderous paintings. Then we shall receive a thousand pounds for reward money and I can buy the new set of maps I've been saving for."

"You have no proper perception of reality at all." Thompson folded his arms over his chest. "Which is quite obvious, since you seem to be stockpiling nets and tele-scopes. You're going to have to hide all your toys when Mother gets back." He gestured at the hat and belt, and

Mira's smile slipped away. She looked as though she was about to snap back at him, but the carriage rattled to a halt just then and she fell silent. After a moment the coachman came around to open the door.

"Mivart's Hotel, young sir."

They disembarked, with Bryony the last to emerge. Outside there was an encouraging lack of running and screaming. People seemed to be strolling hand in hand, or walking past in laughing, chattering crowds.

It seemed they had outrun the chaos, and that the buzz from Oxford Street hadn't reached this area yet. Bryony allowed herself a sigh of relief.

Mivart's Hotel towered above them, sucking up all her attention. It was massive. A solid, multilevel block of tan bricks layered with windows from top to bottom. She straightened her shoulders and yanked on the strap of her bag, determined that whatever happened she was going to track down the elusive bookmaker. He was her best lead: without him, her mission was nearly impossible.

'Well." Mira tipped her head back, the tips of her short hair brushing her shoulders. "Isn't that a splendid sort of place? Like a fairy-tale castle."

"Much too blocky to be a castle," Thompson said. "Let's get this over with."

"You're so very cheerful all the time," Bryony said, making sure her voice was loaded with sarcasm. "It's lovely."

Thompson headed for the front entrance, steps brisk and businesslike. "I shall be sure to only speak about unicorns and rainbows in the future, Ms. Gray."

Bryony tried to stifle a smile as she followed the boy.

They were nearly at the door when Bryony paused to stare up at the hotel, suddenly struck by how much the building towering over them *did* look like a castle. Perhaps it was the sheer enormousness of it all. Or the fact that she finally had a moment to stop and take things in.

It was as if the city of London hit her all at once. It was so much busier here. It wasn't just crowded, as it had been on Oxford Street, with people standing around talking in clumps. No, this street was full of constant motion.

There was noise all around her. Honking, buzzing and creaking, automobiles, carts and buggies. And so many *people*. They leaned out onto the street to yell at cabs, or gusted by in noisy, laughing groups. Someone pushed past Bryony in a rush, and the woman's dress rustled over the bottom of Bryony's own. She didn't seem to notice she'd nearly run into someone.

The buildings here were even taller than they were in her neighborhood. Bryony's face turned hot. How silly she'd been to think those familiar buildings had scraped the sky. The houses on her street would be dwarfed by these ones. They had to be over ten stories high! And there were rows and rows of them.

Bryony squeezed her eyes shut, fighting back the panic.

John Atkinson Grimshaw, born 1836, painted landscapes of the city of London all his life. Died in 1893 without leaving any letters or journals.

When she opened her eyes, the edges of her vision began to blur. The facts weren't going to work. It wasn't enough this time. A strange, smothering feeling crept over her, the sensation that the apartments were leaning in like a crooked picket fence. Any minute now they would collapse in a huge explosion of gray dust and shimmering steel, or they would swoop down and consume her, suck her in and make her a part of the city forever.

What was that dreadful pulsing noise the city was making?

Only the beating of her own heart, she realized, hammering above all the clip-clopping and the roar of traffic. Above the rush of steam hissing as cabbies pulled up to the curb. Above the squeals and laughter of the surging crowd on the sidewalk.

This was nothing like her attic. Her quiet, dim little attic. She longed for it, and in the same moment, hated herself for feeling that way.

Something gripped her shoulders, and Bryony jerked her head back down. She gasped, feeling a little like she was drowning, relieved at the lungful of oxygen that rushed in. Had she been holding her breath? All around the buildings blurred and stretched, the rusty red bricks and the gray cobblestones running into one another like smeary watercolors.

"Bryony?"

"Bry?"

"Thompson, what's the matter with her?"

Thompson's face swam behind his sister, looking a little like a disembodied head. "She's having vapors. Get her inside." He flapped his hand at the buildings around them. "She needs to be inside, quickly."

Mira looped her arm around Bryony's waist and began guiding her to the front entrance of the castlelike building.

"Her face is ghastly pale. What's happening?" Mira's voice was high-pitched with worry, which wasn't helping Bryony feel any better. If Mira—who had flung herself into a room full of monsters to retrieve her notebook—was starting to get anxious, then things must really be grim.

"Nothing serious." It was Thompson who sounded calm now, his voice deep and sure. "Only a bit of a panic. Now, Bryony. You've got to calm down and breathe deeply, all right?"

Bryony nodded, forcing herself to inhale deeply. She would not faint. *Vincent van Gogh suffered attacks of dizziness and ringing of the ears. Visitors at the Santa Croce Basilica in Florence often have fainting spells due to the paintings on the ceilings.*

At last the facts seemed to work, for the throbbing of her pulse in her ears slowed down a little. She concentrated on putting one foot in front of the other and letting Mira guide her straight ahead, until there was a rush of warm air that signified they'd made it inside, and Mira helped her sit down in a cushiony armchair.

They seemed to be in a narrow hallway between the outside doors and the doors to the lobby, where a surprised-looking attendant in a green coat stood beside the front door. When Bryony met his eyes he looked away quickly, folding his white-gloved hands in front of him. His face was composed, as if he were perfectly used to ladies having fits here in the lobby of his hotel. Perhaps he was.

"What was that?"

Bryony blinked, staring down at Mira, who was crouched to the left of her, balancing herself by gripping the arm of the chair. She shifted, uncomfortable, as Mira stared her right in the eyes. "Bryony Gray, you tell me what just happened back there."

Bryony's cheeks burned, and she pressed her lips together firmly. It was terribly embarrassing. Perhaps the siblings would think she was a child, having a fit like that in public. Perhaps they'd be embarrassed to be seen with her.

Thompson hovered behind his sister, clasping and unclasping his hands. "Er, perhaps we should give her a few minutes. Listen, Bryony, there's no need to feel ashamed about that. Likely you've got a touch of the vapors. They're making great advances in the studies of this sort of thing, you know." He straightened up, fidgeting with his collar. "I admit, I've had the odd episode myself."

The rush of gratitude she felt for him surprised even Bryony. He actually seemed to care, and she'd been so beastly to him up until now. Guilt washed through her, making her face feel hot. To think that she'd wished the shepherdess had got him. How awful of her.

"I'm all right." Her voice was shakier than she would have liked. "The same thing happened when I first got out . . . I—the city—" She faltered, her face growing even hotter. Mira's expression had become even darker as Bryony spoke, her mouth drawing down.

"Bryony," Mira said, and her voice was like the rumble of thunder. Low and ominous, threatening a storm. "Exactly how many times have you been out of the house?"

Her throat tightened. She'd swallowed desert sand and her voice had shriveled into a dry little whisper. "Just the once." Thinking about it brought up a wave of lovely memories—the museum, the paintings, the tinkle of champagne glasses—but the horrified looks on the siblings' faces drove the good feelings away. All she wanted to do was melt into the armchair and cease to exist.

And she truly would have torn herself out of Mira's grasp and run away down the street if the pity on Thompson's face had been reflected in his sister's. But when she looked at Mira she was relieved to see only a kind of furious stillness there. A white-lipped, trembling rage that she never expected to see on Mira's face. For some reason, that expression kindled a warmth in her chest that spread right down to her fingers and toes, a happy buzz that filled her stomach. She smiled and shrugged, trying her best to appear casual about the whole situation. "I had my art and my books. It wasn't so bad."

Mira's silent anger finally exploded outward, and Thompson flinched as she called down curses on Bryony's relatives. A long string of terrible things were wished on her uncle and aunt, everything from cold tea to ravens pecking out their eyeballs.

It seemed she did care.

At last Mira seemed to run out of breath, and Bryony stood up, feeling remarkably better. When she did, Mira stepped forward and seized her around the shoulders, pulling her in close for a moment, squeezing her tight. Bryony froze, surprised.

"I'm sorry for what I said earlier, about being lucky, I mean," Mira said, and then she let go and backed away, blushing furiously.

By the time Bryony had recovered herself, Mira had already turned around, heading for the doors of the lobby.

That was probably for the best, because Bryony's face had gone terribly flushed, and her arms still tingled from the strange half hug. Uncle Bernard's idea of affection was a pat on the head when she'd done something that pleased him, and Aunt Gertrude had only ever plucked at her clothing or grabbed at her arms with her pinchy, bony fingers.

Bryony couldn't keep the ridiculous smile off her face as she followed the siblings into the hotel. She even looked straight at the attendant in the green coat as she went past, ignoring the sidelong look he was giving her. Then she was in the center of the hotel lobby and had the chance to really look around for the first time. Mira stayed close, keeping her arm linked through Bryony's as they both stared in awe.

The tile beneath their feet was checkered black and white, and it sparkled, dazzling under the light cast down by six huge chandeliers dripping in diamonds. In the middle of it all was a long, cherrywood desk. Several men in pressed black uniforms smiled as they came in.

Mira grabbed Bryony's hand and pushed her way past Thompson before he could say anything, and the two of them approached the desk. Mira planted herself directly in front of one of the black-suited concierges.

The man's black brows shot up, and his eyes darted from Bryony's disheveled dress and the paintbrush behind her ear to Mira's explorer garb. To his credit he only smiled wider and said smoothly, "How can I help you ladies?"

"Would you happen to know if a man by the name of Constantine is here presently?"

The concierge blinked, and his smile began to look strained. "I'm afraid we have no guest by that name, miss."

Bryony raised one eyebrow in the most disdainful arch she could manage. "But you didn't even look. Surely you can't know every single guest here off by heart?"

"I would remember a name like that," the concierge said flatly. "It's unusual."

He's lying. Bryony tilted her head, studying the man's face, but the concierge only smiled politely. She opened her mouth, about to give him a thorough dressing down, but Mira's hand pressed lightly into her lower back. The other girl directed a bright smile at the concierge, the same fake smile she'd used on Mr. Fiddick. "Three tickets to the tearoom, please."

When the concierge hesitated, Thompson walked up behind them and slid a couple of coins across the counter. Hastily the man behind the desk nodded and stooped down to open a cupboard below the desk, emerging with three pastel-pink ticket stubs.

Bryony made her way up the flight of stairs that led off the lobby and Mira came just behind her, following the signs that said "Tearoom" in elaborately swirling hand-writing. When they finally came to a set of French doors, Mira barely slowed down; she just barged her way through.

The tearoom was every bit as grand as Bryony had expected, the type of place Aunt Gertrude would have loved to be seen in. There were two floors: the main section, a round room with pastel-pink wallpaper and delicate circular tables ringing the outside edges, and a second-story loft that ran all the way around. A dizzying spiral staircase led from the second story down to the main floor.

Since it was nearly lunchtime, most of the tables were occupied, and the gentle hum of conversation filled the echoing space. Bryony scanned the room once before realizing she had absolutely no idea what Constantine looked like.

"Thompson," she said, keeping her voice low. "What exactly does this bloke look like?"

Thompson shook his head, turning to look around the room. "Haven't the foggiest. Father didn't describe him."

Bryony turned to the attendant. "Would you happen to know if a Constantine is here this afternoon?"

The door attendant's smile became wide and fake. "I'm afraid I've no idea, ma'am. Lots of people come in and out, you see."

Bryony exchanged a look with Mira and then said loudly, "We'd like to speak to Constantine."

Her voice echoed around the huge room. Even the people in the balcony turned their heads to look down, teacups halfway to their lips, hands hovering over their sandwich platters.

Thompson cleared his throat, his face turning bright red, his neck growing splotchy. "Sit down," he muttered. "It's clear he's not here. We might as well sit for tea instead of making a scene. Unless you have another plan."

They made their way to a table and, fuming, she waited for him to pull her chair out. Her warm feelings for him seemed to have evaporated, and now she very much wanted to slug him in the side of the head. But Thompson had a valid point: she didn't have another idea. If they left the tearoom now, the only option would be to return home and wait for Uncle Bernard to come back, if he ever did. The idea of sitting alone in the empty house, surrounded by white-sheeted mirrors and paintings, was less than appealing. She couldn't even consider it a possibility at the moment.

Just then there was a loud crash from outside, the sound of shattering glass accompanied by a high, shrill scream of rage, a sound that made goosebumps shoot up both of Bryony's arms and made her back to the beginning of this whole affair. Back to the attic and those black, empty eyes.

The tearoom fell silent, the happy buzz of conversation dying away abruptly. Everyone was craning around to look. For a moment there was only the silence, and at the table beside them a young woman in a pretty blue dress said softly, "What was that?"

Unfortunately, Bryony knew *exactly* what that was.

She spun around, catching Mira's hand and Thompson's sleeve at the same time. "She's here."

Chapter Twelve

A scream from the balcony answered, a shrill sound of terror. Bryony jumped to her feet, muscles tense, ready to run. The crash of breaking glass was accompanied by a sudden frenzy of movement in the upper balcony. There was more screaming, and people flung themselves up out of their chairs, a few running dangerously close to the balcony railings as the crowd from upstairs began rushing for the spiral staircase.

People down below were still seated at the tea tables, necks craning, heads tilted back as they stared at the balcony. A few people began to move for the door.

Bryony stood on her tiptoes, trying to see through the balcony rungs. Dread clenched at her chest.

More screaming from the balcony, and then the crashing sound of china shattering on the floor. Someone had upended a table.

The source of the disturbance was revealed as more people fled the balcony. A woman in a ragged pink dress, fingers crooked into claws as she strode forward, eyes a pair of gaping black holes in a pale, powdered face.

Lady Abney in the flesh. Or, rather, in oils on canvas.

In fact, Bryony was sure she was starting to look a little faded, perhaps because of the great trail of paint she left behind everywhere she went. Still, she was very much alive, and stalking the guests of the tearoom just as a jungle cat prowls after gazelle. Screaming, fainting gazelle who trampled one another and tripped over their own skirts as they rushed for the exit.

The painted Lady Abney was turning over tables, exposing anyone who'd dared to hide underneath, yanking them out by their collars and staring into their faces before tossing them away. A few intrepid gentlemen leapt into her path, but she batted them aside, sending them crashing against the wall and barreling into tables.

Bryony's entire body went stiff. Her feet were rooted to the spot. The painted woman was looking for someone, there was no doubt. She'd been scanning the crowds from the top of the steeple, and now here she was searching the tearoom.

The monstrous Lady Abney tossed another woman aside with a frustrated scream and advanced down the stairs. The black holes of her eyes looked—could they really look?—over the lower half of the tearoom. A chorus of chairs crashing to the ground and shuddering screams masked the sound of Bryony's shaky breathing.

The painted woman stalked forward, leaning over the railing of the curling staircase to look down. That terrible, powder-white face turned this way and that. Then she stopped, frozen like a pointer dog scenting prey. Those eyes, those gaping holes in her face—nothing more than a pair of black pits—were locked on Bryony. Somehow fixed on her and no one else.

Lady Abney sprang up onto the railing, crouching low. She balanced effortlessly, even with the billowing pink dress around her legs. Her hollow gaze still on Bryony, she launched herself forward with a savage howl.

Bryony couldn't move—she couldn't even scream. Her tongue had fused to the roof of her mouth. All she could see was a flurry of pink ruffles and empty black eyes barreling toward her. It seemed to take forever, and she had time to think, *this is the end,* and in that strange, slow moment, not wanting to look at the monster hurtling down and down, she turned her head to look at the stampeding crowd. A split-second glimpse revealed a man standing against the wall, mouth slack with shock, a cigarette dangling from his bottom lip, a violent pink smear of paint blazed across the front of his dinner jacket.

Then someone seized her arm, yanking her backward so hard it nearly wrenched her shoulder out of its socket. There was a dull thud as the painted monster crashed to the floor in front of her, and she scrambled backward, right into Thompson, who still had a firm hold on her wrist.

"Go!" he cried. "Run!"

It was a mad rush for the exit. Thompson led the way, throwing up his arms with a shout as a woman in a frilly blue Sunday dress shoved him into the doorway. He fell against the frame, grabbed Mira and shoved her forward, and then reached back for Bryony.

He caught Bryony's hand just as she was shoved from the side, nearly knocked backward into the tearoom. Mira hooked her arms around her brother's waist and hauled him back, and the three of them became a strange sort of human chain, pulling Bryony through the doorway like a cork from a wine bottle. She pitched forward with a shriek. Going down meant being trampled by the hysterical crowd.

Warm hands caught her arms, pulling her up firmly, dragging her out of the crush of panicked people. Mira smiled at her, and she was so wildly beautiful in that moment, with her hair all tangled and wavy about her face, and her blue eyes glittering and fierce, that Bryony's hand actually twitched toward her paintbrush. What a portrait she would make!

Ridiculous, since they were about to be *mauled* by one of her paintings.

Bryony looped her arms around the other girl's waist and held on. Behind them, someone shouted. Several men advanced on Lady Abney, waving canes and umbrellas. One enterprising fellow held up a pot of tea, ready to throw hot water on the monster.

Bryony tried to run forward, desperate to do something, to help somehow, but Mira tugged her back. "Don't go near her! You can't do anything."

She was right, of course, so Bryony settled for yelling over the screams of the crowd. "Use the tea!"

Chapter Thirteen

"**C**ome on, we've got to go." Thompson tugged Mira toward the exit, which resulted in Bryony being dragged in that direction as well, so she was around the corner and out of sight when they heard a splash and a horrible scream.

She tugged on Mira's hand. "The tea may have worked. We have to go see if it did."

Mira dug her heels in, bringing them to a sudden stop. "Thompson, wait."

Thompson's eye seemed to have developed a twitch. "Absolutely not! We've got to get out of here." He continued to drag Mira forward, out the door and onto the sidewalk.

Bryony was about to protest when there came a faint crash and the distant sounds of bloodcurdling screams from somewhere inside, which seemed to signify that the tea *hadn't* worked. At least, not entirely.

They had reached the side of the road now, and Thompson darted out into the heavy flow of traffic, waving his arms wildly at the nearest cab, a rickety green hansom that pulled over with a series of clanks and rattles that nearly blocked out the noise of the traffic around it. Thompson eyed it nervously, and then jumped at another scream from inside the hotel, diving onto the sagging leather seats almost before the driver brought the carriage to a full stop.

Bryony and Mira jammed themselves into the seat beside Thompson. The cab was so tiny it just barely fit all of them, and Bryony found herself squished between the two siblings.

The cab driver, who had climbed down from his perch, blinked at them and scratched his head through a patched and faded messenger cap. "Sir . . . uh, is everything all right?"

"It is most certainly *not*. Just believe me when I say drive, and drive fast." Thompson shifted forward in the seat, waving urgently at the driver, who continued to stand at the door, his face dumbstruck. "Hurry, man!"

As if to emphasize his words, there came another loud smashing sound from the hotel, and something flew through the lobby window, shattering the glass and falling to the road with a heavy *plonk*.

People on the sidewalk screamed and flung themselves out of the way, revealing a brass kettle wobbling on the side of the road. Several teacups and a plate were lobbed shortly after this, and the crowd began to run into the street in panic.

Thompson lunged forward and snatched at the driver's coat. "Go!"

"Oh . . . yes, sir!" The driver started, wide-eyed, and hurried around the back of the cab, which gave a little shudder and shake as he mounted his seat.

There was a crack and a pop from above, and then the horse started forward, going straight from a walk into a canter, the carriage rattling along behind it. The wheels clunked unevenly over the cobblestones, vibrating every bone in Bryony's body and forcing her teeth to chatter.

She twisted around in her seat, trying to peer out Mira's window. Behind them, the panic was spilling onto the streets. People poured out of the hotel and straight into the road, blocking traffic, running in all directions. Several horses seemed to be on the verge of spooking, tossing their heads, eyes rolling. One reared up and nearly kicked a fleeing gentleman in the head, knocking his top hat onto the cobblestones.

There was a blur of pink and a horrible screech as the painted Lady Abney hurtled out of the lobby and into the crowd, setting off a chorus of screams and shouts and a veritable stampede running for the shelter of the surrounding buildings.

Bryony flinched, quickly turning back around. Her entire body had gone stiff, and both Mira and Thompson looked at her with wide, questioning eyes.

"She's on the street. Just don't look out the window. She can't see us in this mess." She was only guessing, hoping. But it seemed logical.

For a long, tense minute there was only the sound of the cab's wheels bumping over the stones, and Bryony shut her eyes to listen. She could hear the screams in the distance as well as the sound of her heart thumping loudly in her ears.

Thompson let out a relieved breath and slumped back in his seat. "We're around the corner, out of sight."

They were so closely packed together that Bryony could feel the tension leave all of them at the same time.

"What do we do now?" Mira said. "We've hit a dead end. Constantine wasn't there."

"We head home," Thompson said firmly. He leaned sideways, calling directions up to the driver.

Bryony slumped back in her seat, defeated, only looking up when Mira nudged her gently with one elbow, wiggling her brows in a conspiratorial fashion. She hadn't bothered to argue with her brother, but she was clearly trying to say this wasn't over. Did she have something planned? If only they *did* have a secret language!

Bryony had studied the basics of sign language after she'd discovered a book about it on one of the attic shelves. She'd taught herself some basic signs after that—imagine the fun she could have talking about Aunt Gertrude right in front of her!—so how hard could it be to teach Mira some sign language as well? Or her own version of it, anyway. Basic signals should be enough.

If they could sneak away . . .

Already she was beginning to make plans. Someone had to destroy the painted Lady Abney. If tea didn't do it, surely paint thinner would. She bit her lower lip, thoughts racing, but before she could come up with a plan, the carriage lurched to a stop, nearly throwing her headfirst into the wall. Thompson braced himself on the window frame, glaring at the ceiling of the cab. "Why the sudden stop? I nearly thumped my head." He leaned to the side and drew the curtain back. "Ah. Oh, dear."

"What?" Bryony leaned across him, peering through the window. The carriage had stopped about halfway down their street. From here, the top of her roof could be seen, the attic windows dark and empty. Beyond that was the roof of the funeral home, jutting up in sharp peaks and towers. Directly in front of them was a series of hansom cabs, wagons and the occasional automobile, all jamming the roadway, drivers and passengers leaning out the windows to yell and shake their fists at the crowd blocking the street.

No, not a crowd. Bryony clutched the edge of the window so tightly the frame bit into her fingers. Not a crowd, a mob.

The people in the street weren't just standing there; they were shaking their fists in the air. A few were waving crumpled newspapers, and Bryony felt her throat tighten. That article again. Funny that Aunt Gertrude had turned out to be right after all—it *was* causing her trouble. Well, that and Thompson telling the police she had started this. It seemed the crowd from Oxford Street had decided to take matters into their own hands.

Even from their position halfway down the road, the muffled buzz of angry chanting could be heard.

"Come out, Gray!"

"Give us Gray!"

"We know you're behind this!"

Over the clamor came the sound of glass smashing as people dragged portraits and paintings from their houses and into the streets, shattering the glass and breaking the frames to pieces, piling the canvases high in the center of the crossroads. Bryony even saw a few empty frames, probably taken from the museum. One member of the mob must have lit the bottom of the pile with a match, because a fierce shout of triumph arose as the paintings went up in flames, thick black smoke billowing into the gray sky.

Feeling suddenly dizzy, Bryony sat back in the seat. The paintbrush behind her ear poked her in the side of the head, and her arms and legs felt shaky and weak. There was an angry mob outside her house, so big it went halfway down the street, and they were all out for her blood.

Mira was also looking out her window, and her frame went rigid. Slowly she sat back in her seat and leveled a dark look at Thompson.

"*You* caused this, Thompson Evelyn Griffin, and you'd bloody well better help us fix it. She can't possibly go home through the crowd. They'll tear her apart."

Bryony had time to think, *Evelyn?* before the walls of the carriage seemed to lean in and attempt to crush her. She sagged forward, shoulders hunched, gasping for air. For some reason her vision kept fuzzing in and out, and her hands wouldn't stop trembling, in spite of how hard she was gripping the leather seat. Why couldn't she stop shaking?

These vapors—wasn't that was Thompson had called them?—she didn't like them at all. Perhaps if she shut her eyes and thought about other things . . . *Painter Rosa Bonheur was the first female recipient of the French Legion of Honor Award. Peter Paul Rubens was knighted by the king of Spain.*

"Bryony?" Mira's pale hands crept over hers, smoothing over her arms and up her shoulders.

She seized Mira's hands and held on. "They're going to kill me."

"No." It was Thompson who spoke, his voice surprisingly firm. "Nonsense. Mira is right. This is my fault, and I've got to atone for my cowardice."

Mira blinked. "You do?"

"I do," Thompson said, and he squared his shoulders. "So I've got a plan. We'll sneak you in the back, through the basement. None of them"—he gestured out the window at the bloodthirsty crowd—"are going to be looking at the house next door. They're concentrating on your house."

He seemed very sure of himself.

Breathing became a little easier now. She nodded and tried to force a confident smile, though she could feel her lips trembling. Mira squeezed her hands, and Thompson leaned out the window, instructing the driver to turn around and take another street. His voice was confident and firm, admirably so.

The carriage moved again, backing up and then lurching forward, and Bryony had to let go of Mira's hands to brace herself on the seat. "Well," she said brightly, voice trembling only the slightest bit, "it appears I'm famous now."

Mira's eyes sparkled. "Every artist's dream."

"They adore me. Can't you hear them?"

She kept her eyes on Mira's face, and it struck her then that she had everything she'd wished for: an interesting life, the girl next door and fame. She laughed, choking a little as she did so, but Mira joined in, her own laugh high and musical. The sound was enough to make her feel a little better.

After a few minutes, she turned to Thompson and said, "Evelyn?"

Thompson blushed furiously and muttered something about his mother, and since he was being tolerable right now, Bryony didn't push it.

They sat in silence after that. Then the carriage began to slow to a stop, and Thompson leaned out, instructing the driver to go forward a few houses. She sat back in her seat and took a deep breath. They had arrived.

Chapter Fourteen

While Thompson paid the cab, Bryony and Mira crept forward, off the road, to a gap in the hedges that lined the ditch. Her shoes sank into the mud, and Mira, safe in her clunky black boots, had to lend her a hand so she wouldn't fall.

Together they peered through the bristly green shrubs. Straight ahead was the back garden of the funeral home, fenced in by an elaborately curling iron gate. A ways behind them the road was filled with the angry mob, the crowd swelling as more and more people joined. Now that they were outside the chanting was far louder, and the sound sent goosebumps crawling across Bryony's skin.

When Mira brushed her shoulder she jumped, sliding in the mud.

"Sorry," Mira whispered, grasping her arm. "Okay, look, they haven't gone into your backyard or around the side of the house yet, so if we make a run for our house, they shouldn't see us."

Relief filled her, so intense it made her feel a little fuzzy in the head. It was strangely steadying just to see Mira act so completely calm about all of this. Impulsively, Bryony grasped the other girl's hand. "I can't tell you how glad I am you're here. I—I don't think I could do this on my own."

Mira's grin was wide and delighted, and she squeezed Bryony's hand. "And I'm glad I met you, Bryony Gray."

Cursing from behind made Bryony glance back over her shoulder. Thompson was sliding down the embankment, arms pinwheeling as he tried to keep his balance.

"Oh, for heaven's sake." Mira had to drop Bryony's hand to lean back and catch hold of his sleeve, grasping one of the spiny branches of the shrubs in front of them with her other as she pulled her brother across.

"I got mud all over my new shoes," Thompson whispered, his face set in disapproval as he tried to wipe his once-shiny black shoes on the grass.

"Do hush up." Mira turned back to the house. She had her telescope out now, using it to scan the mob in the street. "I've been dying to use my blowpipe. This would be a great opportunity."

Thompson looked aghast. "Your what?"

"You know, a blowpipe. Tranquilizer darts? You'd be terrible on safari, Thompy. Remind me never to bring you." Mira started to reach for her belt and Thompson batted her hand away with a yelp of dismay.

"What? No! You are absolutely *not* tranquilizing anyone."

"Spoilsport." She gave him a sulky look and went back to scanning the street, training the telescope up the road and across the lawn. "All clear. We best go now, before some of them think to walk around to the back."

Quite without warning, Mira grabbed Bryony's hand and shot out from between the hedges, and Bryony had to scramble after her, nearly slipping in the mud. Thompson ran directly behind; she could hear him griping about the mud under his breath. Mira made it to the gate and began fumbling with the lock. Panting, Bryony tried to keep an eye on the small view of the road to her left. Thankfully, the crowd seemed content to stay out front.

Mira opened the gate with a shriek of rusted hinges. "Welcome to the back garden." She smiled, then glanced over as Thompson jogged up, red-faced and out of breath.

"Get inside quickly," he said. "The crowd is starting to get worse. That can't be good."

It was true. The shouting was getting louder, and it sounded as if people were stomping their feet. Bryony hurried into the back garden, past Mira, who slammed the gate shut after them.

The garden was hedged in on all sides by the same green shrubs that lined the side of the road, which gave the backyard a bit of shade and, thankfully, privacy. Of course, it hadn't been private from Bryony's prying eyes. She'd had a perfect view from her attic window. There was a circular fountain in the center, a solemn marble angel presiding over it, wings outstretched. It hadn't looked so big and *stony* from her attic window. The way the statue stared straight at them with disapproval made Bryony hesitate for a few seconds. She pictured it ripping itself off the pedestal and climbing down, thundering toward her, swinging its heavy fists.

"Come on." Mira started forward. The stone angel didn't move.

Whatever was affecting mirrors and paintings didn't do anything to sculptures. And thank heavens for that. The angel would have been unthinkably destructive.

The girls came around the corner just as a tall figure in black stepped out from behind the angel in the fountain. For a second Bryony thought she'd been wrong, the statue *was* moving, and she jumped.

The man wore a long black overcoat—one with a pink paint smear across the front—and a top hat that sat at a rakish tilt. An unlit cigarette dangled from his lips. He had a long, narrow sort of face and dust-colored hair that curled around his ears, and there was something strangely familiar about him.

He ignored Thompson, fixing dark brown eyes on Bryony. He smiled, looping one arm around the statue, as if he and the angel were lovers out for a stroll in the park. "You must be Bryony Gray." He tilted his head to the side, flicking his free hand back and forth, as if he were conducting the chanting of the angry mob. "I've heard so much about you."

"Who are you?" Bryony narrowed her eyes at him, muscles tense, ready to run for the back gate if she had to. "And what do you want?"

The man looked over at the angel and raised his eyebrows, pretending to share an incredulous look. "I know, old chap. She must have a thicker head than you."

Bryony's mouth dropped open and heat flushed her cheeks. Beside her, Mira stared at the man with rapt attention, like he was the most interesting thing she'd ever seen. A flash of irritation went over her. For all they knew the man could be there to kill them.

"I think you should explain yourself," Thompson said sharply, "seeing as you're in our back garden. And I'm going to have to insist you remove yourself from our fountain."

The stranger made a face at Thompson, but he climbed down off the platform, moving quite nimbly for someone in such a bulky jacket. The man stepped into the fountain and strode over to the edge. He either didn't notice or didn't care that the water was soaking his shoes and pant legs. As he walked he flipped open an elaborately engraved gold-and-silver lighter and lit his cigarette, speaking around it.

"I am Charlie Constantine, and I believe you wished to speak with me."

ryony was the first one to speak, after she'd gathered her wits about her—at least, as much as one could when faced with a man who'd popped out of a fountain claiming to be exactly who you were looking for.

"How did you find us?"

The man plucked at the cuff of his suit and pursed his lips, as if he were thinking about whether he wanted to answer. "I have many connections in the book world, my dear. Mr. Fiddick is an old and dear friend."

She frowned, considering this. "All right, then . . . how do we know we can trust you? There are an awful lot of people out there who'd like to kill me."

"How kind of you to associate me with that demented rabble." Constantine, if that's who he was, stuck out his lower lip.

Bryony blinked at him. Surely this man-child couldn't be the mysterious Constantine.

"Let's go in," Thompson said, gesturing toward the back door. "The longer we stand out here, the better chance someone will think to peer through the hedges."

Constantine steepled his fingers, the cigarette still pinched between his finger and thumb, trailing smoke. He gave a thoughtful nod. "Will there be tea inside?"

"We can make some," Mira said quickly. Her face was alight with excitement, eyes wide and fixed on the stranger. She'd even taken out her blue notebook.

As they moved for the front door, and Thompson began to lecture Constantine about popping into people's back gardens unannounced, Mira leaned over to Bryony and loudly whispered, "He's so dramatic. He'll be wonderful for my journal."

Constantine clapped his hands together, loud enough to make the three of them wince, interrupting Thompson's soliloquy. "If you can't do it dramatically then it isn't worth doing at all."

Thompson looked puzzled, having not heard Mira's comment. Much to Bryony's annoyance, Mira's eyes had gone all wide and sparkly, and she looked even more impressed with the man, if that were possible. Bryony merely frowned at him, still not sure what to think. Apparently he had ridiculously good hearing.

He didn't seem to notice them staring. "Lead the way, my dears. I become positively unpleasant when I don't get my mid-afternoon tea, and it's nearly going on three. I should be breathing fire on everyone right about now."

Thompson led them inside, checking back over his shoulder nervously, first at the back gate, and then at Constantine. Mira trailed after the stranger, stealing glimpses as they walked, and Bryony came last, not wanting to turn her back on the man. There was something strange about him. She didn't trust him in the slightest.

And it *wasn't* just because Mira looked dangerously close to running off with him in search of new adventure. Though admittedly, that could have something to do with it.

At the door, Thompson pulled a brass key out of his pocket.

Bryony cleared her throat. "Did you cover the mirrors before you left?"

"Of course we did." Thompson shook his head, expression scornful.

"All of them?"

"Yes, every last spooky one. I've no wish to be murdered." He turned the key and it rotated with a satisfying clunk. For all his protests about covering the mirrors, he didn't step back to let Mira in, but moved inside cautiously, key still clutched in hand. He looked pointedly at Constantine's cigarette. "You can't smoke in here."

"Oh, very well. I just started this one for my entrance anyways. One must always make an entrance." Constantine dropped it, grinding the heel of his boot on the cigarette to extinguish the flame.

The back of the house began with some kind of mudroom. There were shoes lined up on the racks along the walls, and a coat closet that had been left partly open. As Bryony stepped inside, she noticed the doorframe was wider than usual, likely to accommodate people carrying coffins in and out.

Thankfully the room was entirely absent of bodies. There were no mirrors either, and she relaxed a little as she walked farther in, following the others through a short hallway of bare walls into the kitchen. A little plain, perhaps, but fully functional, with a wide basinlike sink, a claw-foot stove and an icebox in the corner.

Bryony's stomach gave an impolite grumble. She hadn't even managed to get one tiny sandwich at the hotel before the monstrous Lady Abney had attacked. There was a long table up against the wall, stained and splintered, but there were chairs around it, and she pulled one out and sat down heavily.

"I'll put the tea on. I know the servants keep it here somewhere." Mira's cheeks were glowing, and she kept darting looks back at Constantine as she flitted around the kitchen pulling cupboards and drawers open.

What did she find so wonderful about him anyway? Bryony's nostrils flared. "We don't have time for tea." Then, without any warning, she found herself blurting out, "How do we know we can trust him anyway?!"

Mira and Thompson both stared at her. Constantine picked at his nails.

"I mean, he could be a nutter, and you've let him in your kitchen because you fancy him some kind of book character!" She fixed her eyes on Mira's face, and her stomach dropped when her friend's expression turned reproachful.

It would have been better if Mira snapped back at her, but she didn't. She just turned away and put the kettle on the stove, busying herself with putting out cups and saucers.

Bryony sank lower on the hard wooden chair and dropped her eyes to the table. How stupid she was being! She was the one who'd insisted on finding Constantine in the first place. Cheeks glowing, she thought about what Thompson's face must look like right now—she refused to look, couldn't bear to. She was acting like a spoiled child again, and she knew it. Throwing a tantrum because Mira was paying too much attention to someone else.

But she couldn't seem to help it.

After a moment the kettle on the stove began to rumble gently. Bryony shut her eyes and listened to Mira banging about in the kitchen. A chair scraped and Thompson said, "Well, it's good to have a moment between the madness."

Bryony opened her eyes. They didn't have time for moments, no matter how guilty she felt about snapping at Mira. She'd been right about that. Paintings were still out there attacking people.

"Yes, tea always makes things more civilized." Constantine stared up at the ceiling, leaning back in his chair, hands tucked behind his head.

"We should speak of the matter at hand," Bryony said pointedly. "As much as I love tea, there are more important things to discuss."

Constantine sat forward in his chair, bringing his hands down by his sides. He looked affronted. "Really? What is it? If there's anything more important than tea, we must put together an expedition and hunt it down posthaste."

Bryony frowned at him. Was he being entirely serious? "Look, there's a dangerous one-armed woman out there, a trail of murderous paintings, and a mob who wants to shred me into little pieces."

Constantine made a show of stroking his chin thoughtfully. "To be entirely honest, Ms. Gray, I'm surprised you let it get this far. It isn't as if you weren't warned in advance."

"I beg your pardon?" She blinked at him.

Constantine opened his mouth, but a high-pitched whistle from the kettle intervened before he could speak, making them all jump. Mira bustled over and threw a cloth over the handle, pouring them all cups of tea before laying out saucers, cream and sugar. Bryony tried to smile at her as the other girl deposited a tray of biscuits in the middle of the table, to show she was sorry. Mira wouldn't look at her.

"Yes, thank you, love. You're truly wonderful." Constantine winked at Mira, and then took his teacup in both hands and inhaled deeply, shutting his eyes. "Lovely."

Impatience was making it difficult to sit still. More than anything at that moment, Bryony longed to smack the cup out of his hands. She took a deep breath.

"I have no bloody clue what you mean about being warned."

Constantine's eyes popped open and he tilted his head to one side, dark eyes fixed on her face. His smile faded. "What? You really have no idea what I'm talking about?"

Mutely, she shook her head. Her stomach was churning, and she tightened her grip on the handle of the teacup. Constantine set his cup in the saucer, the rattle loud in the silence. He looked from Thompson to Mira and back to Bryony.

"Good God, woman. Do you mean to say you never read the book?"

She only stared at him blankly, and it was Mira who filled the empty space. "You mean the book you made, yes? The grimoire?"

Constantine rubbed his temples, brow creased. "Well, yes, but—I mean, no, not that book, the other one." He frowned at Bryony. "Your father's book."

Her mouth fell open, and she lifted one trembling hand to her lips. Words died on her tongue. Her father, the patron . . . it was the first time she'd heard someone talk about him without using a furtive whisper. Her heart fluttered frantically in her throat, in her fingertips.

"My father wrote a book?"

"Not a book written *by* your father," Constantine said. His voice had gone serious, his expression dark. "A book *about* your father."

"Yes, but . . . surely all of that is just fiction," Thompson said, and then quailed when Bryony gave him an incredulous look.

He hadn't mentioned anything about her father up until now. If Constantine weren't here she would have leapt over the table and shook him, the traitor.

Constantine looked miserable. "The book should have been delivered to you."

"To me?" She sat upright, so fast her chair nearly tipped backward. "But I never got anything."

It wasn't a question of how it didn't get to her, though, was it? Not with the way Uncle Bernard behaved, with his secretive, strange ways, and his hoarding of every scrap of mail or missive. The way he refused to tell Bryony about her patron, or what sort of visitors had come calling. If she had received something in the mail, Uncle Bernard would have read it first. And if it had revealed something about her father, information he might use, of course he would hide it from her.

"When was this sent?" she whispered. "Who sent it? My patron?"

"I sent it." Constantine's voice was heavy. "On November 30, almost a year ago today. The night my good friend Mr. Oscar Wilde passed on."

The silence was palpable until Thompson sat back, folding his arms over his chest, expression incredulous. "Oscar Wilde," he said. "As in . . . the playwright?"

"Yes, the playwright," Constantine snapped. "Do you know of any other Oscar Wildes?" He brought the teacup to his lips, but his hands were trembling violently, and he set it back down again and scrubbed his palms on the front of his jacket.

Another silence followed, and Bryony glanced down at her own teacup to avoid staring. It was clear that Constantine had been caught off guard by some sort of strong emotion. After a few seconds he cleared his throat and she looked up again. Constantine smoothed one hand over the brim of his hat and nodded sharply to himself, pressing his lips together.

"Well, no matter. We don't have time to go into all that . . . the facts are that I am the executor of Mr. Wilde's will. Upon his death I mailed two copies of a published novel called *The Picture of Dorian Gray*—to you, and one other." He patted his lips with one of the napkins Mira had set out. "And it appears that you did not receive yours."

"I did not." Bryony squeezed her own napkin in one fist, fury building inside. "I assume there was vital information inside. Something Mr. Wilde wanted me to know about . . . about my father?"

"Indeed there was." Constantine appeared to have reverted back to his old self. The red glow was returning to his pale cheeks, and he made appreciative humming noises as he nibbled one of the biscuits. "These are wonderful, Mira dear."

Mira only blinked at him, eyes wide.

Impatient, Bryony leaned forward, smacking her palm down on the table, making the dishes rattle.

"What really happened to my father? There are rumors going around, aren't there?" She shot Thompson a black look and he winced. "You lot better tell me everything."

Sighing, Constantine put his half-eaten biscuit down. "Look, there were all sorts of wild rumors about your father. Everyone knows them." When she glared at him, he shrugged. "Well, apparently your relatives kept you rather in the dark. Anyways, my point is, some of the rumors were actually true. The man struck a bargain of sorts."

Constantine's face had gone grim again, and now the silence was like an ax hanging in the air above her, waiting to descend with his next words.

"What bargain?" she whispered.

"His soul," Constantine said. "His soul for eternal beauty."

Chapter Sixteen

His soul. Bryony couldn't seem to look at Mira or Thompson, so she settled on staring dumbly at her teacup, still half full. Cold by now, no doubt. She blinked back the tears that were threatening. It would make her sound like a stubborn child if she were to protest, but she wanted to. How she wanted to! To stand on the chair and scream at Constantine, *He wouldn't do that. He's a good person. He's waiting for me in the country.*

He had to be. Or all this was for nothing.

"Ridiculous." Thompson shook his head. "How preposterous. Sold his soul. The man was just a lowlife; it doesn't mean he made some sort of deal with the devil."

Bryony tensed forward, about to snap at Thompson that her father was *not* a lowlife, but Constantine cleared his throat, folding his hands on the table.

"Did I *say* it was the devil?" Constantine said evenly. "No. Oscar didn't seem to know that part. Could have been with an angel, or some force from within the man himself. He was so obsessed with his own youth, with beauty, that the man essentially cursed his entire family with a painting."

A cursed painting? Bryony's head jerked up. "What does that mean?"

"It was during a sitting for a famous artist." Constantine brushed at his jacket. He didn't seem to want to look at Bryony. "When Mr. Gray saw how beautiful his own portrait was, he made a terrible, reckless wish: to trade his soul in payment for eternal life. That all his age and wrongdoings would show in the portrait's face instead of his."

Thompson stroked a thumb over his chin, frowning. "Say we believe you. Why would this be affecting Bryony now? That would have been years ago."

"You have to understand how bargains like this work. Once it's passed down it becomes diluted and twisted, becoming a curse instead of a blessing. A terrible, selfish thing to do." Constantine looked at Bryony at last, his expression sympathetic. "After he died trying to break it, the curse—"

Bryony jerked upright, her hand hitting the teacup. It crashed over in the saucer, but she ignored the slow spread of tea across the tablecloth. "My father is *not* dead."

It was one thing to hear it from the lips of Aunt Gertrude, who had been nothing but spiteful, who had only wanted to wound Bryony with lies . . . but to hear it from a stranger was a different matter altogether. "What proof have you got?"

Constantine faltered. "Well, none really. He disappeared shortly before Oscar's book was published, so I'm just going on what the book says."

"Then perhaps your precious Mr. Wilde didn't know everything," Bryony snapped. When Constantine gave her a long, even look, she sank lower in her chair.

He steepled his fingers. "Perhaps. But as I was saying, the curse wasn't completely broken, not really, just damaged enough that it lay dormant for years. I'm not sure if the curse now resides in that dreadful portrait he kept in the attic for years or in your blood, or both. But the painting vanished some years ago. Which, by all accounts, is not a bad thing, since it took on all of Dorian's old age and all his wicked doings." Constantine shuddered delicately and took a fortifying sip of his tea. "And now we know for sure that Oscar was right. He heard rumors of your artistic ability when you were young, and he was worried. Afraid the curse had somehow been passed down."

Bryony took a deep, shaky breath and picked up her teacup, setting it back on the saucer. "I . . . I wish I could see the painting. If we could find it—"

"Oh, I don't think you'd want to look at it. What with the drinking and the gambling, and all the hearts he broke, I imagine it's truly hideous."

Thompson sat up straight in his chair and made a hissing noise at Constantine, who looked surprised. His eyes widened when they fell on Bryony's face. "Oh dear, yes. I suppose—I *am* sorry, dear." He cleared his throat and fidgeted in his chair, picking fussily at the buttons on the front of his shirt. "I *do* need to learn when to stop talking, don't I?"

A curse. It was hard to wrap her mind around it. Her father had cursed himself—and her, if Constantine was correct.

Bryony blinked frantically, trying to hold back tears. It was almost too much to take in all at once. She wanted to protest everything Constantine had just said. But the part about breaking hearts had brought back the memory of her mother's photograph, how faded she had looked, like someone had stolen something from her. And now Bryony knew what it was.

There was a terrible war going on inside her, between her logical side and the side of her that had dreamed about her father coming to rescue her for years and years. The logical side wouldn't take any of the moonbeams and fairy-dust answers that usually pacified it, not this time. It seemed to know it was no longer an option to sit there and wish.

Perhaps her father hadn't been a saint, but he couldn't be wicked, not truly, and he couldn't be dead. Her father had written that letter to her. He was her patron.

Her stomach roiled. She nearly jumped a foot in the air when something brushed the tops of her fingers, but when she looked over Mira was smiling at her, and Bryony relaxed as the other girl laced her fingers through hers, squeezing her hand.

"Not sure I believe in curses," Bryony muttered, and Constantine gave her an incredulous look.

"And paintings that come to life? You're sure that's completely unrelated?" He sat back and raised a brow at her. "Look, do you at least have the *other* book I sent? The grimoire I dropped off after I left the book about your father?"

Bryony sat up straight and dug into her bag, relieved to be able to at least produce *this* book. "I've got it. My uncle had it, but I snuck into his study and stole it. I . . . you sent it?" Her voice faltered.

Another letdown. All along she'd thought her patron— her father!—had sent this as a gift.

Constantine didn't seem to notice how crestfallen she was. He was busily thumbing through the book, *hmm*ing to himself all the while. "Here." He looked up, stabbing a finger at the page. "I *had* hoped this would serve as a kind of warning to you. You know, urge you *not* to continue painting." Now it was his turn to look crestfallen when Bryony only stared at the page blankly.

There was a drawing on the page, a crude sketch of a woman staring into a mirror with a tiny half-moon hanging over her head. A number of astrological symbols floated around her, and there were notes scribbled in what she thought was probably Latin in the margins of both pages.

"Is that supposed to mean something?" She tugged at the book, pulling it around to stare at the picture. "I mean, now I can see she's looking in a mirror . . ." She sucked in a breath and released it through her teeth, fighting off irritation. "But it's not very clear, is it?"

He blinked at her, and then looked around at Thompson and Mira. "Can none of you read Latin?"

Mira had her blue book out and was furiously taking notes. Now she paused to shake her head. "Mother told the tutor not to bother with me. Apparently there were other, more pressing things." She gestured at the book with her pen. "Now, if you needed me to do a needlepoint or play a particularly dreadful minuet on the piano . . ." She looked over at her brother. "You were taught Latin."

Thompson flushed. "Well, that's a bit rich. It's not as if I had time to read the thing."

When Constantine turned back to her, Bryony glared at him. "I was shut up in an attic, so no, I didn't exactly have the best tutoring. What does it say?"

Constantine let his finger drift across the page. "It talks about generational curses at the beginning of the chapter, and then, just here, mirror curses, which I believe might be related to this one. Acts the same way. Mirrors are already strange when it comes to curses. They tend to reflect whatever the curse does. Rather a bunch of copycats. Of course, I know it seems vague, but you must understand I thought you'd read your father's book." He cleared his throat, adjusting his waistcoat with one hand. His jacket had received the brunt of the paint smear, but there was still a dot or two of pink on his actual clothing. "I know rather more than most about curses, having spent a great deal of time with the fellow who wrote this book. Still, there's a lot I don't know. Why it's only just started now, for example, or why it's spreading the way it does . . ."

"With the paintings themselves," Bryony said eagerly, leaning forward with her hands on the table. "That's how it is, isn't it? They touch something." She waved one hand at his waistcoat. "They got you. When did that happen? Was it the one-armed lady?"

"Does that mean you're cursed now?" Mira leaned back, nearly tipping her chair over.

Constantine waved his hands at them. "Slow, slow— too many questions, ladies." He brushed both hands over his waistcoat and sighed, shaking his head. "Such a shame to ruin a perfectly good outfit." He raised a brow at them. "But yes, to answer a question, she did get me. And in my own house, no less. There I was, minding my own business, crumpets and tea . . . and in bursts this mad one-armed woman. Monstrous creature. Not refined *at all*. Is that any way for a lady to act—"

"Do you know why your house specifically?" Bryony interrupted him, smacking her hands on the table impatiently. She ignored the stern look Constantine gave her. "Was she after you?"

"I don't know." He cleared his throat and adjusted his cravat, refusing to look at her. "She batted me aside and began to rip my house apart. I wasn't about to stay to watch, so I went straight to Mivart's to finish my tea."

She let out a breath, almost a whistle. So the painted woman *had* been looking for someone up on the church tower. She'd found Constantine and chased him all the way to Mivart's.

That left one main question . . .

"What does she want?"

"As I said, I didn't stay to find out," Constantine said, "but I suspect someone sent her after me. I got a rather nasty letter a while ago, telling me to stay away from *you*." He gestured at her with his lighter. When Bryony opened her mouth, a dozen questions already on the tip of her tongue, he shook his head briskly. "No, I don't know who it was from, so don't bother asking. I tried to come around to warn you and was turned away by your uncle at every attempt. And then the letter and the one-armed woman."

He shuddered and brushed at his vest again. "I consider myself terribly brave for even *being* here. Someone is obviously trying to keep me from talking to you at all."

"And you have *no* idea who?" When he shrugged, Bryony had to clench her teeth together hard to keep from growling at him. The only way to stop this was to figure out how it worked and who was causing it.

"What about the other book? The one Mr. Wilde wrote?" Mira said softly, shifting her attention back to Constantine. "You said there were two copies." She leaned forward, chair squeaking. "Does Bry have a relative?"

"Some distant cousin. No rumors about her, though. Doesn't have an artistic bone in her body."

"I have a cousin?" Bryony leaned forward eagerly, nearly upsetting her teacup a second time. Thompson reached across and carefully moved her saucer and cup into the center of the table.

"Yes. I'm afraid I don't know much about her, just that Oscar had me deliver a book to her as well. The woman is some kind of shut-in. Wouldn't even see me, so I had to give it to the butler. Anyway"—he leaned his elbows on the table and peered at her intently—"that's all I know, so don't ask me how to break your curse." He plucked another biscuit from the tray and examined it idly. "It seems to be escalating."

"You don't *say*," Bryony snapped. She started to speak again, about to really lay into the man, but Mira shot to her feet. She reached out and swatted the biscuit out of Constantine's hand. It bounced once on the table and went over the side, leaving a trail of crumbs in its wake.

"Don't you *dare* sit there and eat biscuits and tell my friend there isn't any way to fix this. Don't you *dare*."

Bryony stared at Mira, slack-jawed, and then over at Constantine, who was looking down at the biscuit on the floor, shaking his head sadly.

Thompson sighed and rubbed his forehead, and Mira's cheeks flushed, but she continued to glare pointedly at Constantine, arms crossed over her chest.

He sat back and folded his hands in his lap.

"I didn't say it wasn't fixable. I said I don't know how to fix it." He raised one brow at Mira. "There's a difference. As I said, I know a fair amount about curses, but this one is different. It's morphed . . . twisted. I've no idea how to stop this." He waved one hand in apparent disgust. "Probably Oscar didn't expect any of this to happen provided you were warned not to paint actual people. Of course, there is one natural conclusion, but . . . I don't know if it will work."

"The painting," Thompson said. It was the first time he'd spoken in a while. To Bryony's surprise, his eyes were sparkling the same way Mira's did when she was intrigued by something. "That's how we solve this thing. Destroy the painting of Dorian Gray."

"Precisely." Constantine nodded. With a sideways look at Mira he leaned forward to take another biscuit. "That does seem logical, doesn't it?"

"But we don't know where it is." Bryony's voice was tight with frustration. "Uncle Bernard never mentioned a painting. I mean, we have some . . ." She let her words trail off, thinking hard about all the portraits in the house.

It was doubtful the cursed painting was a pastoral scene or something. "What does it look like?"

"It's a simple portrait," Constantine said, "and if you'd seen it, you'd know. It's ruined, slashed halfway down the middle from when . . . " He winced. "From when your father stabbed it."

"When he tried to break the curse?"

"He tried," Constantine said gravely. "Oscar claims it killed him." When Bryony grimaced he shrugged apologetically. "I'm sorry. I don't know if that's true or not. Your father disappeared after that."

Bryony took a deep breath and tried to gather her thoughts. "Well, I went all through the house, and we certainly don't have it. I would have noticed if one of the paintings had a big slash through it." She curled her hands into fists under the table.

"If you don't have it, perhaps your cousin does," Mira said. "Maybe it was passed down to her instead."

Yes. She sat up straight, heart thumping. "Do you still have the address?"

Constantine drew a breath in through his teeth. "After a year? Of course not." He stood up, brushing crumbs off his jacket. Bryony watched him take up his hat, her stomach filled with lead. That was that then, a dead end. The only new thing she'd learned was that she was cursed. And it didn't take a genius to think that one up.

"But no need for an address, dear. The woman lives in a great big tacky house on the corner of Claridge Street. As far as I know she hasn't moved. You can't miss the blue-and-yellow trim." He shuddered. "Positively criminal. I believe you'll need me to drive." He clucked his tongue at them. "But tomorrow, yes? It's just starting to get dark, and I won't have a bunch of children running around in the middle of the night when there are murderous portraits about. Mira, my dear, you wouldn't happen to have a spare bedroom?"

Bryony was so overwhelmed by all of this new information that she barely noticed as Mira led Constantine out of the room, chatting excitedly the entire way. There was a long stretch of silence, and it was just Bryony and Thompson at the table.

"I don't like leaving it until tomorrow," she said at last. "But I suppose he's right. It isn't safe out there in the dark."

Thompson shifted in his seat, tapping his fingernail on the side of his teacup, frowning. "It isn't safe in the light either. I don't like any of this, to be honest."

Of course he didn't. Bryony was about to say something when there was a clatter and a thump from the doorway. Mira was back, and she appeared to have just bumped into the doorframe trying to walk and write in her notebook at the same time.

None of them was quite ready to go to bed as early as Constantine, apparently, and Bryony—desperate to distract herself from thinking about her father and the curse—suggested to Mira that they put together a list of hand signals, a bit like that secret language she'd been thinking about earlier. To her surprise, even Thompson had seemed interested, saying that doctors in the Opium Wars had signaled one another with Morse code. Apparently it fooled the enemy.

A mere few hours ago, she would have shot back that *he* was the enemy, that the language was just for her and Mira, but Thompson had looked so eager that she gave in almost at once. It was strange to see him agreeing with her, and she'd warmed up to him a few degrees more.

So she'd taught them both the limited sign language she knew. And they added a few new signs of their own making.

Eventually they ran out of patience with the process, but Bryony had been quite happy with their results. She'd grinned, and signaled at Mira, *Us smart*, beyond pleased when the other girl dissolved into a fit of giggles.

But then it was quiet again, and all she could think about was her father.

Bryony pressed her forehead to the table, eyes shut tight as she listened to the sound of Mira opening and shutting cupboards and the gentle rumble of the kettle working itself up to a boil. The dull shuffle and thump of boots on the floor meant that Thompson was still pacing back and forth.

Everyone seemed positive that her father was dead, but how could they be sure? If he *was* dead, then who was the patron? Had she read too much into the letter? Maybe it really had been an error.

It is my greatest hope that Ms. Gray will someday regard me as family.

It had to be a hint. Some kind of code. It had to mean her father, didn't it?

Plus, if her father was alive, did he truly have no soul? Everyone seemed to think so.

But then, everyone thought she was unstable too. Her aunt and uncle had seen to that. So what was to say her father wasn't similarly besmirched? Perhaps her relatives had gotten to this Oscar Wilde person too.

It was up to her to expose the lies. To discover the truth about her father and whatever had caused this curse.

There was still something extraordinarily suspicious about Uncle Bernard's disappearance. That was something she should talk to Constantine about in the morning. They would have to start searching for him, perhaps after they retrieved the painting.

"A little tea is always nice before bedtime."

She sat up as Mira came over and filled her teacup straight from the kettle, sending a spiral of steam up to bath her face. Bryony smiled and murmured her thank you, placing her hands over the warm porcelain cup.

It would all be fine. She and Mira would uncover the truth and find her father, proving him innocent. Then they would all go live in his house in the country and have lovely adventures together. That would make Mira happy. And Bryony would paint it all as it happened.

Mira went back to the counter, and there came the slam of cupboards and clink of china, over which Thompson said, "Can't believe how early that chap goes to bed. You'd think he was ninety. Anyways, hope he knows how to drive a funeral carriage. It's the only thing we've got for tomorrow morning."

Even through her own frustration Bryony couldn't help but smile, picturing them riding about town in a funeral carriage. Wouldn't that be strange?

A sharp cracking sound cut into her thoughts, followed by a scream from Mira. Bryony shot up so fast her head spun. Mira was facing the stove, grappling with something—the kettle. She was gripping the stove with one hand, struggling to pull herself away. There was something stretching out from the kettle, a flare of quicksilver arcing out, wrapping silver tendrils around Mira's wrist.

For a moment, Bryony couldn't move. Thompson was standing on the other side of the kitchen, eyes bulging, feet rooted to the ground. Mira shrieked again, high and shrill and so full of terror that it sent a bolt of fear straight through Bryony. She hurtled forward. Grabbing Mira's shoulders, she pulled her backward. Thompson leapt into action then, yanking the kettle away from his sister, wrapping his hands around the metal base. He flung the kettle across the kitchen.

Bryony caught herself just before staggering into the table, keeping her grip on Mira's shoulders. Across the kitchen, Thompson gave a strangled cry of pain, clasping both hands to his chest. Mira's blue book lay open on the floor, pages crunched and torn, and next to it the kettle lay on its side, boiling water pouring out of the top, steam billowing out around it. Bryony stared at it with wide eyes, chest heaving. It didn't move or change.

From this far away it just looked like . . . a kettle.

Still, she seized the cloth Mira has been using earlier and darted forward, throwing it over the kettle without looking too hard at the shining metal surface. Mira must have been holding the handle with the cloth earlier, and it had draped down over the kettle. Bryony bit her lip hard, eyes watering. She should have noticed, but she'd been so preoccupied with Constantine.

Returning to the counter she grasped Mira's arm, gently turning her around. The other girl's eyes were filled with tears, and her entire body was trembling. There was something different about her, something that made Bryony's blood turn cold. Her face. Mira's perfect, heart-shaped face. It had changed.

A faint dusting of freckles had appeared over her nose and cheeks, and her face was the slightest bit narrower. On either side of her mouth fine creases had appeared, so faint that no one would notice unless you were standing nose to nose.

Mira blinked at her. Tears spilled out over her cheeks and trickled down to her chin, and she said in a small, trembling voice, "I dropped my book."

It was hard to catch her breath. Bryony shut her eyes and forced herself to think clearly.

The Mona Lisa *is painted in oils, on a cottonwood canvas.* The Last Supper *took three years to complete.* Vermeer's Girl with a Pearl Earring, *painted in oils on a 17.5-by-15-inch canvas.*

She took a deep breath.

Still holding Mira's shoulder with one hand, Bryony reached out and touched the girl's face with shaking fingers. Had Mira gotten older?

There was a groan from the other side of the kitchen as Thompson staggered over to the sink and ran his hands under cold water, but she couldn't look away from Mira's face. The change was subtle, but it was there. Was this what happened to the people who'd sat for her paintings?

The years had been sucked out of them? It was starting to truly register now. The pile of ash; the mummy in the art gallery.

This was all her fault.

"Mira," she breathed, and then her voice failed her completely, words sticking in her throat. *I'm so sorry.*

Mira's lips trembled. She shook her head.

Another groan from Thompson at the sink. He was resting his elbows on the side, hands palm up, letting the water run over his fingers, which were bright red and already blistering.

Mira took a sharp breath and released it, turning to the sink. She took her brother's wrists, examining his hands.

When Thompson saw her face he went white. "You . . . you're . . ."

Bryony couldn't see the look Mira gave him, but it was enough that he fell silent.

"You're right," Mira said. "This is too dangerous."

Thompson only shook his head, and Mira clasped his arm, her voice a whisper. "But that's why we have to find the painting."

Thompson looked down at his sister's face, and he pressed his lips together, brow creased. Both of them looked shaky, on the verge of collapse. Mira reached up and touched her own cheek, tentatively, as if she were afraid to find out what had happened.

"We've got to stop this."

Chapter Seventeen

T he next morning Bryony discovered that there was a very good reason that nobody except dead people rode in the backs of funeral carriages. The ride was unusually bumpy, seeing as there were no seats in the back, and she pressed her hands to the wide glass window, trying to brace herself. Her body ached from being continuously tense for the last ten minutes.

By contrast, she could hear Constantine whistling cheerfully up front. He'd been thrilled to drive the funeral carriage, exclaiming how very fashionable he would look perched atop it.

She didn't think much of his taste, if she were honest. It was a huge, black coach—long and rectangular, to fit a coffin—with glass on all four sides. The walls were draped with heavy red curtains on the inside, and sharp red spikes jutted from the rooftop at all four corners. It was a wicked-looking thing, ornately threatening, and not something she'd like her dead body to be transported in at all, never mind her perfectly live one.

But it wasn't as if they had a choice, and besides, there

didn't seem to be anyone to gawk at them as they rolled past. The crowd in front of Bryony's house appeared to have moved on, leaving the street full of empty carriages and piles of burned and broken picture frames. Not only did it make it difficult to navigate with the carriage, but it was also eerie. The city seemed . . . abandoned.

Every street they traveled through seemed to be worse than the next. Most were in shambles, some crowded with overturned carriages and buggies, automobiles abandoned in the center, many with engines still running. In the market square the stands had been knocked over and the roads were crowded with bruised fruit and vegetables. More than one building along each road was in flames or just starting to smoke.

Down the next street and the next. There was only the odd person here or there, sometimes running, ducking from one upturned carriage to the next, and sometimes cowering in doorways and on balconies, trying to stay out of sight. The blare of sirens could be heard non-stop, even through the thick glass of the carriage, and Bryony's stomach tied itself into knots as she pushed the red velvet curtains aside and peered out the window, pressing her face to the glass.

She kept a lookout for the painted monsters, but she didn't really expect to see any. It looked as if they'd already been through. They seemed to be spreading through the center of the city, now most likely heading for the outskirts, the wealthier neighborhoods, which was exactly where their carriage was headed.

Neither Mira nor Thompson seemed to have much interest in looking out the windows. They were both white-faced and silent this morning. Last night, Mira had managed to find an old medical kit in the bathroom. The kit had been covered in a layer of dust, but it contained a roll of bandages, among other things. Constantine, who'd been awoken by Mira's scream, had tried to help, chattering about salves and tonics and how he'd read a book about burns one time, but Mira had insisted on wrapping Thompson's hands herself, blinking back tears all the while.

Meanwhile, Thompson had kept trying to play doctor in spite of his burned hands, diagnosing Mira with shock and telling her to lie down. When he tried to look more closely at her face, she insisted she was fine, and that he should lie back and rest. Each was anxious about the other, as if they were determined to out-worry one another.

And all of this—the entire wretched situation—was Uncle Bernard's fault. For keeping her locked up. For disappearing the moment everything started. For not telling her about whatever this strange power was. Or curse, as Constantine had said. Whatever it was.

She took a deep, trembling breath, reaching back to pluck the paintbrush out of her braid, smoothing her fingers over the polished wooden surface. Just for something to hold on to. When she found Uncle Bernard, he would regret it. He was a horrible, wicked man for lying to her and for keeping Mr. Wilde's book from her. And especially for forcing her to paint when he knew what might happen. That this thing, this . . . curse, might hurt people. That it might spread.

And now it had, and she was the one responsible.

Even as the carriage rocked forward, Thompson kept his bandaged hands pressed to his chest, bracing himself with his feet. He kept glancing back over, eyes fixed on Mira's face, a deep crease between his brows. Still, no one spoke, and Bryony couldn't bear the silence any longer.

She cleared her throat. "We'll find the painting. And then . . ." She hesitated, not wanting to say it. "Then maybe you two should just go back. I'm sure my cousin will help me."

That was a complete lie. It was far more likely this mysterious, reclusive cousin would take one look at her and toss her out on the street. Whoever this woman was, she hadn't tried to contact Bryony once. In all likelihood she wanted very little to do with her scandalous family. And who could blame her?

"We shall see," Thompson said, but he didn't look at her, only at Mira. Her complexion had improved slightly. Her face was no longer sheet-white, and the freckles didn't stand out as much anymore. She almost looked herself, though she didn't smile.

"I'm not sure I want to go back to the house." She looked at Bryony, who felt her chest tighten at the raw fear in the other girl's eyes. "When that . . ." She faltered. "When the reflection touched me . . . I felt it start to suck something out of me. It was about to drain me." Her voice shook. "I could have ended up like those people, the ones at the museum."

Bryony shuddered, trying to push the memories away. She didn't want to think about the pile of ash or the crawling mummy. It had been better—more comforting—when she'd thought they were monsters.

To think that she'd been so entranced with Mira's beauty, so obsessed with the idea of painting her. Her father's curse really *did* run in the family.

And now this had happened.

"I won't let anything hurt you. I promise." She leaned forward, boldly taking the other girl's hand. Mira didn't pull away, much to her relief. "And you're okay. It didn't touch you long. You barely changed."

"How much older do I look?" Mira straightened up abruptly, eyes wide and alarmed. "Mother's already talking about having my coming-out party early, for my fourteenth birthday. And then she'll be free to marry me straight off to that horrible Sir Albert. Do you think I look older?"

"Certainly not enough to be noticeable." The relief was almost enough to make her knees weak. If Mira was worrying about something as ridiculous as debutante balls, it probably meant she was back to her regular self. "And I'm sure a coming-out party wouldn't be that horrible."

"Not quite as bad as becoming a shriveled mummy." Mira turned to look at Thompson. "Which I would have been if you hadn't grabbed me. You were very brave back there, Thompy."

For once, Thompson didn't protest the nickname. His cheeks flushed red at the compliment, and he fixed his eyes on the window, looking pleased with himself. "Yes, well. Um, did you get your notebook before we left?"

Mira sat up straight. "Oh no, I—"

"I've got it," Bryony said hastily. She was already digging into her bag, pulling out the blue notebook. When she handed it over, Mira gave her a watery smile, relief flooding her face.

"You rescued it from the floor?"

Bryony nodded, face flushing. "It was sitting in a puddle though. I hope it's okay."

While Mira tried to smooth out the wet and crinkled pages, Thompson leaned forward, peering out the window past the curtains. "Looks like we're nearly there, at least. We're on the right street now."

"Good." Bryony settled back in the seat, determined not to appear frightened even though her chest was slowly tightening at the thought of approaching the house. "I'll go knock and explain who I am. If she lets me in, then everything's fine and you two can go home."

Mira frowned. "I'd rather not leave you with some stranger. What if this woman paints things too? Perhaps she's got an attic full of murderous portraits."

"Constantine said she doesn't have a creative bone in her body, so it's safe to say she doesn't paint," Bryony said.

Mira arched a brow at her brother. "Maybe an attic full of murderous stick people then, but—"

"We'll wait." Thompson was playing with a bandage that had come undone. "I'm curious to see this painting anyway. To tell the truth, I've often wondered what really happened to your father. Surely this *Picture of Dorian Gray* is mostly fictional."

Bryony gripped the paintbrush so hard it creaked. "I think it is. I think he's still alive, out there somewhere.

He has to be." She hesitated. "But, will you tell me about the book? What's in it?"

Thompson grimaced. "Good heavens, I haven't read it. And even if I *had*, it's not something a civilized person admits to."

"Well, then, what have you heard—"

Just then the carriage gave a lurch, tilting her forward in her seat.

They were picking up speed.

Thompson pushed the curtain aside and they all leaned forward to peer out. The streets were no longer filled with upturned carts and carriages; in fact, they were fairly normal, save for a large amount of traffic coming through. This was rather a surprising sight after the deserted streets they'd just been on, and Bryony leaned forward, pressing her hands to the glass.

Constantine had encouraged the horses into a brisk trot, to keep up with the other traffic. Everyone seemed to be driving rather faster than usual, perhaps fleeing the more chaotic parts of the city.

They were in a much finer neighborhood now, and the farther they went down the street, the more extravagant the houses became, growing from narrow little buildings to medium-sized houses and then mansions with wide, wraparound porches. On top of that, the signs of chaos had vanished completely, as if nothing had touched this neighborhood at all.

"They haven't been here yet," Bryony said. "Or at least they haven't been spotted here yet."

"These houses are enormous." Mira tipped her head

back, pressing her face so close to the glass she left a nose print. "Far bigger than ours. Which one do you think your cousin lives in?"

"Look for the trim." Bryony craned her neck, trying to peer up as far as she could as they passed by. "Constantine said it's tacky. What did he say, blue and yellow?"

"Oh, I think that's it." Thompson's voice was excited. "On this side, look here. It must be the one, we're slowing down."

She slid across the seat to peer at the house, and Mira crowded behind her. The carriage kept going, moving away down the street, and Bryony was about to reach up and thump the top of the roof again when it began to pull over and slow to a stop. In the sudden quiet they could hear the other carriages passing them, and the sound of Constantine whistling to himself up front. It made sense not to park directly in front of the house if they were going to scope out the place, Bryony had to admit.

"Oh my," Mira said. She had the telescope out and pressed to her eye already. "Constantine is right, it *is* ugly."

"Poor taste in color hardly matters . . ." Her words trailed off. There was a man going up the walkway toward the house, dressed in a long black jacket and bowler hat. Perhaps her cousin had company, or her husband was returning home.

"Here, can I see the telescope?" Bryony nudged Mira, who handed it over, looking pleased with herself.

When she pressed the brass scope to her right eye the house and walkway came into sharp focus. The man had paused on the steps of the house. He dug into his jacket pocket, pulling something out. It was hard to see from across the street, but she caught a glimpse of gold, and noted the way the man peered down at the object. A pocket watch, maybe.

She frowned, pressing closer to the window, the hairs on the back of her neck prickling. The way the man walked, how he hunched his shoulders up to his ears . . .

At that precise moment, the man turned to wave away his carriage driver, who'd been sitting by the curb in front of the house, and she got a good look at his face. The black caterpillar brows, the red nose, the narrow eyes set in a pudgy, pale face. Her heart stopped.

"Uncle Bernard?"

ome foolish impulse made her clap her hand over her mouth. As if merely speaking his name out loud—even shut up in the carriage and a hundred feet away—could somehow attract his attention. Hastily, she grabbed the curtain and jerked it back over the window.

She'd had brief suspicions, fleeting thoughts, but this . . .

When she at last sat back, breathing a little harder than she probably should have been, Thompson and Mira were both staring at her in shock.

"That's your uncle?" Mira's blue eyes were wide.

"Why is he at your cousin's house?" Thompson frowned. "I thought you didn't know about her."

"I don't . . . I *didn't*." Bryony glared at the curtain, tempted to draw it back halfway, to see if he'd gone inside yet. "But clearly he knows. Add it to the list of things he didn't tell me."

"So . . . what's going on then?" Thompson looked down at his bandaged hands, brow creased in thought. "Your uncle must have read the book. Perhaps he guessed your cousin might have the painting as well."

"Then they both know how to fix this," Bryony said slowly. "If Constantine is correct, and the painting is the key to breaking the curse."

"But neither of them has done it, or told you about it." Mira picked at the fabric of her dress, her eyes far away. "So does that mean they don't want to fix it? That they want it to keep spreading?"

"I'm not sure." Bryony didn't want to think about that; it made her skin crawl. "Look, whatever it is my uncle and this cousin of mine are doing . . . I don't like it. I don't trust him." Had she really ever trusted him? No, certainly not. Aunt Gertrude had been a persnickety old bat, but at least she'd been predictable. Who knew what the man was up to?

"But we still haven't got a choice. We've got to get our hands on that painting, or we just sit here like dummies while London falls apart around us," Mira said.

"Right," Thompson said miserably. "What's the plan then?"

Bryony folded her arms over her chest. "I'm going to break in."

Thompson made a sound of protest, but before he could say anything, there was a dull thumping from the front of the carriage. Constantine was kicking the front wall with his heels. Bryony flicked the curtain back again, peering out the window.

Something was happening on the front porch. A figure burst out of the doorway, pushing past a woman in a blue dress, crashing into Uncle Bernard. He went down, arms and legs flailing. There was a tangle of petticoats and bright blonde hair and a single flailing arm that landed on him. It slowly uncurled and sat up, revealing a pale face and a pink dress. Black holes for eyes.

The Lady Abney monster was sitting atop Uncle Bernard, trying to claw his eyes out, by the looks of it. Bryony watched all of this happen in the space of several seconds, eyes wide.

Then the woman in the blue dress moved through the doorway and reached out to snatch a handful of the monster's shorn hair. The woman dragged Lady Abney back toward the door, and the one-armed creature struggled half-heartedly, still reaching for Uncle Bernard. The woman in the blue dress shoved the monster inside. Then she turned back to Uncle Bernard, who was slowly climbing to his feet, clutching the railing with one hand.

Bryony leaned sideways, trying to make out the woman's face properly. There was something vaguely familiar about her, but she wasn't close enough and half of her was obscured by the post in the middle of the porch. The woman said something, gesturing at him with a dismissive flick of the wrist. Then she stepped back and shut the door in his face. For a few moments Uncle Bernard stayed where he was, staring at the door. Then he brushed off his coat with shaking hands and yanked the door back open, striding inside before slamming it shut behind him.

Bryony pulled the curtain into place and leaned back in her seat. Nobody said anything in the stunned silence, until Thompson finally sighed.

"Blast it all. This just got even more complicated, didn't it?"

Everyone jumped as the back door opened and Constantine launched himself inside, narrowly missing Thompson's left leg as he threw himself down and arranged himself cross-legged on the floor of the carriage, cupping his chin in his hand. "Well, that was most interesting. I nearly had the vapors when I saw that horrible monster. Luckily, I pulled my hat low and slouched. I'm a magnificent actor when I don't want to be seen." He tilted his head and stared at Bryony. "It seems your cousin was the one who sent that thing after me . . . perhaps she knew I was going to warn you."

"This changes things." Mira was hunched over in her seat, furiously taking notes in her blue book. "What does that mean?"

"She controlled it," Thompson said darkly. "That can't mean anything good. How did she manage that, do you think?"

Bryony was silent. Her cousin had somehow ended up with the monster that *she* had painted. How exactly did that work?

"One thing is clear," Thompson said, regarding Bryony gravely. "You can't sneak in there. That thing will rip you to shreds."

He was probably right. She shivered, hugging herself. The last time she'd been face-to-face with it, back in the attic, all she could think about was the way it looked at her with those empty eyes . . . hideous. It left her alone after that, as if it had been driven to leave the attic. To seek out—what? It wasn't wise to count on that happening again; it was far more likely that next time she got close it would attack.

"We need to think." That was all she wanted to do at the moment, just sit and think quietly until her head stopped spinning.

For a few seconds that was all they did, though she kept expecting Thompson to blow up and declare he was taking them all back home. Finally Mira shifted in her seat and cleared her throat. "How do we fight it?"

"Not you," Thompson said. "You're not putting yourself in any more danger."

"That's getting old, Thompy." Mira rolled her eyes.

"Do stop calling me that."

Bryony chewed her thumbnail. Aunt Gertrude would have scolded her and smacked her hand for such an unladylike habit. She moved on to her other thumb. Back at Mivart's Hotel, a liberal application of Earl Grey tea hadn't destroyed the monster. But judging by the gargling scream, it had resulted in some kind of damage.

It stood to reason that paint thinner would be even more effective. As much as it pained her to admit it . . . as much as it made her feel sick at the very thought . . .

"We have to go back to the house."

"Right." Constantine clapped his hands, startling all of them. "You're the boss. Home then? Break for midmorning tea?"

Bryony shot him a cross look. Everything was always about tea with him. "You've just had breakfast."

Constantine shrugged. "Well, one can never have too many breakfasts."

Thompson looked relieved. "Finally you're making sense. We should just go home, and call the police."

Mira shifted in her seat, and Bryony turned, startled, to find the other girl shaking her head in dismay.

"What—"

"*Please* don't say you're calling it off, Bry. We can do this!"

Bryony blinked. "I'm not calling it off. Don't worry. I'm *never* going back there. Not to stay." Was she saying it to reassure Mira, or herself? She wasn't entirely sure. "Look, I've got a plan." Bryony clutched the bottom of the window frame and pressed on before anyone could interrupt. "We need a few things." Perhaps white paint and a few more brushes. She glanced down at the paintbrush in her hands and then stuck it back into her hair. Thicker brushes were needed for this job. If paint thinner didn't work, blotting the creature out might.

Mira's expression relaxed into a smile, and surprisingly, Thompson didn't protest.

"Smashing." Constantine fished into his pocket and pulled out his gold-and-silver lighter, producing a cigarette from the sleeve of his jacket. "Let's head out."

He tipped his hat, the top of which ended up clunking hollowly on the carriage ceiling, since there was barely enough room for it while it was on his head, and then he slid over, shoving the doors open with his feet.

Thompson shut the doors behind him, waving his hand in front of his face at the trail of cigarette smoke. "All right. Back home. We'll help you get your supplies, and then you're quite on your own, I'm afraid."

No one argued with him this time, mainly because everyone knew without saying so that it simply wasn't true. Even Thompson folded his arms over his chest with a resigned sigh, as if he'd merely said the words out of force of habit.

The only sound for the next few moments was the rumble of the carriage wheels. If she sat there in nervous silence, she was bound to think about the attic again, to worry that she would walk into that place and never come out. That something would come over her and she would stay there by choice. That perhaps her relatives had brainwashed her so completely . . .

But no, that was ridiculous.

To distract herself, Bryony leaned forward and pulled the curtains aside. To her dismay, they'd only traveled several houses down and now appeared to be slowly coming to a complete stop.

The street ahead was packed with even more traffic, ramshackle carriages wedged in right next to packed trolleys. There was even a stopped trolley bus on the side of the street, and the driver had climbed out and begun to smoke, gesturing at the traffic in irritation.

Bryony pressed closer to the window, breath catching in her throat, dread already pulsing in her chest. "Blast! This isn't good."

There were no signs of paintings anywhere, no smoke rising except in the very far distance, and no screams . . . but still. It couldn't mean anything good. It couldn't be a simple traffic jam, could it?

Mira and Thompson both leaned forward to look, and Mira fidgeted where she sat, tapping her boots against the wooden floor with dull clumping sounds. "What is it? Is it the paintings? Do you think they're coming?"

"Another mob perhaps?" Bryony had chewed her nail well past the tip of her thumb now.

"If it is, that would mean they know you're in this part of town." Thompson went to rub at his forehead, and then grimaced, holding his bandaged hands away from his face. "Not good at all."

At last the carriage pulled up short. The one in front of them, another hansom being pulled by a dust-colored pony, was stopped completely, parked beside a luxury automobile piloted by a cross man with goggles perched on his head. Ahead of that, there were more carriages, all down the road, until the street turned the corner, and Bryony was willing to bet there were more after that.

"I'll go check what the holdup is." Thompson slid across the seat and shouldered the door open. Constantine, it turned out, had already jumped down and was in the middle of an animated discussion with the driver of the hansom cab in front of them.

Bryony leaned forward, straining to hear the conversation through the open door.

"Blocked off all the way to Cherry Street, you say? Do you know what the problem might be?" Constantine pushed the brim of his top hat back with one finger and tapped the ash off his cigarette, his face unconcerned, as if it were merely a casual inquiry.

The second driver shrugged, leaning back against his cab. "Well, I reckon it's all exaggeration, but here. Picked this up on me way over." He thrust a bundle of crumpled newspapers at Constantine, who took it with a tip of his hat.

All down the line, drivers and passengers were crowding in the street, and there was a buzz starting miles down the road, the hum of excited conversation that grew and swelled as it came nearer.

Bryony practically had to squash her face against the glass as she attempted to read over Constantine's shoulder. All she could make out was the headline: *Quarantine*.

Constantine's mouth dropped open as he skimmed the article. His cigarette fell to the road, trailing a wisp of smoke, embers scattering over the stones. He turned to Thompson, who was standing just behind him, and his expression was grim.

"It's not good," he said. "I don't believe we'll get through this way. They're saying there's a quarantine on."

Bryony shot out of the carriage, shoes clattering on the steps. "A quarantine!"

She'd read about quarantines before. How they helped to contain things like smallpox. This was serious business. "If they're quarantining parts of the city, then it must be spreading fast."

Constantine, whose face had gone very pale, shook his head and carefully folded up the newspaper, drawing in a deep breath before saying, "Not just parts of the city, darling. London. The entire city of London."

Chapter Nineteen

"We've got to get this carriage backed up before we get stuck in this mess." Constantine started for the front of the carriage, fishing another cigarette out of his sleeve, and Bryony wondered for a brief moment, in spite of everything, exactly how many of them he had hidden about his person.

Reluctantly, she backed up toward the carriage. "We haven't any relatives in the area to stay with. What does the paper say about it anyway?" A tight, painful knot formed in her chest, spreading down into her stomach.

"That paper said it's a plague." Constantine whisked the lighter up to his mouth and lit the cigarette, puffing once before continuing. "Says they're finding people all shriveled up like mummies." His brow creased. "Strangest curse I've ever heard of. What is it trying to *do*?"

"Well, it's certainly not a plague. I've studied them all." Thompson straightened his shoulders and puffed his chest out, flipping one hand carelessly, as if he weren't troubled at all. Bryony was fairly certain she saw his eye twitch. "I'm studying to be a doctor, you know."

Mira had been leaning out the door of the carriage to listen, and now she added, "Thompson is right; he did study them all. He was sure he had the Black Death for a week, and he still sleeps with his plague mask under his mattress."

Thompson's chest deflated, and he shot his sister a look of irritation.

The traffic wasn't moving an inch, and Bryony could feel the frustration mounting as the noise from the crowd grew louder. Horses and buggies ahead of them were attempting to turn around in the limited space. Carriage doors slammed and voices called out over the buzz of gossip. Groups of people, couples and families with young children had climbed out of their carriages and were making their way down the sidewalk. It seemed that more and more people were abandoning their coaches. The crowd in the street was growing rapidly.

And then the screaming started.

At first it was so faint it could have been anything—a seagull's cry from the Thames River, perhaps, or a spooked horse whinnying. All the same, the three of them went tense, exchanging a long look. Mira spoke in a hushed, trembling voice. "Is that—"

"Back in the carriage," Constantine said tersely, and none of them argued.

Once she was settled inside, Bryony had to squint to see out the glass wall properly.

Columns of smoke began to appear in the distance, too black to be from chimneys, and the keening wail of a siren started up.

"She's here. It's her again." Bryony shot up, as much as she could with the ceilings so low.

"Stay put!" Constantine's voice came through the thin wall of the carriage, muffled and full of dismay. "It's a complete mess up ahead. We won't get through."

The sound of glass shattering and frantic screaming could be heard clearly through the hearse's thin walls. People were climbing out of their carriages to stare down the road behind them. Some were already pushing forward, moving away from the noise as quickly as they could.

A high, terrible shriek split the noise, louder than the screaming and decidedly more frightening. A chill dropped down Bryony's spine, and she turned around, pressing one hand to the glass, already knowing what she was going to see.

The lady in blue must have let the painted monster go, or she'd gotten away.

Sure enough, a splash of pink appeared in the distance in the middle of the street. Moving fast, parting the crowd before and behind. The screams flared up as the pink thing drew closer, and before long she could make out the painted Lady Abney. Behind her came an assortment of horrifying creatures.

The shepherdess was there, seizing anyone within arm's reach, staring into their faces before tossing them aside with an angry screech.

The twins came next, still locked arm in arm as they had been in their portrait. They placed their white hands on the side of an ornate gold-trimmed carriage, tipping it over with one shove, sending it crashing onto the street.

194

The screams of the people inside mingled with the twins' high-pitched giggles.

There were others—the wicked-looking baron for one, stomping his way around carriages and buggies, smashing in the windows. And running through the crowd, launching herself from the top of one carriage to the next, was a sour-faced Queen Victoria, her crown crooked on her head, her billowing skirts flowing out around her. She whacked through the tops of the carriages with the scepter she carried in one hand, leaning down to shriek at the passengers.

The paintings were getting closer and closer. It was either get out and risk being crushed by the panicked crowds, or stay in the carriage and hope the glass remained intact. Around them the crowd began heaving, rocking the carriage back and forth, a tidal wave of people behind and in front of them, running and screaming, shoving one another out of the way.

From somewhere above came a terrific crash, and then the wicked baron was there, looming above one of the carriages he'd turned over, no more than ten feet away. Bryony stared in shock, hands pressed to the glass as the baron punched through the wooden door of the carriage and hauled out a terrified young man. The man thrashed in the baron's grasp, screaming and slapping at his attacker's arms. The bizarre thing was, the baron was him. Or at least their faces were the same. They had the same sharp chin and the same ears that stuck out like flaps on either side of their face. The same dark, curly hair, a little bit too long at the top and too short at the sides.

The wicked baron placed his hand on the man's chest and a look of intense concentration came over his terrible, painted features. The man stopped struggling, his entire body going stiff. Lines and wrinkles appeared on his skin as his face began to shrivel like a prune. In contrast, the painted baron's features only seemed to grow sharper, like he was slowly becoming more real.

Then the crowd was in the way, blocking her view.

Bryony pressed her back against the glass, feeling her head start to swim with the familiar beginnings of panic.

She took a deep breath.

The first art was on cave walls thousands of years ago, engravings and paintings done in red ocher and black pigment. The earliest paintings often depicted hunting scenes.

Slowly she opened her eyes. They should go, escape before one of the paintings spotted them inside. Bryony opened her mouth to say so, but an angry howl rose up, drowning out everything else. It was coming from the wicked baron, though Bryony couldn't see over the crowd.

There was silence inside the carriage for a moment. Mira and Thompson huddled in the corner, eyes wide and terrified, but Bryony's mind was working furiously.

The baron had found his double and crumbled him, but the painting didn't seem happy about it. It sounded . . . angry.

She pressed her palm to the glass, staring out eagerly. "They only ever want their double," Bryony breathed. "But . . . he didn't *just* want the double."

Mira and Thompson only stared at her.

"Didn't you see it? The painted baron touched the real one, but it wasn't happy when he crumbled." Her hand flew to her mouth. "I think . . . I think it's still trying to be the original curse. My father pledged his soul. I think they want *souls*."

Bryony's excitement surged. She sat up straighter, spoke faster, her words tumbling over one another. "The curse is still trying to perform its original purpose, what it was made for. But it's broken, so it doesn't know how. Instead of sucking the soul out and immortalizing the subject of the painting, it's sucking the years away."

Mira's eyes went even wider. "That's why it's spreading. It keeps failing. It's trying to fulfill its original purpose."

"This is just going to get worse and worse." Bryony gripped the strap of her bag, her fingers white. "I have to go back."

Thompson sat up so fast he hit his head on the top of the carriage. "What?"

"This is my father's fault. My family did this, and if my cousin has that painting, I have to find it. Now. I can't wait any longer."

Thompson and Mira both shouted as she slid forward and kicked open the door, jumping down onto the pavement. Heart in her throat, Bryony plunged into the writhing crowd before anyone could stop her.

Thankfully Constantine didn't notice; he was far too busy shouting at a couple of men trying to climb on top of the carriage.

Bryony attempted to elbow her way through the frantic crowd, a task that quickly proved nearly impossible. She only moved forward a couple of inches at a time, and was stepped on and elbowed every few seconds.

Finally she settled on letting the crowd push her forward. Luckily, they were flowing back toward her cousin's house anyway, even if she couldn't cross the street yet.

She could see the bright pink of the painted Lady Abney in the near distance, a splash of color in the panicked crowd, and she kept her head down and tried to dodge between people, finding an open space here and there. Some of the mob had spilled over the gates and hedges and into people's yards, and the crowd was much thinner here. At last, Bryony found herself able to break away from the crush. She ran, ignoring the stitch in her side, fixing her eyes on the house at the end of the road.

Several minutes later, and thoroughly out of breath, she was at the gate. She looked both ways up and down the road, peering into the yard in front of her. There was nobody there or in any of the windows of the house, and the crowd was far too busy panicking to notice one small girl slipping uninvited into someone's front yard.

Once her feet were on the porch her heart started to slow its frantic beat. She was here; there was no going back. She had to find the painting and put a stop to all of this. She curled her fists at her sides, jutted her chin in determination and slid her fingers over the cool door handle. The lock gave a neat little click, and to Bryony's surprise, the door slid smoothly inward.

The front hallway beyond was lit by several lanterns in sconces along the wall, which was done in eggshell-blue wallpaper. There was a gaudy crystal chandelier overhead. Just beyond that, in the very center, was a red-carpeted staircase. And beneath it, the dim entrance to a hallway.

Bryony bit the inside of her cheek. Did she dare venture up the staircase? Or was it better to try the hall first? She crept forward, trying to step as lightly as she could in her boots.

The hallway then.

The light was dim in the corridor, and what looked like framed pictures hung on the walls between each door that Bryony passed. Luckily, some enterprising individual had thought to drape a thin cotton sheet over each painting, though there was one lying facedown in the middle of the hallway, shards of glass glittering in the carpet. Bryony skirted carefully around it.

Surely none of these could be the painting of Dorian Gray. It had to be locked away somewhere.

She paused at one of the doors, hand hovering over the knob. Where would she, Bryony, hide a valuable painting if she had one?

This place was even bigger than she'd realized, and her heart sank at the thought of trying to search all of these rooms without getting caught.

She was just turning the knob, fingers trembling slightly on the cold metal handle, when there came a gentle scuffle from somewhere nearby.

She froze, heart pumping in her ears. It had to be the cat, or the house settling, or—

The scuffling sound came again, directly behind her.

Bryony turned—too slowly, far too slowly—just as someone snaked an arm around her throat. From behind, a cold, wet cloth crushed her nose and mouth, suffocating, trapping her breath in her lungs.

She couldn't breathe, not properly, and something flowery filled her nostrils, overwhelming in its cloying sweetness. Stars danced, the hallway lights flickered and blurred together to form a glittering daisy chain. Though she desperately tried to bring her hands up to knock the cloth away, they hung limply by her sides. She was a puppet, and someone had cut her strings. Her eyelids were weighed down by stones, dragging down and down as she struggled to keep them open. She pictured herself opening them and bursting into consciousness, kicking and screaming. Instead, her eyelids finally slid shut. Her thoughts became jagged, coming in bright spurts and then drifting off, and slowly the panic in her chest eased.

What had she been worried about? How silly.

The last thing she saw before the darkness came was the warped silhouette of her attacker stretched across the wall like a faceless portrait.

Chapter Twenty

When she opened her eyes, the darkness didn't retreat. Was it night already? Had she drifted off?

Bryony groaned and struggled to sit up. Her mouth tasted fuzzy and sour, and her temples throbbed in time with her heartbeat.

For a second the room seemed to spin, revolving in slow, lazy arcs. Her stomach tried to lurch up into her throat and she forced it back down. Panic was sinking into the edges of her consciousness, and instinctively she fought against it. It was important to keep a level head about this, to focus.

Giorgione: Renaissance painter killed by the plague in 1510. Rococo artist Antoine Watteau succumbed to tuberculosis in 1721. Pietro Aretino died of a laughing fit in 1556.

Not the best subject, of course, but it was what popped to mind. And surprisingly, it worked. The panic receded and Bryony breathed deeply in through her nose. She stayed where she was, hands gripping the sides of . . . what? A couch? Yes, definitely a couch.

The room stopped revolving and swam into view,

allowing her to assess the situation properly. There were boxes and trunks neatly organized along each wall. One corner—the corner she found herself in—was furnished, complete with a cot, a small kitchenette and the couch she was currently lying on.

Bryony dug her fingers into the fabric of the couch and bit back a scream of frustration. She'd started out at the beginning of all of this trying to find her freedom and her patron, and had met with nothing but dead ends and trouble. And now here she was, trapped in another room and all alone again.

Slowly she drew herself more firmly upright, head throbbing harder than ever. Her stomach gave an angry rumble. It felt like something was eating away at her insides, and she groaned. How long had she been out?

She swung her legs over the edge of the couch, and her feet hit a cold cement floor. Flinching, she stared down at her bare feet.

Who had taken her shoes, and why?

The answer was obvious—*so I can't run*—but it wasn't something she cared to think about. After a moment of sitting, which she told herself was solely to collect her bearings and not a case of fear-based paralysis, she stood up slowly—very slowly—on shaky legs.

The room was empty. So perhaps this depressing little setup was meant for her. From one prison to another. The thought made her mouth taste sour, and she drew in a deep, shaky breath.

It wasn't going to happen.

Bryony wouldn't be trapped in here forever. There was

no way Mira would give up on her. She and Thompson and Constantine would come. And Bryony's patron had to be out there looking for her somewhere, didn't he?

But she might as well try to get out on her own. First things first: explore the surroundings and assess her best chance of escape.

Now that her vision had adjusted, she could see the source of the dim light filtering into the room. It was coming from a staircase on the far side, leading up to a door.

So this was a basement. She looked around more intently. A few of the suitcases and trunks looked very new, and there was a big oak grandfather clock, still ticking away, pushed up against the wall.

But . . . there was something slightly different in one corner. A couple of boxes had been knocked over, their contents—paperbacks with faded, crumpled covers—spilled out over the floor. There was a wide smear of bright paint beside one of the boxes, and Bryony held her breath as she moved closer. Her hands trembled, and she clenched them into fists to stop the shaking.

That color . . . that brilliant pink that had become so horribly familiar. The painted woman had been here, in this very basement.

The image of the monstrous Lady Abney flinging herself at Uncle Bernard came back to her. She didn't hear any noise from the crowd outside, which either meant the basement walls were very thick or that hours had passed and the crowd had gone.

The most logical thing would be to find a weapon. But when Bryony cast about for a convenient cricket bat, or

perhaps a croquet mallet, she found herself at a loss. Everything was in bags and boxes, which were stacked on top of one another.

She chose the nearest box and tore the top open. Folded silks and satins, discarded clothing, useless. The next box held shoes, the next a series of grim-looking rubber plague masks. Bryony growled under her breath, about to slam the box shut, when something glittered near the bottom, a sliver of glass just wide enough to reflect her face. She gasped and jumped backward, slamming the flaps shut.

Breathing heavily, she sat absolutely still for a moment. Thankfully, she hadn't seen her reflection, not properly. Slowly she climbed to her feet and eased the flap of the box back open, reaching one hand down, gingerly searching for the piece of glass. It had looked sharp, and so she was very careful. But she wanted it *because* it looked sharp. It was better than nothing.

There. Her hand closed around something that felt like a mirror, cool and smooth under her fingers, biting into her skin the slightest bit. She eased it out, taking care to flip it over so the back was pointed upward.

The doorknob rattled.

Bryony snatched her hand back, dropping the bit of glass into her dress pocket, and darted back toward the couch. If someone was coming to check on her, she wanted the element of surprise. The door squeaked open. She burrowed into the couch cushions, curling up on her side. Footsteps on the stairs, loud boots clumping down. This was how she'd been lying when she woke, wasn't it? She couldn't remember.

The footsteps clumped all the way down and stopped, and she squeezed her eyes shut and forced herself to take deep, even breaths. Scuffling noises followed as someone approached, accompanied by a sharp clicking sound.

Bryony frowned as the shuffling drew closer. That sound was so familiar. Her eyes flew open, just as a deep voice said from above her.

"It's no use, Bryony. I know what you look like when you're pretending to sleep."

ncle Bernard looked the same way he always did. She wasn't sure why that seemed strange, but she'd almost expected him to have grown a long mustache since she'd last seen him—one he could twirl while he laughed—or to have begun dressing all in black. After all, he had known about the curse and hidden it from her. He had let Aunt Gertrude get eaten by the mirror, and he was in league with a woman who controlled a monster.

But he didn't look different, or particularly evil. He just looked sweaty.

For a moment, neither of them said anything. They both stared at one another unblinkingly, Bryony in shock and Uncle Bernard in nervous silence, fiddling with his pocket watch.

At last, he cleared his throat. "I really didn't mean for any of this to happen. I hope you know that, Bryony."

She pinched her lips together and stared harder at him. Uncle Bernard cleared his throat again, rubbing his hand over his brow. He seemed to be sweating even more profusely now.

"I mean, of course I realized some of this would happen. The curse kicked in as soon as *she* triggered it." Uncle Bernard waved a hand at the ceiling. "We had to be sure it was working. But then it spread." Out came his handkerchief, an embroidered one Aunt Gertrude had monogrammed for his birthday. He mopped his forehead with it. Did he even feel bad about Aunt Gertrude?

He stuttered and then continued. "I didn't see that coming, so I take it upon myself to end this." With trembling hands, he reached into his jacket and pulled out a very sharp-looking letter opener. It was long and silver with an ivory handle shaped like a swan.

Even in the dim light it glittered, and fear clenched her heart tightly and thrust it up and up, almost out of her chest. Blood rushed in her ears.

"I read the end of the book. Skipped the beginning. All I really need to know is how to stop it." Uncle Bernard's brown eyes were wide and sorrowful, and he slowly sank down on the couch beside her, still keeping a safe distance, keeping his motions slow and careful. Like she was a stray cat he was afraid to spook.

Her mouth was dry, but she forced herself to speak. "How did it end?"

"Are you sure you want to know?" Uncle Bernard said softly, and he stared down at the letter opener in his hands. "Your father died, and he stopped spreading death and misery around. The curse was broken." He was clutching the letter opener now, and his jaw clenched and unclenched.

"I wish everyone would stop saying that! He's not dead! I know he's not." Bryony glared at him. She slipped one hand into her pocket, fingers brushing the sliver of mirror. "What did she do to start it?"

Uncle Bernard looked up from the letter opener, startled. "What's that?"

"The curse," Bryony said. "What did she do to trigger the curse?"

Uncle Bernard shrugged. "Well, I suppose I can tell you." He glanced toward the stairs. "She's out." He lowered his voice, still glancing at the staircase now and then as he spoke. "She brought the painting over to the house. The original one, of your father. She said to hang it somewhere near you, that the curse was probably generational and the painting would trigger it again. Said you and the painting were two halves of a whole. If I brought it close enough, the curse would be triggered, awoken from where it lay dormant in your blood, and in the canvas." His eyes were wide. "It's terrible . . . the painting, I mean. I couldn't bear to look at it so I had a mirror put over the top to disguise it. I thought maybe destroying it would break the curse, but . . . but *now* . . . now I can't find it." His voice shook and he clenched his meaty fists in his lap. "I knew I shouldn't have accepted her so-called hospitality. While I've been staying here, she went to the house. The painting needs to be destroyed, but she took it. When I went back . . . it was gone."

The cursed painting—the very thing they were looking for—Uncle Bernard had put it behind the mirror he'd hung in her attic.

Bryony felt sick. She'd stood right in front of that mirror with no idea of what it had been hiding. She'd been inches away from it. She could have stopped this before it started.

So she really had triggered it. Or . . . her cousin had, indirectly.

It made a lot of sense when she thought about it. Everything had started to go wrong after Uncle Bernard brought that awful mirror into the house. That was why the paintings had started going funny. And why her attic had been in shambles when she'd returned from the art gallery, why the mirror had been removed from its spot above the fireplace . . .

And if that wasn't enough to make her head spin, it sounded as if her cousin thought she was actually *part* of the curse. *Two halves of a whole.*

It all fell into place.

"So," she said, and her fingertips brushed over the sharp edge of the mirror in her pocket. It had occurred to her that she didn't actually have to stab her uncle with the jagged shard of glass. The mirror had other uses. "Why does she want this? The entire city has been quarantined. People are being shriveled up like raisins and turned to dust."

Uncle Bernard looked miserable. He smoothed his fingers over the handle of the letter opener, staring down at it. He wouldn't look at her. He really was a coward. "I don't know," he muttered. "She won't tell me anything— aside from saying that this has turned this city on its head, and that change is good because it means opportunities."

"In other words, she isn't letting you in on her plan." She leaned back, eyeing the distance between them. How fast would he be able to reach her if she pulled the mirror out? It had taken only a few seconds for Mira's reflection to grab her, but who know if that would work in this case.

"How does she control it—the woman I painted?" Bryony asked. "She's got the real Lady Abney locked up somewhere in this house, doesn't she?"

Uncle Bernard shifted uncomfortably on the sofa. "Well, I . . . I don't really keep track of what she's doing anymore."

Bryony gave him a narrow look. He was a terrible liar.

"And why did you let her trigger the curse?" she said, and Uncle Bernard flinched. "What was in it for you?"

He began to play with the letter opener again, and Bryony's right hand twitched, ready to pull out the mirror. But not yet. She had to know first.

"You must understand, dear." A hint of his normal, oily tone was returning now. As if he were sliding back into an old and comfortable suit. Because he was about to explain something, and Uncle Bernard prided himself on explaining things. "Your curse is not a curse . . . not really. It's a gift. And we could use it." He flashed a wide, white smile, eyes glittering. "I had great plans. We would work for the King himself, you would paint his enemies and I . . . we would be famous. Made wealthy for our service to the country. I had to see if it would work. Can you imagine it, Bryony?"

"Yes," she said, her voice flat. She could imagine it. It would just be another version of what she'd done for the past few months, only the attic would be fancier, and the people sitting for her would be the generals of opposing armies and royalty from countries with which they were at war.

"I didn't realize it would get so out of control." Uncle Bernard's shoulders slumped. "Who could have predicted it would affect mirrors the way it has? That it would be so widespread? She thinks it might be because the painting was damaged some time ago. The curse is leaking, or some such thing. It's not working the way it was meant to. And now all my wonderful plans . . . ruined!"

"A terrible shame for you," Bryony said sharply, and his face went dark.

"Yes, well. You might think badly of me, niece, but as I said, the only thing for it now is to put a stop to all of this." His fingers tightened around the letter opener, and he raised it slightly. "Sacrifices must be made. I'm terribly sorry about this."

"I am too," Bryony said, and she yanked the mirror out of her pocket and pointed it directly at Uncle Bernard's face.

He only blinked at first, and then he must have realized what it was, because he pushed himself backward off the couch with a strangled shout. He fell heavily onto his backside on the concrete floor, eyes popping open wide and still fixed on the mirror.

In her hand, the sliver of glass jerked. She stiffened but held on, the jagged edges biting into her fingers. Something long and silvery shot out of the other side of the mirror and wrapped itself around Uncle Bernard's throat like a quicksilver boa constrictor.

She couldn't watch.

Even with her eyes squeezed shut, she could feel the mirror jerking. It wasn't any heavier, and she could hold

211

it in one hand, technically, but the movement was unnerving, and she wrapped both hands around it and held on tightly. Scuffling and grunting filled the room, and then the sound of gasping, loud and raspy breathing. That had to be enough; she couldn't bear it anymore. Uncle Bernard was vile, but this was too much like slow torture, from the sound of it.

Her eyes flew open.

There, in the middle of the room, was an old man, hunched over and grappling with what looked like a silver snake. The man barely looked like Uncle Bernard anymore; his face sagged all over, so deeply wrinkled it was hard to see his beady eyes. The silver snake curled around his throat more tightly as he clawed at it, his mouth open wide. Only wheezing gasps came out.

Horrified, she gripped the mirror tightly in one hand and yanked on it. There was a sharp pain in her hand as it resisted, and a thin trickle of blood ran down her wrist. It was impossible to force the thing back into the mirror! Perhaps it would turn on her once it had crumbled Uncle Bernard to dust.

"Stop!" she yelled, and it finally gave, snapping back into the mirror so fast that she pitched forward, stumbling until she finally caught her balance and steadied herself on the arm of the couch. The glass smashed to pieces as it hit the floor, and shards of glittering mirror skittered across the cement, reflecting her face over and over. Bryony flinched when the reflections all lifted their arms, pointing straight at her. In that moment, she knew what they wanted.

Her soul.

She grabbed wildly for the nearest box, upending it, sending silk scarves and gloves and odd bits of linen tumbling to the floor until the glass was covered, until she could no longer see her own face reflected anywhere.

After a second of thought she darted forward and grabbed one of the nearest pieces of fabric, a silk handkerchief that had drifted over one of the smaller shards. Carefully, she wrapped the sliver of mirror and put it in her pocket. It made her nervous to have it so close, but at least she had something, in case she had to use it again.

The basement was silent. Neither she nor the new, older Uncle Bernard said anything, only looking at one another. Finally, he let out a rasping cough and said loudly, "What am I doing here? Where's Gertrude? Is someone at the door?"

Chapter Twenty-Two

"What a dump this place is. Bryony, be a good girl and take me home." Uncle Bernard was turning in circles now, taking in the basement with watery blue eyes.

So, he'd locked her up in the attic for the last six years, abducted her, nearly stabbed her with a letter opener, and now she was expected to be a "good girl" and take him home. It was tempting to just turn around and leave. She scowled up at him. "It would serve you right if I left you here."

"What's that, dear?" He was already doddering toward the stairs, back stooped, muttering in a cracked voice. He clearly wasn't himself anymore.

"I said, it's nice weather here." It seemed he was completely senile; most likely, he didn't remember anything he'd done. Walking away now would be like abandoning a box of puppies.

And if her conscience wasn't enough in this case, there were a number of far more logical reasons not to leave him behind, the first being that he was her legal guardian. She was already down an aunt, after all.

Bryony sighed and hurried over to him, taking him by the elbow gently. "Come along, let's get you up the stairs."

"Yes, yes." The old man huffed. "You know, you're my favorite granddaughter."

"Niece." Bryony bit her lip. He was going up the stairs so slowly it was painful. He had said her cousin was out, so she would probably be back soon, though the state of the streets would slow her down. In any case, her return could prove bad for Bryony and her newly senile uncle. No doubt the woman would be furious to learn he'd let her escape.

But there was no hurrying the old man. He was concentrating very hard on his upward progress, the wrinkles around his eyes growing even deeper as he frowned. He clutched her arm with one hand and the railing with the other, wheezing with each new step.

It was unspeakably frustrating.

Over the dull *thud, thud* of his footsteps and the light tapping of her own, a very faint noise started up from some faraway corner of the house, a rhythmic thumping sound. Bryony froze, foot hovering in the air above the next step, clutching Uncle Bernard. He didn't question their sudden stop, and seemed only to be relieved for the rest period.

The thumping sound stopped, and Bryony held her breath and clutched the railing tightly. Then it started up again, quiet but growing slowly louder. It sounded as if someone were playing war drums, but badly, and on and off.

"Uncle Bernard," she whispered, and when he didn't answer she said it louder, a whisper-shout. He blinked at her.

"Do we have to go on the stairs again?"

No point in telling him he was still on stairs, and that he would have to either go up or down soon. "No, not yet. Just stay here, all right? Don't go anywhere until I check if the coast is clear."

He nodded and clutched the railing, mumbling under his breath. He'd be fine until she got back. Bryony crept the rest of the way up the stairs, wincing as they squeaked underfoot.

The thumping continued, and she paused at the top of the staircase, fingers curling around the doorknob. Her insides felt quivery, like that horrible raspberry jelly Aunt Gertrude used to give her. She twisted the doorknob slowly, grimacing when it clicked. But it wasn't as if a tiny noise like that could be heard above all the thumping that was going on.

The door wasn't locked, and as she pushed it, it swung slowly open. The thumping paused again. Beyond the door was what looked like a kitchen, a glimpse of a sink and a counter and a shiny tile floor.

Perhaps if she ran she could make it out before anyone stopped her. She felt a pang of guilt at the thought of leaving Uncle Bernard behind, but she could bring help back if she made it out. She could fetch the others.

A quick glance back once showed her that Uncle Bernard had grown bored and begun making his way back down, one stair at a time. Good. He could stay in the basement.

The question was . . . sneak, or run for the exit? She settled on a sort of combination, poking her head around the doorframe first to check if it was clear, and then scurrying over to the table in the middle of the kitchen. As soon as she reached it, the thumping started up again, and Bryony dropped into a crouch beside the counter, heart beating furiously. She pressed her back to the drawers, balancing on the balls of her feet. The position was extremely uncomfortable, but she stayed there and listened, barely breathing. The strange thumping was still muffled enough to sound far away, and it was still irregular, starting and stopping in bursts. As if someone was banging on a wall or a door.

If it was the real Lady Abney, she should probably rescue her. But there was always the risk of running into the painted one on the way there.

She couldn't go investigate without a weapon.

Bryony darted a look around the kitchen. She hurried forward as quietly as possible, yanking open first one cupboard and then the next. Canned pickles and jars of preserves. Not exactly what she was looking for.

The next cupboard was more promising, and Bryony snatched one of the glass jars off the shelf. It was filled halfway with white powder. She screwed off the lid, checking nervously over her shoulder as she did so, and dipped a finger in to touch it to her tongue.

Baking soda.

Another quick search revealed several jars of black liquid—vanilla and molasses, probably—and one near the back that held clear liquid. Bryony snatched up that one, unscrewing the top and sniffing. Vinegar.

She grimaced at the smell, then tipped in a bit of the vinegar, jamming the lid of the baking soda jar on tightly before it could fizz up over her hands. She shoved it deep in her pocket.

There, at least she had something now. But it would go flat eventually, so she had to do this fast.

Scurrying forward, short breaths, quiet steps. At the kitchen door she pressed her back to the wall and peered around the corner. A long hallway spread out in front of her, dimly lit with flickering gas lamps. Squares of black cloth covered large portions of the wall, places where portraits or mirrors were covered up. Bryony felt a jolt of recognition, remembering the portrait lying facedown on the rug. It was gone now, but there was a faint dent in the carpet. This was the same hallway, which meant the front door was just ahead.

The dull thumping continued overhead, growing louder as she crept down the hall. Instinctively she stayed close to the wall, though the jig was up if anyone turned the corner and stepped into the hallway. There was nowhere to hide.

At the end, the hall opened up into the same foyer she'd been in before, and for a moment she stared at the door, torn. She could get out of here, just . . . escape.

But she'd come here for a reason.

The noise from overhead only seemed to be getting louder. Someone was in trouble up there, needed her help. Bryony took a deep breath and set one foot on the staircase.

She took the steps two at a time and was greeted by another short hallway at the top. This one branched off in two directions. To the right was a wide, empty parlor, warmly lit and decorated with salmon-colored wallpaper and slender standing lamps. Though the couches and chairs were beautiful—all dark carved wood and plush, velvety cushions—they were punctuated by horrible, red-and-orange tasseled cushions with the late Queen Victoria's face embroidered on them. Bryony grimaced and went left instead, which led to another set of stairs, this one with a narrow door at the top.

The thumping sounds were coming from behind the door.

Someone was being held prisoner.

She remembered Uncle Bernard's expression when she'd asked about the real Lady Abney, how guilty he'd looked. It had to be her.

She swallowed, throat dry. Muttering uneasily to herself, she climbed the staircase and paused in front of the door. It was as if the person on the other side had heard her, for the thumping stopped abruptly.

She cleared her throat, smoothing her sweaty palms against her dress. "Lady Abney?" Her voice was small, tremulous in the silence. Another long pause, and then the thumping on the door resumed, louder this time. She jumped.

Lady Abney had to be trapped inside, maybe tied up and unable to yell for help. She reached for the doorknob. It couldn't be unlocked, could it? She'd have to find the key, or pick the lock somehow, or . . .

The doorknob turned, and the door creaked outward a few inches. It was dark on the other side.

"Lady Abney?" A rustle from the other side, and Bryony stepped closer. "Hello?"

The door crashed open, smacking her face and shoulder, sending her backward, and she shot one hand out, grabbing for something, anything to stop her fall. Her fingers snagged the railing, slipping, ripping her nails back in a flash of white-hot pain. But it was enough to slow her down, and she finally caught the rail and felt herself swing sideways, slamming her back into the wall on the fourth step, knocking her head as she came to a stop.

Vision swimming, she sagged forward, still clutching the railing, gasping for air. She couldn't pass out. Not here in the middle of this house.

William Blake, watercolors, born in 1757, died in 1827. Thomas Lawrence, pastels, born in 1769, died in 1830.

Gradually the darkness began to recede, the stairs beneath her feet coming into focus.

A dragging, scraping sound came from the top of the staircase. Slowly she turned her head, grimacing at the pain the motion sent shooting through her neck and shoulders. A splash of pink. Blonde curls that looked as though they'd been hacked off at the root. Gaping black eyes.

Bryony stiffened as the painted Lady Abney dragged herself the rest of the way through the door with one arm. She was definitely faded now. Patches of her were lighter than the rest, and a great portion of the bottom of her dress seemed to be missing, but still she kept coming.

Bryony's entire body hurt, throbbing as if it were one giant bruise, and the staircase was still swimming in wavering circles, but a very insistent voice somewhere in the back of her mind kept repeating: *Get up. Run.*

Allan Ramsay, chalk drawings, 1713 to 1784—

Grasping the railing, she levered herself up, and then nearly collapsed as the staircase spun faster around her.

She was going to die. This was it. The painting *she'd* created was going to shred her into confetti and throw her around the house just for fun.

She cleared her throat. Maybe she couldn't move without passing out, but she could still talk. The painted woman hadn't bothered to stand. She slid down the first few steps on her belly, wiggling like some kind of hideous fish out of water, leaving a thick trail of paint behind her. Her one arm reached for Bryony with grasping white fingers.

"Stop." Bryony slid down one step and then another, so hastily she nearly fell backward, and though her temples throbbed from the effort of speaking loudly, it seemed to work. Lady Abney paused on the third step, and just as it had done back in the attic on that very first day, her head tilted to one side in consideration. Perhaps all the paintings would do what she said, just as the mirror had.

The thought made her a feel a little sick, that monsters like this would obey her because . . . because she was one of them. But better that than having the one-armed woman crush her like a bug.

It was hard to concentrate with Lady Abney staring at her. The way her mouth gaped open—a black, endless maw—made it look as though she were always screaming. And her *eyes*. Her eyes were almost worse. So endless and dark that there might be some intelligence glittering deep inside, like a diamond at the bottom of a well. But you couldn't be sure until you got close enough. And by then it would be too late for whoever was looking.

Bryony shuddered. Terrifying as the creature might be, perhaps she could be reasoned with. Slowly, she reached for her pocket. If she could keep the thing distracted long enough to grab the jar . . .

"I know what you want." She slid one hand inside the pocket of her dress and wrapped her shaking fingers around the lid of the jar, slowly unscrewing it. "I'm your creator, and . . . part of you . . . part of this curse. I can give you what you want. A soul." Sweat was starting to soak her collar and collect along her brow. Opening the jar with one hand was harder than she'd expected.

The painted woman stayed still, considering, much as one would stare at an insect that had wandered across the breakfast table, pondering whether to swat it with the newspaper or a slipper.

The lid came loose, and Bryony straightened up, triumphant, just as the painted woman moved, scrambling to her feet, swinging her fist into the wall with a crack, splattering paint across the steps, spraying speckles of beige oil paint across Bryony's cheeks and neck.

Bryony flinched back with a yelp, struggling to pull the jar out of her pocket—was it caught on something?—as the monster moved down another step, head tilted, face thrust forward.

It should have been impossible to read the monster's expression, but Bryony was getting the distinct impression that she had only seconds left. All her clever talking was useless.

The jar was slippery, and she nearly dropped it. Something splashed on her hand and her skin tingled, but she couldn't look away from the monster's face. A little voice in the back of her mind screamed, *Do it now!*

Her fingers tightened on the cold surface of the jar. The stairs shrieked as the painted woman flung herself forward, scrambling down the steps, closer and closer.

Bryony drew the jar back and then flicked it forward, a scream rising in her throat. The liquid arced up, glittering milk-white droplets under the lights. It splashed across Lady Abney's face.

The monster's neck snapped back and she writhed, her horrible scream ringing through the stairwell. Already the baking soda was working; there were huge, foaming spots on Lady Abney's face and shoulders, and the paint smeared and ran. One of her black eyes seemed to be liquefying completely, seeping into the rest of her face, turning her white skin into a mess of muddy brown.

Bryony splashed her once more before retreating, inching down stair by stair since she didn't want to risk falling. She kept her eyes on the painted woman, who seemed to be melting slowly from the top downward. Great trails of paint had begun to run down the steps, rivers of pink and black and beige, muddy mixtures of all three blending in the middle.

Bryony reached the last step just as the painted woman finally collapsed, swimming in a pool of blurry brushstrokes until she was nothing more than a giant puddle in the center of the staircase, slowly spilling over and down the steps to the growing mess at the bottom.

There was paint all over Bryony's left leg, and all down the back of her dress, and she couldn't have been happier about it. She felt like laughing, propped up against the wall at the bottom of the stairs, the empty glass jar lying at her feet.

She shut her eyes and breathed deeply. The air smelled like paint, of course, and chemicals. Now to find a way out of this place.

Bryony's eyes flew back open as a thought occurred to her.

She *could* just look for the painting now. As appealing as escaping was, this seemed like too good an opportunity to pass up, now that she was here. She could put an end to all of this. And if the monstrous Lady Abney had been kept up there in the attic, perhaps it was because she was guarding something. Like the painting. It was worth a try. If it wasn't there, well . . .

She'd think about that later.

This had to be done fast. Bryony pushed herself off the wall with both hands, climbing to her feet, ignoring the shooting pain in her head. She made it up—gripping the railing, swaying slightly, but still triumphant. Then a cold, haughty voice from behind froze her insides, and the triumph crumbled.

"Bryony Gray, you certainly have a flair for making a mess."

Chapter Twenty-Three

The woman standing over her had on a very frilly lavender dress, and a hat was perched on her golden curls. There was a cameo pin on one side of her collar, the lumpy outline of the late Queen etched in white stone. As Bryony watched, the woman pulled white tea gloves off and pursed red lips at her. It was Lady Abney's friend, the beautiful one, Lady Plumberton. The one she'd wanted to paint instead of Lady Abney. What was she doing here?

"Lady Plumberton?" The words came out squeaky. The blonde woman arched a brow at her.

"Oh, you can call me Lottie, dear. How lovely of you to drop in like this." She chuckled, low and mean. "I sent our little painted friend everywhere after you. All over London, over to that silly Constantine chap's place, the tearoom. But you kept giving her the slip. And now you show up here. It really is too fantastic for words."

"*You're* my cousin?" Bryony frowned, feeling as though her brain was still playing catch-up.

A shuffling sound jerked her attention away momentarily, and a man came into view in the hallway behind Lottie.

He was round-faced and weak-chinned. His cravat was crooked, and his hair was slightly ruffled at the top, as if he'd been hurrying after her.

"Lottie, dear. She'll find her eventually . . ." Upon seeing Bryony, his voiced trailed off and his face lit up. "Ah, there, you see? A happy ending after all."

"Quite, my dear." Lottie clasped her hands together delightedly.

Bryony was starting to put two and two together, and she didn't like what it equaled. "You don't have a twin, do you?"

Lottie tittered. "Silly girl. Of course not. Your uncle set up the appointment so I could assess your particular talents. Now, where is he, by the way? He and I must have a little chat." Her narrow blue eyes swept over Bryony, and then up and down the hallway. "Hiding somewhere, no doubt."

"Yes, I suppose." Hopefully, Uncle Bernard would stay put. She would rescue him once she found a way out of this mess.

"We'll deal with him later." Lottie looked over at the stairs, at the river of paint, and pouted. "You've destroyed my fun, you know that?" Lottie swept forward, skirts rustling, seizing Bryony's arm very tightly just below the elbow. "Well, never mind. I was getting bored of her anyway. Come with me, little sister."

Bryony stumbled, so surprised she barely protested, allowing herself to be dragged down the hallway, deeper into the house. "Sister?" she sputtered.

Lottie smiled prettily down at her. "Oh yes, half sister,

to be precise. Mr. Wilde was mistaken. Our father had two daughters. But I was kept . . . a secret."

Her brain felt fuzzy with shock, and she opened her mouth and shut it several times before she was able to form a proper sentence. "What? But . . . I've never heard about you. Uncle Bernard never . . ." Bryony let her words trail off. Lottie's cheeks had begun to redden, her pink mouth turning down in a scowl. She looked as though she might explode.

Instead, she sniffed and said, "Yes, well, everyone knows *you're* his daughter, because your uncle did nothing but feed the rumors. He was smart; I'll give him that. The moment he knew you had any talent for painting he began sparking people's interest. And so you started getting famous for your portraits. I didn't get so lucky."

"Lucky?" Bryony stared up at her, aghast. Why did people keep *saying* that? "I was shut up in the attic for *six* years. My relatives told everyone I was unstable."

Lottie nodded sharply, eyes glittering. She had loosened her grip a little, but she still didn't let go, steering Bryony firmly down the hall. "You think that's bad? I grew up a servant. A *servant*, Bryony. My grandfather couldn't bear to admit I was my father's daughter, so he pretended I wasn't related to him, that his precious daughter never had me. The day my mother—my weak, useless mother—gave birth to me, my father left her, and her heart was broken. She didn't fight it after that. I suppose it was just . . . easier to give in to madness. Then Grandfather had her committed." The scorn was plain on Lottie's face. "And I was given a *new* mother. Our scullery maid." She gave a sharp,

227

mirthless laugh. "Did you know, he finally admitted I was related to him? But it took him years, and by then it was too late. He was going senile."

Lottie's eyes were swimming with unshed tears, and her voice was low and bitter. "We were both treated badly, and now we're going to get ours."

Bryony only nodded, concentrating on keeping a straight face to mask her disappointment. Some small part of her sympathized with Lottie, knew just how unfairly they'd both been treated. But that didn't justify her triggering the curse.

Just her luck to search high and low for a family member only to find one who was completely *mad*.

"Anyhow," Lottie said. "Don't you worry, I have a plan. Things have been going beautifully so far."

"How did you control that thing? The painting. You've got Lady Abney locked up somewhere, don't you?"

Lottie shrugged. "I've studied curses extensively, but they're unpredictable. It was a guess that the painting would come looking for Prudence, and I was right. My only real gamble was testing to see if I could bargain with it, or if it would just rip my arm off before I got a word out." She winked. "I'm an excellent gambler."

"And what did she want from her?" Bryony said, hoping Lottie would let something slip about the curse, about how to break it. "Her soul, by any chance?"

"You're a Gray, all right." Lottie stopped in the doorway of the huge plush parlor Bryony had seen earlier. "We're smart, the Grays." She sank down on a blue velvet fainting couch, patting the seat beside her, and Bryony had to fight back a couple of the grouchy-looking Queen Victoria pillows to actually clear a space.

"Now, I'd like to discuss our plans. That's why I sent your uncle back to get you after he got spooked and ran when the mirror finished off your aunt." She shook her head. "The man is so small-minded; he couldn't accept the fact that the curse might have spread a bit."

"A bit?" Bryony nearly shouted, pushing herself off the fainting couch.

"Heaven's sake, don't raise your voice," Lottie said sharply. "You don't see royalty shouting, do you?" She leaned forward and tugged the bellpull hanging just to the left of the couch. "Let's call for some tea. I can't discuss anything without tea. Grandfather only imports the best from India."

Bryony's heart lifted a little bit. Perhaps this grandfather would be home any minute to put a stop to this. To rein in the childish tyranny that Lottie seemed to radiate from every pore.

"And where is he?" she inquired politely. "Away on business?"

Lottie cackled. "Yes, away on business at Bedlam. Ernest and I had him committed."

"You had your grandfather thrown in the asylum?" Bryony said, horrified.

"Well, he was mad. He kept denying me everything," Lottie cried. "And worse than that, he was *old*. All covered with wrinkles and always blabbing on about things that happened ages ago." She shuddered. "I simply couldn't have him around anymore. I couldn't bear it. Anyways," she said, her face suddenly dark, "he seemed to think it a perfect place to send my mother. So I think it's only fitting that he joined her. Don't you?"

Thankfully, the tea came at that moment, delivered by a woman in a white apron, who deposited the tray on the table and disappeared without a sound. Bryony couldn't seem to form words, only a few outraged sputters.

Lottie fixed wide blue eyes on her. "Be polite and drink your tea, little sister. If we're going to redeem our family name, I must teach you how to behave in public." She frowned. "You're not *actually* unstable, are you?"

Bryony ignored the question, even though doing so was far ruder than not drinking her tea. "And how on earth do you expect to redeem our family name when half of London is in ruins because of us? There's an entire mob out there searching for me; it's probably gotten a lot bigger by now." She wiped sweaty palms on the front of her dress, and her fingers grazed the small bundle in her pocket. She'd forgotten about the mirror. She could use it on her newfound sister, but after seeing what it had done to Uncle Bernard . . .

Besides, Lottie *was* her half sister; it didn't seem right to try to kill her without at least giving her a chance. Perhaps she could be reasoned with. At the moment, Lottie wasn't coming at her with a letter opener. It was possible she could be talked out of whatever mad plans she had brewing.

Bryony slid her hand into her pocket, hoping it looked like a casual gesture. "And how will you stop all this? You'll do something with the original painting, won't you? Stop it from being so strong, somehow. That's how you triggered this in the first place."

Lottie's smile disappeared. "I said not to worry yourself, dear."

There was a dangerous edge to her voice, but Bryony pushed on. "We can't very well talk if you won't tell me your plan, can we?"

Lottie leaned back against the couch, folding her arms across her chest. "I'm going to throw a party tomorrow night, where we'll make an announcement. All the most fashionable people will be there. That's when we'll explain the Gray family curse—and how we'll stop it. We'll be heroes."

Bryony stared at her. So, Lottie *was* planning to stop the curse.

But . . . after all that? After all that she'd done to trigger it, to spread it, even knowing what would happen? It felt like there had to be more, that there was something Lottie wasn't saying.

"That's it?" Bryony said, as casually as possible. "That's your entire plan?"

Lottie's smile wavered, and for a split second some indiscernible emotion passed over her face. Then it was gone, and she beamed and waved one hand at Bryony. "Don't worry your head about the details, sister. I've been planning this for weeks. Nobody is going to ruin this for me."

She was definitely hiding something.

"No one is going to show up to a party." Bryony gripped the handkerchief in her pocket so tightly the shard cut into her fingers through the cloth. "There's a quarantine on. People are worried about murderous paintings and being mummified by their mirrors, not what sort of dress they're going to wear."

"I'm calling it a quarantine party, like a masquerade party but with plague masks. Victoria always did say improvisation is the mark of leadership." Lottie clapped her hands, wicked glee etched across her face. "There's going to be dancing, and quarantine-themed party favors, and when the big finale comes, you're going to paint someone. It's perfect!"

For a moment, Lottie's words didn't register. Then it sank in. Bryony collapsed back onto the couch and stared at her sister, aghast. "Wait, what? I can't paint someone else."

"Of course you can." She didn't seem to notice the dazed look Bryony was giving her. "It will show them exactly what we can do, in case they doubt us."

The tea had gone cold anyway, so Bryony slammed it down on the saucer with a crack, glaring at the woman sitting across from her. "You're clearly insane, and I'm certainly not going to follow along with your plan."

Lottie stood up so quickly that Bryony jumped, nearly pulling the mirror out of her pocket. "I'm your big sister, and your legal guardian once we get your uncle out of the way. You have to do as I say." She looked triumphant, as if Bryony would have to obey simply because she'd said so.

"And to think they call *me* unstable." Bryony folded her arms over her chest. "I'm not going to do anything you say."

Lottie turned sharply, dress swirling around her. Her face was a thundercloud. Then she fixed her eyes on the window and her anger melted away abruptly, replaced by a wide, fake smile.

"We'll talk more about this later, dear." Lottie clasped her hands together and smiled sweetly. "Now, what have you got in your pocket?"

Bryony started. "What? I don't know what you mean."

Lottie's eyes glittered dangerously. "I'm not stupid, darling. Your hand keeps drifting to it, like you're thinking of pulling something out. Ernest!"

Ernest must have been listening at the door, because he shot into the room almost immediately, an ugly smile on his face.

Bryony reached for her pocket, but Ernest was faster. He lunged across the room in one step and seized her wrist so tightly she could feel the bones grinding together. He didn't even seem to notice when she screamed at him, kicking his shins, swinging at him with one fist. With his other hand he reached into Bryony's pocket and fished out the bundle of cloth.

"Ah yes. No doubt something you found in your ransack of my kitchen, you little thief." Lottie wrinkled her nose at Ernest. "Be a dear and throw that out."

Ernest slid it into his pocket and gave Bryony a smirk.

"It's just past dinner, sister darling. I'll have the servants bring you something. You'll sleep here in the parlor for tonight, and tomorrow I'll have them make up your bedroom. You'll take my old one, I think. Welcome to the family."

Lottie shut the door sharply behind her, leaving Bryony standing in the center of the room, listening as the key clicked in the lock.

———

For the first few hours she paced the room, trying to determine how she might get out. There were two entrances to the parlor. Both doors were locked, of course, and she had nothing on hand to pick the locks with. When she tried the windows, shoving the frilly pink curtains aside, she found they didn't open at all.

Eventually a servant came, a solemn-looking woman who bustled about in complete silence, laying out a tray of food and arranging an armful of blankets on the couch before lighting a fire in the grate. She didn't look at Bryony once.

After the servant had gone, locking the door behind her, Bryony settled herself on the fainting couch in front of the fire. Wrapping herself in the scratchy wool blankets, she picked at the dinner on the tray—cold chicken and potatoes. She felt very tired all of a sudden, her eyes drooping as she watched the flames flicking at the wood in the fireplace. She wouldn't sleep, though. She couldn't.

She had to find a way out.

Chapter Twenty-Four

T he sound of shuffling and thumping somewhere below snapped Bryony awake, and she blinked, dazed, staring in utter confusion at the fireplace in front of her. The fire had burnt down to embers now, flickering orange behind the grate.

Memories of the previous day hit her all at once, and she groaned and fell back against the arm of the couch. She hadn't meant to fall asleep, but watching the flames had made her so very drowsy.

She stared at the ceiling for a moment, trying to prepare herself to get up and face whatever it was that Lottie had planned for today. The shuffling and clunking below was growing louder. It sounded like there were a lot of people down there, probably servants preparing for her sister's insane party.

The door clicked, and Bryony scrambled up so fast she felt dizzy.

Lottie bustled in, placing a silver breakfast tray on the table beside the door. She was wearing a daffodil-yellow dress with a lacy, white neck this morning, and she looked insufferably cheerful. "Good morning! Ready for the party tonight, dear sister?"

Bryony frowned. "I told you. You can forget it. I'm not going along with whatever you've got planned."

An expression of pure fury crossed Lottie's face, there and then gone in a second. Then she was back to beaming again, and Bryony bit the inside of her cheek. This was the second time she'd seen a glimpse of Lottie's true temper.

Lottie strode over to the parlor doors and threw them wide open. "Ernest, good morning, dearest. Bring our new guests in to see my darling sister."

Bryony sat up straight in her chair as Ernest appeared in the hallway. Stumbling in front of him was a very white-faced Thompson and a furious-looking Mira.

"Say hello, you two." Ernest prodded Thompson in the back, shoving him into the parlor. He tried to do the same to Mira, but she was already throwing herself forward. Flying across the room, she caught Bryony in a crushing hug, pressing the side of her face to Bryony's.

"I thought perhaps you were dead," Mira whispered. "I'm so sorry, Bry. We tried."

Bryony kept her voice low, her mouth next to Mira's ear. "Constantine?"

"We don't know. We got separated in the crowd."

Ernest smirked at Bryony's look of shock. "They made it rather convenient. We caught them in the upstairs rooms. Snuck in one of the back windows by climbing a tree. Rather clever until they left the rope dangling out the window." He frowned down at Mira, who turned without fully letting go of Bryony and pulled an awful face at him. "I don't like this one, Lottie. She's rude."

Bryony tightened her grip on Mira's arms. When she made eye contact with Thompson, he gave an apologetic shrug.

"Sit," Lottie said, gesturing imperiously toward the couch. "All of you."

When Ernest took a step forward, fist raised threateningly, they complied. Bryony sank down onto the sofa, Mira still clinging to her side.

"You've got your friends back. Aren't you happy, dear?" Lottie smiled at her, honey-sweet. She was insufferably pleased with herself. She nodded at Mira. "I think the littlest one will go first."

"What?" Bryony stared at her.

"*Pardon*," Lottie said primly. "Ladies do not say *what*. And I mean that if you don't cooperate, I have a lovely mirror I've had to store in the attic that needs polishing. For some reason, none of the servants will go near it." She was looking right at Mira, and Bryony squeezed her friend's arm tightly, as if they might try to sweep her away right then.

"You won't get away with this. My patron knows I've come looking for him. He's going to realize something's wrong when I don't show up."

Lottie tittered, her hand fluttering up to her mouth. She widened her eyes dramatically. "Oh dear, your patron?"

Bryony gave a curt nod, limbs trembling as she tried to keep her anger leashed. "He'll come for me."

"Of course he will." Lottie's voice went softer, almost a whisper, and she crept forward on her tiptoes, reaching out to snatch Bryony's chin in her hands. "Your precious patron, with his little house in the countryside with the white-on-gray trim."

Bryony jerked back, pulling out of the woman's grasp, heart beating furiously against her ribcage. "How—how do you . . . ?"

Lottie's eyes glittered, and a smile slithered across her face. "All that talk of how creative you are, how wonderful. Ridiculous!"

The patron's letter.

"You read my letter," Bryony sputtered, outraged. "Uncle Bernard showed you—"

"Don't be daft." Lottie straightened up, blue eyes narrowing to slits. "I know you're smarter than that. I *wrote* it. So, yes, I know it off by heart. Your uncle started putting me off. Wouldn't deliver you directly to me, even after several weeks of trying to convince him, so I took matters into my own hands." She laughed. "I knew it was rather a long shot, but your uncle did tell me you had a tendency to plan your little escapes. I *did* hope my letter would drive you to try again." Lottie smirked. "Of course, I didn't realize you'd search out that dreadful Constantine, but I suppose he ended up delivering you straight to me anyways, didn't he?"

"That's a lie," Bryony protested angrily. "He was helping me."

"Was he, though?" Lottie raised a brow, her expression smug. "What do you even know about the man?"

Bryony could feel her mouth hanging open. She snapped it shut, thinking furiously. Constantine *was* the one who had led her here. He'd told her this house belonged to her cousin. Then he'd vanished when they'd needed him most.

Was it possible he'd been in on this with Lottie the entire time?

The thought of this betrayal, the shock of it, was enough to suck her breath away.

"It's not true." Her voice was barely a whisper.

"Don't be sad, darling. The man is a lowlife." Lottie smiled at all of them in turn, as if they should all be as delighted as she was. "And it all worked out in the end. Now, Ernest dear, shall we go have breakfast?"

Ernest smiled thinly and nodded. "Of course, darling. Let's leave your new sister and her friends to their thoughts, shall we?"

They shut the door behind them with a bang, and Bryony slumped backward on the sofa, feeling as though someone had deflated her. Her arms and legs felt like jelly, and somehow heavy and light, all at the same time. Everything she'd believed was a lie. Constantine was probably helping Lottie. Her father had been a terrible person, and her patron . . .

Lottie. Lottie was her patron.

No. There *was* no patron. It had all been a complete lie. And that meant that the end of the book was true. That her father was dead. Constantine was right; that was how the story had ended.

Tears welled up in her eyes, hot and stinging. Beside her, the couch shifted slightly as Mira leaned over and wrapped something around Bryony's shoulders, something warm and soft. A blanket, and on top of that, Mira's arm, looped about her shoulders, holding her firmly, as if she were afraid Bryony was about to fall to pieces.

And she did think she might just shatter, right there in the middle of the ridiculously frilly parlor with all its foolish Queen Victoria pillows and royal crest teacups. For so long now, she'd held on to this one thing to get her through the darkness. To escape the lonely nights in the attic. To fight the small, cold spot inside her that wanted to give in to the sadness. And now she knew it was all a lie. A false hope.

She'd made up stories about her father in her head. Dreamed he was a sailor, a soldier, a secret spy for the King. But the patron, *her* version of her father, had never really existed. He'd been a fictional character created by Lottie.

All she'd wanted was a father. Or, if the patron hadn't been her real father, a kind of surrogate father. Just some kind of family. Even a substitute one.

And Lottie had torn that out of her grasp. She would never have a family now. Not really. She tried to concentrate on breathing, in and out, to feel her chest rise and fall. It felt like the room had narrowed down to a pinprick and she was in the center of it, like looking backward through a telescope to that one tiny spot of nothingness.

Her shoulders caved inward and she hunched her back, wanting to retreat into herself, to curl up like a snail and shelter herself from the danger of ever dreaming again. Of ever hoping again.

"Bryony?" Mira's voice was small and tentative.

"I can't believe I fell for that." Her voice came out in a sob, the words catching in her throat. "What an absolute *numpty* I've been. Dreaming of living with my patron in the country." Tears burned hot tracks down her cheeks, and she didn't bother to wipe them away.

Mira's arm tightened around her shoulders. "It isn't your fault. She's far sneakier than any of us imagined."

Thompson had been pacing back and forth in front of the fireplace, his face and neck blotchy. Clearly he was uncomfortable with her tears. But now he stopped and nodded vigorously. "You can't blame yourself, Bry. She's absolutely conniving. I never would have thought her to be so clever." He shoved his hands into his pockets, eyes glazing over in thought. "She's clearly deep into a kind of psychosis. I believe she thinks she was a personal friend of the late Queen's. Or perhaps she even think she *is* royalty. I'm not entirely sure yet."

Bryony blinked, and then reached up and rubbed some of the tears away. That was the first time Thompson had called her "Bry," and he was doing what he always did with Mira, diagnosing things. It seemed to be his way of caring. Her chest lifted a little.

"I just feel foolish," she admitted. "I was so determined to find my family that I let myself daydream about it for weeks."

Mira shifted, moving closer on the couch until their knees touched, until Bryony was completely tucked into the circle of her arm. "Did I ever tell you the story I read once, about an intrepid explorer who ran all about town searching for her family?"

Bryony actually smiled; she couldn't help it. Something about Mira trying to tell her a story at this moment in time, when they were locked in a psychotic woman's parlor, didn't surprise her. She sighed and shut her eyes and let her head rest on Mira's shoulder, just for a moment. "No, I don't believe you have."

"Well, as I said, the silly thing ran all over the place, searching for her family, without realizing that all along they were there with her, searching with her, because they were her true family, not by blood but by everything else in the world. And they would do anything for family. Even chase made-up fathers, just for her."

Bryony's eyes popped open in surprise, and then, slowly, a wide smile spread across her face. "This girl, she sounds like a great big ninny."

Mira's shoulders shook with laughter. "She is, a little. But they love her anyways. And did you know that one of her family members, the boy who started out a terrible coward at the beginning of the adventure, was the one who led the daring break-in in order to rescue her?" She gave Thompson a sly, sideways smile, and Bryony looked over at him in astonishment.

"He did?"

Thompson blushed brightly and ducked his head. "Yes, ah . . . and, well, people change. But now her family had better figure out what to do next, right?"

Bryony straightened, hastily rubbing away any remaining tears. While she felt a bit sheepish about the breakdown, her chest also felt strangely full, as if her heart had swelled up to twice its normal size. It didn't feel broken anymore.

"Yes, we need a plan. But first there's something I have to do."

She steeled her nerves and moved to the fireplace, reaching into her breast pocket to fish out the letter. *The letter.* The one she'd read again and again, the one she'd dreamed about reading, the one she'd obsessed over.

Mira came to stand beside her. Bryony could feel the other girl watching her as she held the letter over the flames. Her hands shook, even though she knew it was all a lie, and her stomach twisted itself into knots.

While she stayed frozen, uncertain, Thompson shuffled up and stood on the other side of her. Both siblings were silent.

They didn't need to say anything. They were there.

Bryony slowly uncurled her fingers. The letter drifted down and settled on the coals, and the paper blackened and curled at the edges before the flames licked through the center and sent the words crumbling in on themselves.

At last there were only a few words left, slowly disappearing in bright sparks and black spots: *Greatest hope . . . regard me as family.*

She didn't need to. She already had one.

After a few more minutes of silence, Bryony straightened up and squared her shoulders. "I think I might know a way to break the curse."

Thompson's brows shot up, and Mira nodded eagerly. They both stared at her, waiting.

"But first you need to know a few things." She told them everything that Uncle Bernard had said, how he'd tried to stab her with a letter opener—here Mira growled and said she'd like to return the favor—and how the cursed painting had been hidden behind the mirror in Bryony's attic. About Lottie, who was not, in fact, a cousin. She'd had a sister all along. A sister who had terrible plans to have her paint someone. And lastly, how she, Bryony, was actually part of the curse.

It took a while for it all to pour out, and when she was finally done, she felt better. For a few minutes all three of them sat in silence on the couch, staring down at the ugly Queen Victoria cushions Mira had pushed to the floor.

"All right," Thompson said finally, and his voice was firm with resolve. "So we find the painting and destroy it."

Bryony straightened her shoulders. "That's the plan."

"But . . . Bry," Mira said, "you do realize if you're part of the curse—" She cut herself off, her face pale.

Thompson nodded, his expression grim. "It could be the same for you. Constantine said that destroying the painting destroyed your father. We could destroy the painting and you could be . . . connected."

"It occurred to me." Her mouth tasted sour, and she dug her fingers into the fabric of her dress.

Mira's face grew white, and she stared at Bryony. "I don't like this. We have to find another way. Hide the painting. Lock it away."

"Hiding it might not be enough," Thompson said.

"Then we bury it! Throw it out the window! Lose it at sea!" Mira blurted out.

"It won't work." A heavy feeling of dread settled over her, and with it, a sense of resignation that had been coming for a while now. "We don't have time to find another way of doing it, and we can't hide it. It might resurface in a few years and this mess would begin all over again." She straightened her shoulders. "We find the painting and destroy it so there's nothing left. There's nothing else for it. And now we know what we have to do."

"We do?" asked Thompson.

"Sort of." She folded her arms and tried to look confident, even though her stomach felt squirmy. "I've got a plan."

The plan was simple, and after she'd explained it, Mira and Thompson both just stared at her. It wasn't particularly clever; in fact, it relied on a lot of things happening a certain way. If anything went wrong, they would have to improvise.

"When the chaos hits, you two make a break for it. Head for the attic."

"And if it's locked?" Thompson raised his brows. "Now that her pet monster has melted into a pool of goo she's probably going to keep the painting locked up."

Bryony smiled. If there was anything she was good at, it was unlocking attic doors. Primarily from the inside, but how different could it be?

"We need something to pick the lock." Bryony reached out and plucked one of the leather pouches from Mira's belt. It contained three very long and very sharp metal darts.

Thompson looked horrified, but Mira gave him a wide smile. "See? They come in very handy sometimes."

Thompson flinched when Bryony tried to hand him one. "Aren't those poison?"

Mira rolled her eyes. "Of course not. I don't actually have any tranquilizer."

"Well, thank the good Lord you have some sense at least."

"They wouldn't sell it to me. It was terribly vexing."

Thompson began to sputter again, and Bryony jumped in before he could get anything out. Speaking quickly, she explained how to jimmy the lock. She didn't think it would be too hard, even for Thompson, who looked rather pained at the mere thought of breaking and entering. This was an old house, so everything could probably be opened with a skeleton key.

She tucked the dart into her pocket, pinning it to the fabric inside so it wouldn't stab her in the stomach. Thompson did the same, though he looked dubious. That left Mira with the remaining dart. If they got separated, they would all try to continue with the plan: destroy the painting by any means necessary.

"All right," Thompson said. "Say we make it to the attic. What happens if—"

He didn't get the rest of the sentence out. There was a flurry of footsteps from the hall and then the door crashed open with a loud whump. Lottie stood in the doorway.

"I'm not interrupting anything, am I, darlings?"

Chapter Twenty-Five

Lottie was dressed in a long black gown and delicate lace gloves. Her hair was piled on top of her head, blonde curls punctuated by glittering red rubies. Draped around her neck was a very odd-looking leather plague mask. Black tubes dangled from the mouthpiece, and the eyes were buglike black lenses. The whole apparatus looked like a bizarre set of goggles.

But the thing that really caught Bryony's eye was the heavy-looking silver tiara that rested on top of Lottie's hair. It sparkled under the gaslight as the woman turned her head this way and that, her movements slow and deliberate.

Her sister twirled around, and Bryony gave a sigh of relief. She'd thought for sure that Lottie had somehow heard all of their plans through the walls. But now it appeared she had simply burst in to show off her ridiculous outfit.

When Lottie caught Bryony looking, she smiled coyly. "Do you like the crown? It's rather pretty, isn't it? Wait until you see the upgrade, though."

"Upgrade?" Bryony frowned. Did this have something to do with whatever her sister was planning?

"For the ceremony tonight, silly!"

Bryony's mouth worked, but nothing came out.

All the Queen pillows and teacups and paintings . . . and an "upgrade" to what? A better crown? Was Lottie planning to crown herself tonight? How absolutely ridiculous.

"You're mad."

Lottie smiled sweetly. "Ready for your debut, baby sister? The servants are going to get you cleaned up for the coronation. You've got to look like a princess if your big sister is going to be the next Queen of England."

Bryony stood up from the couch as gracefully as she could manage, smoothing her hands over her dress. She immediately regretted it as the metal dart pricked her thumb. She darted a quick look at Mira and Thompson, and then away again, before saying, "I'll make you a deal."

Lottie's face brightened. "So, you're ready to start being reasonable? How smashing!" Ernest appeared at her elbow, and she whirled around clapping her hands. "Oh, Erny darling, she's going to make a deal with us. Isn't that splendid?"

A slimy smile crawled across his face. "That's more like it." He turned to look at her, and Bryony shuddered. It felt like he was mentally assessing her, to see if she was going to be a problem or not.

Lottie clapped her hands again. "Now, what sort of deal? When we rule all of England, we're going to have loads of money, of course, but you'll have an allowance. You're still a child, after all."

This was so outrageous that Bryony nearly lost her

temper on the spot. They *were* planning to use her as a threat, and Lottie was going to make some kind of wild claim to the throne. Before she could open her mouth, she caught sight of Mira standing behind Ernest and Lottie. She was shaking her head ever so slightly.

The plan would be ruined if she gave Ernest a piece of her mind.

"Here are my terms," she said, doing her best to match the demanding tone that Lottie always seemed to use. "First of all, my friends stay with me. They get to attend the party tonight."

A stroke of genius struck at that moment, and she blurted eagerly, "*And* they get to dress up too. In masks like yours. It isn't any fun if they don't. And you'll lend Thompson a nice suit and everything."

Ernest looked affronted. "I beg your pardon? My suits are all custom-made. They won't fit . . ." His voice trailed off when Bryony narrowed her eyes at him.

"If my friends aren't having fun, then I'm afraid I simply won't be inspired to paint tonight."

Ernest huffed, indignant, but Lottie was staring at her silently, head tilted.

Had she guessed that the costume request was a way to make sure Thompson and Mira blended in with the crowd? Quickly, she added, "And I want to be made duchess of something."

That got their attention. Both Lottie and Ernest started disagreeing angrily.

"Certainly not!"

"Outrageous!"

Lottie collected herself quickly, clasping her hands together, a sweet smile spreading over her face. "My, you're a sharp bargainer. How about this? We agree to give you a weekly allowance. How does that sound? Ten pounds?"

"Fifty pounds," Bryony retorted, "*and* you buy me a wardrobe of pretty dresses." It was an utterly ridiculous thing to say, but it was also exactly the right thing, for Lottie's cheeks flushed and her eyes lit up.

"All right, I agree to your little bargain. We'll go shopping tomorrow afternoon. Oh! I've always wanted a little sister to dress up. Now come along, dear. You'll love the costume I bought you for the party. I had your uncle send me your sizes last week." She seized Bryony's hand and began to tow her from the room.

Reluctantly she let herself be led away, shooting one last wide-eyed look at Mira and Thompson over her shoulder. Clearly, her new sister had been planning this for a while.

Shopping with Lottie sounded like torture. But Bryony wouldn't be here tomorrow, not if her plan worked (or even if her plan *did* work and destroying the portrait destroyed her along with it). She swallowed hard, trying to push the thought away.

And on top of everything, she still couldn't shake the uneasy feeling that Lottie threatening to crown herself wasn't even the worst of her plans. Her sister wasn't just obsessed with royalty; she was fixated on their father. On the Gray family curse. There had to be more.

So what else was she planning?

If the idea of shopping with her new older sister had been repulsive, getting ready for the party with her turned out to be far worse. The room she showed Bryony to was done in garish shades of pink and purple, and it had a child-sized bed with a silk canopy draped overhead. On the walls hung pastel drawings, scrawled depictions of horses pulling carriages and bejeweled crowns, and a rough charcoal sketch, a poor rendition of the Queen's profile.

Lottie floated around the room, reaching out to touch each drawing. "I was quite talented as a child. Perhaps not as good as you." She smiled graciously down at Bryony, as if paying her a terrific compliment. "But I did it for pure enjoyment of my subject." She paused at the charcoal outline of the Queen, running one fingertip down the edge of the crinkled paper. "Our birthday is coming up, you know—May 24." She giggled, eyes fixed on the drawing, face distant and dreamy. "That's when I knew we were the same, she and I. After Grandfather told me I had the same birthday." Her face went dark. "During one of his moments. He was hot and cold, that man. One day I was his granddaughter and he would shower me with gifts; the next day I was a servant again."

Bryony swallowed past the lump in her throat. Lottie was so unpredictable! She was almost afraid to speak, but dozens of questions were burning inside her. "You lived with your grandfather. But did you . . . did you ever meet our father?"

Lottie wheeled around to stare at her, eyes wide, and Bryony flinched. But then the woman's cold expression melted into a smile. "You've inherited those startling blue eyes of his. Did you know that?"

Bryony went very still, hardly daring to breathe as her sister reached out and cupped one hand under her chin. Lottie's fingers were soft and warm, gentle, and she tilted Bryony's face up.

"I never got to meet him," Lottie said, "but I found a picture amongst Mother's old things. They were shut away in a box after she was sent away, but I found it. I kept it in the attic. I used to love hiding things there. All my secret treasures." She dropped her hand from Bryony's face and stepped back, and the smile slid away. "When Grandfather found the picture, he burned it."

"I know what it's like." Bryony kept her voice to a whisper, afraid of shattering whatever this was. Whatever kind of moment they were having. "Never being allowed to speak of him, or ask questions."

"Yes. Forever a dirty little secret, our father. After he disappeared, and that man sent me the book, I found his house. I went through it to salvage what I could before they auctioned everything off, but those vultures at the bank had nearly stripped it clean. There was precious little left for us."

"Is that when you found the painting?"

For a moment Lottie held her eyes. She didn't deny that she had the painting, or tell her to be quiet, and Bryony felt her hopes rise. She could talk her sister out of whatever it was she was planning. They could leave all this madness behind, hide out somewhere the rumors couldn't reach them. Together. Like a family.

She was about to say something—she wasn't sure what—when Lottie blinked rapidly and snapped upright. "It was a lonely childhood, but I always had dear Victoria to talk to." She smiled beatifically up at the drawing. "She was strong. Born to be royalty. As am I." She turned back, clasping her hands as she stared dreamily at Bryony. "How I would dream about us as sisters, Victoria and I. The lovely parties we would have."

Bryony's heart sank. She'd only witnessed a tiny glimmer of her real sister, and now the madwoman was back. The one with all the insane plans.

It was possible Thompson's diagnoses about Lottie were correct, that the woman was delusional. But if that's what they were, her delusions were uncomfortably familiar. Hadn't Bryony dreamed about being friends with Mira? About painting Mira?

Perhaps this sort of madness ran in the family.

And if anyone had told her it was all just a delusion, she would never have listened. So it was unlikely Lottie would either. She'd have to stick to her own plans instead.

At least Lottie had more or less confirmed Bryony's plan, which depended on the painting being hidden in the attic. She'd been positive that Lady Abney had been guarding something, and now she was sure of it. If Lottie hid her "treasures" there, that's where her father's painting would be.

Another thought occurred to her as she stared at the pictures on the wall. The first thing she'd noticed was how very terrible they were, but it was also worth noting that none of them were coming to life and trying to climb down from the wall. Now, perhaps the curse didn't run to drawings, just paintings, but somehow she doubted it . . .

It seemed if the subject wasn't lifelike enough, the curse wouldn't work.

Bryony bit the inside of her cheek hard. That probably explained why Lottie needed her in the first place. She was too bad at drawing to make the curse happen herself.

"Look, look, Her Highness and the generals are having tea." Lottie giggled again, flapping her hands toward a low table set in the corner of the room.

The table was made up with five place settings, set with delicate china teacups and saucers. On each seat was a glass-eyed teddy bear, all of them very old and saggy. One of the bears was wearing a paper crown, another sported a drooping mustache made of black yarn, and the others had on top hats and cravats.

"I decorated this room with everything I would have loved as a child," Lottie said rapturously. A second later, though, her face went dark. "*If* I hadn't been restricted to the servants' quarters, that is."

Lottie turned away from the tea party abruptly, nearly running into Bryony as she stomped back toward the bed. "But now it's yours." Her smile was back just as suddenly as it had disappeared, brightening her face. "Just look at the bed. Isn't it darling?"

Bryony wanted to say that her feet would hang off the end, and that the décor was more vomit-inducing than darling, but she pressed her lips together firmly and forced herself to stay silent.

Lottie swept about the room, gushing over how adorable Bryony would look in the frilly new dresses they were going to buy her, and pointing out an extremely creepy shelf of porcelain dolls they were apparently going to have tea with at some point. The idea of Lottie, a fully grown adult, crouched around a doll-sized table pretending to have tea was somehow both horrifying and completely unsurprising.

While Lottie went on and on about how pretty everything was going to be, Bryony tried to keep her nausea hidden. Her sister had obviously inherited their father's obsession with extravagance and beauty. Perhaps both of them had, though she preferred things to be less . . . pink.

There was a rope pulley near the vanity table in the corner, and the woman yanked on it repeatedly until a frazzled-looking servant rushed in.

"Bring lunch up to her rooms. And give this child a bath! She smells like poor people." She wrinkled her nose, and Bryony shook her head in disbelief, glaring at Lottie as she bustled toward the door. "Get her into her costume and down to the ballroom by 9 p.m. sharp. It won't do to miss her own unveiling!"

As the doors crashed shut behind Lottie, all Bryony could do was stare. She felt a little bit like she'd been picked up and whirled around by a hurricane, and had just now been set back down.

What followed was a hot bath and a very long, painful session tugging out the knots in her hair with a silver-backed brush. Then the maid—a timid woman with mousy brown hair who said nothing the entire time—helped her slip into the outfit that was laid out on the bed. It was a black silk dress with an overabundance of lace at the cuffs and collar, and an eerie white-and-black cameo pin at the center of the breast. The pin was a trifle alarming; the woman's profile was raised, like she was about to come bursting out of the broach, and she had a toothy smile on her face that made her look slightly deranged.

Even stranger was the mask Bryony was meant to wear around her neck, the same type she'd seen on Lottie earlier—black glass goggles and tubes sprouting out of the mouthpiece like bug antennae.

She wasn't sure what this party was going to be like, but she was certain she wouldn't enjoy it.

everal hours later, the servants had brought both lunch and dinner and cleared away the plates, and Bryony had hardly touched anything.

There was no mirror to preen in front of, no way to twirl around and watch her dress swirl out, but she could look down and see the black silk and chiffon move around her legs, and the lacy black slippers that peeped out from beneath the hem. She could feel the cleverly braided pattern at the back of her head and the curls that brushed her cheeks. She had, somewhat reluctantly, left her favorite paintbrush on the vanity table, since she had no doubt Lottie would have some remark about it if she kept it behind her ear. That aside, she would have felt pampered, perhaps even enjoyed being the center of attention. She'd almost never been allowed to dress up, unless she'd been about to paint one of her uncle's clients.

But dread curled at the bottom of her stomach, waiting to bloom like a poisonous flower. She couldn't let it paralyze her. "I'm ready."

The maid led her down several hallways and staircases, past any part of the house that had seemed familiar.

The farther they went, the darker it became. The dim light from the candelabras seemed to be sucked away by the crimson-patterned wallpaper, and shadows stretched and jumped along both walls. To make matters worse, the hallway was lined on both sides with dark-sheeted paintings. No doubt there were more than a few murderous Queen Victoria portraits lurking behind the black velvet drapes, and Bryony flinched back every time they passed another covered painting. She half expected something to come bursting out.

Still, she tried to keep calm and memorize the way back. Once she created her distraction, she and Mira and Thompson would have to get up to the attic fast. In her dress pocket the reassuring shape of a tiny glass bottle she'd taken from the vanity bumped against her leg now and again. She'd emptied out the perfume and filled it with kerosene from the lamp in the center of the teddy bear tea party. The maid had looked askance at her while she did it, but hadn't said anything. When Bryony had requested a matchbook, the mousy woman, lips pressed together tightly, had nodded toward a black tin box high on the shelf beside the fireplace. It had been out of reach, but a chair from the tea party table had solved that.

She kept going over the plan in her head, and every time, it seemed less likely to work. As they made their way down a final stretch of hall, the sound of a waltz began to seep through the walls, as well as laughter and the buzz of conversation. The party was in full swing already, and now it was time for her sister's mad plan: the coronation of a false queen.

It still didn't add up, though. How exactly did this fit in with the curse Lottie had triggered? She seemed obsessed with their father, but what did he have to do with queens and coronations? There had to be something more going on. If she could just think clearly, if she could concentrate. If only she had Mira and Thompson with her . . .

"My friends?" Her voice came out shaky, and the maid's smile was actually sympathetic.

"Already inside."

At the end of the hall a set of double doors was being monitored by a solemn-looking pair of footmen, their faces grim, arms folded across their chests. It hadn't even occurred to her that the door might be blocked. How on earth was she going to get by them on her way out?

The worry gnawing at her stomach was growing, and she curled her fingers into fists to stop her hands from shaking. Her plan had so many holes in it, so much that could go wrong.

The maid nodded at the doormen, one of whom nodded back, stone-faced, and stepped sideways. The door glided open.

Instantly a wall of music washed over her, and the lights made her blink, startled. The ballroom was only a little bigger than the lounge at the art gallery had been, and every bit as fancy. She found herself at the top of a double-sided marble staircase, staring down at the party. Three chandeliers hung from the ceiling, dripping in glittering teardrop crystals. The floor was so polished the marble shone. It was shocking how many guests were packed into the ballroom, all dressed in sweeping black and gray dresses and tuxedos. And every last one of their faces were covered by the same type of bug-eyed plague mask that Bryony had around her neck. It was like watching shiny black beetles waltzing in circles. A shiver dropped down her spine and she hunched her shoulders, frozen at the top of the staircase.

Costumed performers scattered throughout the ballroom were entertaining the guests. The actors were painted in liquid silver, their motions fluid as they pivoted around one another. It was either a dance or a play, since once in a while one of the dancers stopped to pantomime something. The nearest performer echoed the movements of one of the guests, placing his hands on his hips when she did, waving one hand just like her. Then he lunged forward, stretching out one hand toward her, and the woman shrieked with nervous laughter and backed away. They were supposed to be mirrors, Bryony realized, and her skin crawled.

On the other side of the room a troop of actors was dressed in old-fashioned outfits and framed in painted gold wood. They pulled horrible faces at guests as they walked by and reached out of the frames toward them. The guests danced away, laughing.

Movement to the left caught her eye. Ernest seemed to melt from behind the door, appearing out of nowhere with a hiss like a deflating balloon. "Get ready, girl. Don't stand there like a buffoon." He leaned closer and muttered in her ear. "Smile."

Bryony forced a smile just as all of the shiny bug people turned toward the raised dais at the end of the room. At least they weren't looking her way. From the edge of the dais a woman stepped forward. She raised her champagne glass with a dramatic flourish. Her purple-and-black dress sparkled as she moved, and Bryony realized she had seen that pattern somewhere before, in a picture in one of her textbooks. The Queen had worn something almost exactly like that on the day of her coronation. Well, that was a bold statement, to be sure.

Lottie's mask was accentuated with a cluster of black feathers that stood out sharply against her blonde hair. A chair sat in the middle of the stage, not a throne but almost, with elaborate curling arms and red velvet cushions. Beside the chair was a short pillar, on top of which sat a smaller cushion, a dome-shaped crown rising up from it in glittering majesty. It looked exactly like Queen Victoria's.

The murmur of conversation died away as Lottie's voice echoed around the ballroom. "Welcome, darlings! Thank you all for coming to my ball! London may be under a quarantine, but there's no stopping us from having fun, is there?"

A cheer went up, glasses were raised in a toast and Lottie beamed with pleasure. It was alarming that there were so many shallow, ridiculous people in London. Who could attend a party during a citywide crisis?

"I'm sure we're going to have an absolutely smashing time of it. I mean really, darlings. You might say this party is fit for royalty!"

That got a laugh from the crowd, a malicious, sly kind of titter that washed through the room like a wave of toxic sea water. Bryony's fingers tightened on the railing and her heart began to hammer even harder in her chest.

She glared at the crown on the cushion, and at Lottie, and felt Ernest shift beside her.

"For heaven's sake, don't scowl so," he hissed near her left ear, and she almost swatted him. Hopefully he wouldn't be glued to her side all night; it could prove a real problem. Palms clammy, she watched as Lottie swept her arms out in another flourish. The chatter died away almost instantly, though there was still a faint buzz of anticipation in the air.

The blonde woman paused dramatically, sweeping one hand toward the stairs, her eyes now fixed on Bryony's face. "And now, as all of you know, Ernest and I have a very big announcement. But first . . . an introduction."

You mean a threat. Bryony's stomach plunged.

Ernest stepped closer and, to her distaste, slipped one arm through hers. The gesture probably looked gallant from the outside, but he squeezed her arm very tightly in his, trapping her more than escorting.

Lottie continued. "Today we welcome a new family member and unveil an incredible talent. It's a name you may be familiar with. Please welcome my little sister, Ms. Bryony Gray."

The band struck up a loud, brassy waltz as Ernest began to make his way down the ballroom stairs, never once relinquishing his grip on her arm. It was either match his pace or risk falling down a very long flight of marble stairs. The crowd turned, masks swiveling toward them, hundreds of shiny, empty eyes fixed on her. Like giant, horrible insects. The music was blaring, drowning out the noise of the crowd. But there had been a reaction to her name, a surge of movement through the crowd that swept from one end of the ballroom to the other. The guests nudged one another and lowered their faces to their neighbors, masks wiggling back and forth as they whispered. What were they saying about her as Ernest paraded her past?

She shivered and tried not to look at them, fixing her gaze on the decorations. Sparkling black and gray statues punctuated the crowd here and there, masks fixed over their faces, limbs twisted in a parody of movement. As they passed by one of the statues, it quivered ever so slightly. She nearly stumbled, and Ernest yanked her onward.

Goosebumps crawled up both arms. Not statues then, but servants painted to look like statues.

As they neared the long dessert tables, she spotted several of the black-suited butlers stationed at each end, each carrying a flat tin of something that looked suspiciously like paint thinner.

Somewhere in that sea of strangers were Mira and Thompson. Unless Lottie had lied to her. Stomach fluttering, she scanned the crowd, trying to pick out two familiar figures. Thompson would be hard to spot, since he was nearly the same height as everyone else. But Mira would probably be shorter than most of the adults. Best to look for a slight figure with unfashionably short hair. Halfway across the ballroom she still hadn't seen them—at least, she didn't think she had. There were multiple short women in long black dresses.

Someone moved abruptly as she walked past. A short, dark-haired woman who wore her hair pinned back behind the mask straps. She turned her head, and one of her hands twitched, ever so slightly, tapping the ring finger to the thumb twice, so fast it was barely noticeable.

It was the sign for *ready* . . .

Bryony sucked in a sharp breath and pressed onward, trying to look as if she was facing straight ahead while still darting glances out of the corner of her eye. Now she knew where Mira was. And beside Mira, a figure in a black tux stood very close. Thompson. When she made eye contact with him he dropped his gaze down to his hands.

He signed . . . *when you are.*

Laughter bubbled up in her chest and she had to force it down, pressing her lips together to keep from smiling. Behind them stood a serious-looking man in a black suit. They had a guard.

The urge to laugh vanished as quickly as it had come.

A guard was going to mean problems.

Plague masks turned, tracking her progress up to the dais, her own goggles bumping rhythmically over her collarbone with each step she took. It almost would have been better to have the mask on, to watch all of this through cold, black glass. Instead, her gaze darted wildly across the crowd, catching on the still figures of Thompson and Mira each time. Mira's hand twitched, as if she was trying to suppress the urge to sign something else, lest it become too obvious.

Bryony smiled slightly, keeping her hands down low, smoothing them together in what could have been interpreted as a nervous gesture. What it really meant was *all right*, which wasn't the perfect sign, nor particularly accurate, but at least it would let them know she'd seen them.

Now she and Ernest were directly in front of the dais. She could see the glitter of the lights bouncing off the jewels in the crown, and Lottie's face beaming down at her. The platform she was standing on was fenced in, with a neat little gate blocking the stairs. Lottie reached down and swung the gate open, stretching one hand out to help her onto the platform. Bryony took it reluctantly. The woman's smile became wider and froze in place, and she spoke through her teeth. "Smile, dear, we have an agreement."

She was right about one thing. It was important to make them think she was still cooperating.

Forcing a smile, she mounted the steps as gracefully as she could with Ernest still trailing after her, and tried not to flinch when Lottie turned her to face the crowd. Her sister made a chopping motion with one hand and the music cut off abruptly.

A light smattering of applause answered, like rain hitting the surface of a pond. But the most noticeable sound was the buzz, people murmuring behind their hands, darting glances at one another. Her name was on everyone's lips. She shifted uneasily, and her smile became fixed in place. Frozen and unnatural. They definitely knew her name.

"Now, many of you may have heard of my little sister," Lottie crowed. Her face was flushed, eyes glittering as she addressed the crowd. "And many of you have heard rumors about her particular talent."

The buzz had been growing steadily louder, but now it dropped away. In the silence, the gentle clink of glasses chiming could be heard.

A wave of Lottie's hand, and the musicians started up again. The golden curtains at the back of the dais rustled and swayed, parting briefly to allow a pair of servants through. They shuffled backward onto the dais, both moving very carefully, balancing a large wooden easel between them. Her easel back home had been terrible, a rickety old thing that Uncle Bernard had picked up at an estate sale, and it had wobbled constantly, until she'd propped the left leg up with *Madam Grundy's Book of Proper Manners and Correct Conduct*. Aunt Gertrude had grumbled loudly that at least she was getting *some* use out of that book.

This easel was beautiful. Dark cherrywood with a tray for paint attached. A pang of longing hit her, so intense that it felt like something swelling in her chest. It wasn't the proper time to be thinking about how pretty the easel was, but she couldn't help herself.

As the servants set up the canvas and paints, Lottie turned to address the crowd again.

"And now, for a demonstration of the wonderful and unusual talent of the Gray family, my sister will paint none other than yours truly! Please enjoy the champagne and sweets as you watch the picture slowly come to life on the canvas."

ryony stiffened, panic freezing her to the spot. She was going to be forced to paint Lottie. Not some unfortunate random partygoer, but Lottie herself. *This ruins everything.*

Her sister *wanted* to be painted. Now she knew what she was planning.

The realization was a punch to the gut, making her breath hitch and stick in her throat. This little gathering had nothing to do with being queen. Lottie wanted eternal life. She was going to pledge her soul.

The plan had been for Mira and Thompson to create a distraction, something that would go on long enough for Bryony to paint. But she'd expected her sister to run from the portrait, not embrace it. The chaos was supposed to give them time to escape.

The music swelled after Lottie's announcement, drowning out the malicious little giggle at the end of her sentence. She may have thought her tasteless joke went over people's heads, but Bryony didn't think that was the case. A few in the crowd began to murmur again, and several people at the front backed up hastily, masks swiveling from Bryony to the easel and then back again. Beside the dessert tables the paint-thinner-wielding butlers began to move forward, weaving their way through the crowd to stand at the ends of the dais, silver tins held in front of them.

The majority of the party guests, however, didn't seem at all bothered, and their attention drifted away almost the instant Lottie stopped talking. The chatter picked up again; laughter and the clink of plates and glasses echoed around the room.

Numbed by the callousness of these people, Bryony allowed herself to be led over to the easel. Ernest pressed down firmly on her shoulders, forcing her to sit. Paints were already laid out on the pallet, brushes lined up in rows along the tray beside it.

And such brushes! Even through her dread, she experienced a little shiver of delight when she picked up the first brush. For a few seconds she simply held on, imagining herself sitting somewhere nice, perhaps by a riverbank somewhere. She would paint cotton-white clouds above a portrait of Mira, who would sit with her back against a big oak tree, bare feet on the grass. Lost in her favorite book.

The grip on her shoulders tightened. "What's the matter, girl?" Ernest's voice was a low growl in her ear. "These people are here to see you paint."

Bryony turned her head slightly, fake smile still in place though her mind was working frantically, trying to rethink her entire plan in a manner of seconds. "She has to know this might not work. The curse is malfunctioning. It might tear her soul to ribbons."

"Of course she's thought of that. We've taken precautions." Ernest gave her a thin smile, gesturing at the butlers standing beside the dais. "She's figured out how to test it first."

A test. Surely that couldn't be good. She darted a look out at the ballroom and dropped her voice to a whisper. "How?"

"None of your concern. Now stop talking and paint."

"I cannot work if you hang over my shoulder like that."

Ernest muttered, but he backed off, and she turned in her seat to dab her brush in the paint, using it as a chance to peek at him. He was still within sight of the canvas.

She had to figure out a way to stop this.

Her earlier conversation with Lottie was coming back now, the way her sister's drawings had looked. The warped face of the queen. *If it's bad enough, the curse won't work properly.*

It was enough to trigger an idea.

Hands shaking, she reached for a vial of paint and then stopped. The paints were familiar. The long, graceful glass bottle, the dark wooden cork in the top. The way the paint was so richly colorful.

Her patron. Of course.

Face burning, she tried to steady her hand, drawing the paintbrush across the canvas. It didn't matter now, though she felt foolish for dreaming about it the way she had, for convincing herself the patron was her father. She'd pored over that letter in the attic for days, dreaming about being adopted by her patron, about going away to live with him. How ridiculous that her wish had been granted in this fashion.

Over her shoulder a rustle of fabric made her back stiffen. Ernest was practically breathing down her neck. He was going to watch her, which was fine, if a bit nerve-wracking. She'd prepared for that. Time to start from the ground up. It was an unpleasant feeling, rather like rubbing all the hairs on your arms the wrong way. But desperate times called for a little anarchy, didn't they?

The dais first, slowly appearing on the canvas in wide brush strokes. Once in a while she looked up, scanning the ballroom. The two figures in the corner were now one, just Mira in her plague mask, swaying a little bit to the music, hands folded behind her back. Where had Thompson gone? Ah, there he was, pushing his way back through the crowd with a glass of punch in each hand. It was actually easier to spot him with the stern-faced doorman following him so closely. Good.

On the canvas things began to take shape—the bottom of Lottie's dress, the ruffles and pearls along the edge.

"Why is it from the ground up?" Ernest's voice was laced with suspicion. Her shoulders tensed, and she had to force herself to keep painting.

"Just leave her, darling," Lottie said. "Lord knows these artist types are always strange."

Her ears were burning now, and she longed to snap at both of them. Her aunt and uncle had forever been discussing her as if she wasn't there. It had driven her mad. But there was no point in starting a fight before she put her plan in motion.

"How long will this take?" Lottie asked. "I'm eager to get to the good part." Without waiting for an answer, she turned to wave at the crowd, leaning over to talk to someone who'd approached the dais.

Bryony scowled. She'd never painted anyone who moved around so much.

It was odd to feel so many eyes on her as she worked. Only her uncle and aunt had ever watched her paint. But now, even though much of the crowd wasn't paying attention, there were still quite a few people who were standing around idly chatting, wine glasses clutched in hand, gazes continually drifting her way.

It made her itch, like there were tiny black beetles skittering over her skin.

Here and there a fancier mask or dress stood out, and occasionally the glitter of diamonds under the light punctuated the sea of black. In one corner a tall man in a golden mask stood very still, staring directly at her. When she made eye contact, he smiled and lifted a lighter to the cigarette in his mouth.

Her breath hitched. Even from where she stood she could tell the lighter was gold and silver. It had to be Constantine.

That meant one of two things. One, he had somehow found out that her cousin—sister, she had to remind herself—was having a party, and he had come in costume. Or two, what Lottie had told her hadn't actually been a lie . . . he'd been in on this with her the entire time.

In any case, she couldn't afford to think about that right now.

She painted fast, now onto Lottie's collar, her neck, her chin. Ernest was still standing right beside her, and it was making her break out in a cold sweat. The new plan wasn't going to work if Mira and Thompson didn't come through. Luckily, the timing could still work if they went through with their part of the original plan. Without it, Ernest would see what she was doing right away. Raising the handle of the paintbrush to her lips, she bit the end, brows furrowed. A few people tittered from the ballroom floor. It was a habit that Uncle Bernard had said—in a display of good-natured indulgence—made her look like an eccentric artist. And one that Aunt Gertrude had slapped her hand for, because *she* said it made her look like a beaver.

She brought the brush away from her lips, dabbing it in the gray and then the white. Background it was, then. At least until the next stage of the plan. Already she could see Mira out of the corner of her eye, edging sideways toward the dessert table. Her mask was turned toward the tower of champagne glasses sparkling under the glittering lights. Bryony bit back a grin. Mira had picked the perfect thing. Having that tower crash over would be the perfect distraction.

Lottie had swept over to Bryony, and now she sighed loudly over her left shoulder. "Ernest, start the ceremony now. I'm bored. I didn't realize how terribly *long* she would take to paint me."

"Of course. Couldn't stick to an actual *schedule*, could we?" Ernest muttered to no one in particular and then waved at the band, who shifted from a slow waltz to a brassy rendition of "God Save the King." As the music played,

Bryony couldn't help thinking that her sister was probably changing the lyrics to "Queen" in her head. The black-suited butlers ceased their lurking beside the dessert tables and moved toward the sides of the room, standing in front of the double doors. Meanwhile, a solemn-faced man in a gray suit climbed the stairs to the dais and whisked the crown and pillow up, kneeling before Lottie with a dramatic flourish, lifting the cushion up to present her with the crown.

The audience seemed to love it. They clapped and murmured appreciatively, nudging one another with whispers and soft laughter. Most of the audience seemed amused, and a few people near the front bowed mockingly.

Couldn't Lottie tell these people had come to see her make a fool of herself?

Bryony stiffened as Ernest stooped down and growled through his teeth. "You don't need to put in all that detail." He looked like he was about to say more, but a great flare of music sounded just then, and he turned to look as Lottie lifted the crown up, placing it delicately on her puffy hair. Then she sat in the thronelike chair, arranging her skirts primly as she did so. All the while she smiled demurely out at the crowd, as if she really were Queen Victoria, come back from the dead to reclaim her throne.

Perhaps she thought she was. Destined to be an immortal queen.

The music swelled again, and the murmurs from the crowd increased, the noise blurring together in a rising crescendo. Then it dropped off suddenly, and Lottie's voice echoed around the room.

"And now," Lottie said grandly, "for something even *more* spectacular."

The crowd hushed, waiting with bated breath.

Lottie folded her hands in her lap. "You came here today for one thing: your own selfish entertainment. I see many of you are my neighbors. People who I know talk about me behind my back, the so-called high society. You came to see if Mad Lottie would go through with actually crowning herself the new Queen. If I was deluded enough, perhaps, to think I really *was* the Queen. And you have seen that today, ladies and gentlemen. Congratulations."

Her voice rang out around the room, and in the space between one sentence and the next, a metallic *snick* could be heard.

Bryony stiffened, brush hovering over the canvas.

The butlers beside the doors had locked them, slipping brass keys smoothly into their suit pockets. The crowd began to mumble again, but the noise dropped off when Lottie spoke.

"My friends. You're here with me today because I intend to live forever. But I'm afraid I'm going to need your help." Her hand fluttered to her face and she tittered behind her fingers. "Now, once we get started, I suggest you simply step aside. They're only going to want one thing, so most of you needn't worry. We pride ourselves on our manners, so don't shove."

Ernest strode forward, shutting the gate at the top of the dais stairs. At the same time, the butlers at the exits moved sideways. There were seven of them, Bryony counted, and each came to stand by a red velvet tapestry on the wall, one hand poised to lift the corner. Perfectly rectangular tapestries, she realized. The best size to cover up portraits.

Was this it then, the test Ernest had been talking about? Was her sister really reckless enough to set paintings loose in the middle of a party?

Her heart stuttered in her chest, paintbrush flying back to the canvas. She had to finish the painting before something terrible happened.

Lottie's voice was smug. "Before you, you will see seven portraits. Seven portraits of seven people here in this room tonight."

She thrust a finger out toward the audience. People had started to murmur to one another. A few had pulled off their masks, and several began to make their way through the crowd, as if they intended to leave.

None of this seemed to bother Lottie in the slightest.

"And now, I would ask that the subjects of the paintings freely pledge their souls. Or risk being shriveled up like Egyptian mummies. Not pretty at *all*. The curse is particularly touchy since my darling father messed it all up, so you need to be *very* clear what you want. If you are clear, it should work." She tapped one finger on her chin, still smiling. "I think."

There was a dusty *whoosh* as the butlers whipped the velvet from the walls, followed by a chorus of horrified gasps. Bryony didn't look up. She kept her head bent in concentration, jaw clenched. Every instinct inside her was balking at the thought of creating another monster, her skin crawling at the very idea of painting something so hideous. But she had no choice.

On the canvas, a particularly ugly face was taking shape under her brush.

It had Lottie's fine lips and chin, and Ernest's thick brows and long nose; the actual face shape was a strange mixture of the two.

It was hard not to stop and stare at the chaos below. Between brushstrokes she darted glances at the ballroom floor, where the paintings had slowly begun to tear themselves from their pictures. The crowd backed away, shrieking and stumbling over one another. Thankfully, Ernest was watching the ballroom as well, his back to her.

Bryony kept painting.

The partygoers had crowded together, stepping on one another in their attempts to get away. But of course, the portraits were on all sides, which resulted in people colliding with one another in the center of the ballroom.

One portrait was nearly all the way out, a woman in a cream-colored dress with ridiculous puffy sleeves. Her torso spilled out over the frame and she howled with rage, clawing at the floor, dragging herself out the rest of the way.

Grinding her teeth, Bryony tried to paint faster.

A second painting tore one arm out of its canvas, a portrait of a man in a black tuxedo, his blond hair slicked back. He managed to get his head through, and his expression was twisted with rage as he struggled, gnashing the air with his teeth like a madman.

There was a terrible shriek from the middle of the crowd, and Bryony winced. A man identical to the one in the portrait was scrambling for the door, elbowing gentlemen and ladies alike as he tried to push past the butler.

One last brushstroke, a dab here and there. There! She was done.

For a moment nothing happened. She was surrounded by the sound of screaming, of glass breaking, of shouting.

She had failed. These people were going to be turned to dust because of her.

And then . . . on the canvas, Lottie's red smile slowly stretched wider.

Never had Bryony thought such a horrifying spectacle would make her so happy. The painted figure came into sharper focus as it slowly stepped closer, and Bryony actually laughed, so filled with relief that her plan had worked. It had actually worked! Ernest turned, frowning at her, and then he gasped, stumbling back a step. On the other side of the platform, Lottie was too occupied with the scene unfolding on the ballroom floor to notice anything.

The portrait of the woman with the puffy sleeves had finally dropped to the floor on her hands and knees and launched herself forward with a howl.

The strange figure on Bryony's canvas stretched closer, pushing one hand forward, punching a fist through the surface of the painting with a ripping sound that echoed in Bryony's ears and sent a chill zipping through her. It was hard not to just stand there and gawp at it. Still, as the painting pushed its way through, first an arm, then a shoulder, she backed away.

Below, more people were storming the exits, slamming into the doors, crushing one another against the walls.

Lottie smiled at the crowd and raised her arms, about to say something. At that moment, though, Bryony's canvas gave a very obvious wobble on the easel, nearly tipping over. Ernest shrieked in dismay and jumped back another step, and Lottie's head snapped around, her furious gaze fixed on Bryony. "What did you do?"

Bryony gripped her paintbrush tightly and took another step back. The plan had been to flee down the steps after the portrait got out, but now the gate was closed.

More of the torso emerged from the painting. Now Lottie's chest and stomach, the fluffy dress rustling as it emerged—all attached to a very strange face.

The canvas shook on the easel, and Bryony jumped back as it finally tipped over, hitting the marble floor with a smack. Finally, the painted monster clawed its way forward, until its entire upper torso was out.

It was chaos on the ballroom floor, people smashing into tables and slipping on broken glass and pools of champagne. The sound of savage howling seemed to be everywhere at once, echoing from the ballroom's vaulted ceilings. Five of the seven paintings had now managed to rip themselves out of the canvases, plunging into the crowd, throwing people aside in a frenzy.

A thunderous crash followed, and one of the ballroom doors caved outward under the crush of people. Almost instantly the hole in the door was flooded with hysterical guests attempting to cram themselves through. The wash of people was so great that the other door gave a stiff cracking sound and splintered off its hinges.

A high, shrill scream of outrage pierced the noise.

Lottie's crown had slid forward, tilting sideways to cover the glass eye hole in her mask, but it didn't seem to bother her in the slightest. She stomped over to the gate and threw it open, bellowing at the crowd. "Don't you dare! Don't you dare! I didn't say you could leave."

Mira and Thompson had disappeared into the chaos, and Bryony hoped feverishly that they had managed to slip out.

The painted monster was on its feet now. It studied Ernest, head tipped to one side. An enraged shriek came from the steps of the dais, and the creature's head snapped around.

"What did you do? That's not me at all!" Lottie crouched on the steps, her face full of outrage. She shoved the crown up with one finger and it slid right back down. "Why is it looking at Ernest like that—Hey, you!" She snapped her fingers and the painted monster's head swiveled. It stared at her.

"That's right," Lottie started to say, and then shrieked as it turned back to Ernest again. "No! Not him, you fool!"

Ernest's face had gone parchment-white, and he headed for the steps, shoving Bryony and Lottie out of the way as he went. The painted monster tensed and then leapt forward, tearing after him.

"No!" Lottie shrieked, waving her hands. "Come back! I pledge my soul!" One of the butlers seemed to have noticed Lottie's distress, and was attempting to shove his way through the panicked party guests. He only managed a few feet before he was shoved aside, and vanished beneath the crowd.

Bryony took the chance to make her way down the steps as quickly as she could, pushing her way into the writhing crowd. Even in a state of total panic people spotted her and drew back, their expressions filled with horror. As if she would paint them on the spot. Though it was useful to have the press of bodies part before her, quite as if by magic, it was also a bit disconcerting to be looked at with such terror. In fact, it made her feel ill. But she didn't have time for pangs of conscience. She had to get to the curling staircase across the room, to get out the way she'd come.

On stage, the painted monster barreled toward the steps, and Lottie shrieked a teakettle-pitched scream and launched herself after it, grabbing the bottom of its dress, still screeching, "I pledge my soul! I pledge my soul!"

The monster staggered. Still shaky on its feet, it fell down the last few steps, paint smearing on the marble, dragging the screaming Lottie down after it.

Bryony turned away from the spectacle, putting on another burst of speed. The adrenaline pumping through her limbs seemed to make her twice as fast as usual, and the staircase was only a few feet away now.

She darted behind a couple of the gray-painted "statues" who both looked askance at her, eyes wide and white in their ash-colored faces. Then a heavy hand came down on her shoulder, jerking her backward. Her shoes squeaked on the marble as Ernest's face loomed above her, his expression enraged.

No. He couldn't ruin everything now; she was almost halfway through her plan. She struck at him with both fists, teeth grinding, furious. Ernest clutched her shoulder more tightly, pinching her skin. Over the noise of the crowd a fierce howl sounded, and a blur of blue velvet crashed into Ernest, grabbing for his coat. It was one of the paintings, trying to wrench Ernest around to see his face.

Bryony yanked her arm away, ripping it out of his grasp. She had no choice; she let herself be pushed forward by the crowd flowing out the side doors.

The hallway was dimly lit by hurricane lamps along both walls, and, luckily, all of the paintings here were covered by thick curtains. The ballroom guests streamed straight ahead, toward the exit, still shrieking and sobbing, and Bryony peeled off from the crowd as quickly as she could, stumbling into the first empty corridor she could find.

It was weirdly quiet, the noise growing more muffled the farther from the ballroom she walked, and the rest of the walls were stark white and bare, stripped of their mirrors and paintings. It was almost eerie. At the end of the hallway the corridor branched off, one side leading into what looked like a coatroom and the other into a massive library.

Blast! She was completely lost.

Chapter Twenty-Eight

The directions she'd tried to memorize on the way to the party were completely useless, since she'd run out the wrong door. Hopefully, somewhere in the house, Mira and Thompson were having better luck. A thump, followed by muffled cursing from down the hall, made her freeze. Holding her breath, she strained to listen.

Footsteps coming closer. It was either the coatroom or the library.

The coatroom was good. There were loads of coats she could hide behind, and it would take Ernest ages to look through them all. Then again, if she could make him search through all of them while she went the opposite direction, it would be even better. Mind racing, she reached down and yanked off one of her silky black slippers. Black diamonds glittered under the gaslight as she threw it onto to the ground, and it rolled and came to a stop in the middle of the coatroom floor.

There. Turning, she darted into the library, glancing around, frantic. There was another door on the other side of the room, between two towering bookshelves. A study maybe; it would have to do. Bolting forward, she flung herself at the door, praying it wasn't locked. The knob twisted under her fingers but wouldn't turn, and her shoulder crashed into the door.

A thump from the other side made her jump back, and then a muffled, hysterical-sounding voice shouted through the door. "Hello? Who's there? I demand you let me out!"

So this was where they had the real Lady Abney stashed away. "It's locked." She pressed her face to the door so the woman could hear her better. "Do you know where the key is?"

"The desk!" the voice screeched. "Is there a desk? I heard him pull out a drawer. Hurry and get me out!"

The desk was in the corner of the library, scroll-topped and made of polished cherrywood. She hurried over, raking a quick look across the cluttered surface. Nothing, just papers and an ashtray full of stubbed-out cigars that still smelled faintly of smoke. There were multiple drawers, and she yanked the bottom one open, heart sinking. It would take her ages to go through them all. If Ernest was close behind her—

There! In the right-hand corner of the bottom drawer something glittered, dull silver in the gaslight. She shoved papers out of the way, revealing a skeleton key rattling around. That had to be it! She snatched it up with a cry of triumph and ran back to the door. It took several tries to fit it in the lock, since her hands were shaking so much. It didn't help that Lady Abney shouted the entire time.

"Did you get it? Are you unlocking the door? Let me out, hurry!"

"Be quiet," she snapped, and the woman stopped talking abruptly. It was shocking, really. A metallic click broke the silence, and Bryony grinned. "I think I got—"

The door burst open, catching her hip and shoulder, throwing her backward. A great mass of pink ruffles and rustling chiffon shot out and blurred by her, making a break for the door of the study. Lady Abney's arms pinwheeled as she ran, and her high-pitched squeals of indignation echoed down the hall a full ten seconds after she was out of sight.

Bryony shook her head and groaned, climbing to her feet. A fine thank you that had been. Perhaps Lady Abney would run into Ernest and keep him busy. One could only hope.

Now, to find a way out of here that didn't involve going back the same way she'd come. Shouldn't there be a secret passageway behind one of these bookcases? The mystery books in her attic had agreed on that much, but there had only been two of them.

After a couple of seconds of searching, she found another door. Not a secret at all, since it was right there, in plain sight between two of the bookcases. It proved to be unlocked, and behind it was another long hallway. She pressed the door shut as quietly as she could. Hurrying down the hallway, she rounded a corner and collided with something or someone. Someone with a lot of sharp elbows and knees, who hissed at her in alarm.

"Ouch! Hello?" the voice said. "Who's that? You can't go zipping 'round corners like some kind of demented ferret. You've bruised my knee."

The voice, deep and velvety and utterly proper, was familiar. She squinted through the shadows. "Constantine?"

She blinked as a light ignited in the darkness. Constantine's face was suddenly there, illuminated in the orange flame of the gold-and-silver lighter he held, and looking a little as if it were floating in midair.

"Ah, yes. Bryony! So glad I found you. Mira and Thompson and I, we split up to look, or rather . . . it wasn't voluntary, but—"

She stumbled backward, keeping a sensible distance between them. "How did you know to dress up? Did you lead me here on purpose? Are you in league with her?"

"What?" Constantine looked horrified. "Absolutely not! In league with that horrible woman and her tacky sense of fashion, I *ask* you."

He looked so insulted that Bryony almost believed him straight away. She frowned at him, chewing the inside of her cheek, trying to search his face for some sign he was lying.

"How did you know it was a masquerade then?" She gestured at his suit and mask.

"Your relative, lovely woman." An indignant sniff in the darkness. "I spent ages looking for you after the panic died off. Went back to the house to recuperate and found she'd actually had the cheek to send me an invitation. Do you know . . . I recognized the handwriting. That bloody woman is the one who sent me the letter warning me off months ago. And then, to add insult to injury, she told me it was a masquerade, but my mask doesn't fit in at *all*."

"It's not a masquerade," she said impatiently. "It's a quarantine party. But that's hardly—"

"A quarantine party! How intriguing. What do you think she's—"

"Constantine," she growled, and he jumped, the orange light flickering in his hand.

"Oh, very well. You shouldn't interrupt, you know, it isn't polite."

Honestly. She bit back a retort. He was unspeakably annoying, but she was at least relatively sure he wasn't working with Lottie. Still, she'd been sure of other things too, and they'd all turned out to be wrong.

"I . . . I don't know if I should trust you. She said you'd led me here on purpose."

Constantine's face fell, and he looked almost hurt. "Well, I can appreciate how that looks, but the woman is a liar. And besides, I don't see that you have a whole lot of choice right now." He flicked one hand in the direction from which she'd come. "I'm your only ally at the moment."

He was right. She didn't like it, but he was right. "Look, the painting is in the attic. I'm completely lost in this big, stupid house, and I've no idea where my friends are." Her voice went all high-pitched at the end, and she pressed her lips together firmly. Getting hysterical wasn't helping.

"Where is the attic located then?" Constantine shook his head. "I mean, on top of the house, clearly. But the entrance—"

"I don't know." She wrung her hands, face flushing. Why hadn't she paid closer attention to her surroundings?

She was usually so good at remembering things. "There was a kitchen, and then past that another hall, and stairs."

"Stairs covered in great whacking paint stains, perchance?"

"Yes!" She nearly danced on the spot. "Yes, that's it! That's where I melted Lady Abney—well, the fake Lady Abney. Lead the way."

"Yes, absolutely." He hesitated, glancing down, smoothing his fingers over the lighter in his hands. "Look, you can trust me, I wasn't lying about that. But I also haven't been entirely honest with you. Before we go I should tell you something. I've been meaning—"

Before he could continue, the clatter of footsteps came from down the hall. They both froze, and then Constantine plucked at her sleeve and whispered urgently, "Quickly, behind that hideous fake plant over there. I'll hold them off."

She nodded, scurrying over to the nook in the hallway, a small space that hosted a narrow oak side table and, beside that, what looked like a fake umbrella tree. She slid behind the plant, wincing as one of the wide leaves poked her cheek. It occurred to her, as the footsteps drew nearer, that she had effectively backed herself into a corner.

There were no more plans. No more mirrors in her pockets. Her sleeves were empty of aces. This one was up to Constantine, whom she didn't even fully know if she could trust. The idea was a little alarming.

Constantine had flicked off the lighter and plunged them into dimness again. Voices came from around the corner, whispering but still loud enough to hear clearly.

"You said you knew the way."

"To the parlor! I said I remember the way to the parlor."

"That's not even on this floor! I told you we should have carved markings in things along the way, like Isabella did in the Congo."

"One can't go about hacking away at things like some kind of uncivilized—"

"Mira!" Bryony shot out of her hiding place so fast in the darkness that she half ran into the plastic tree. It tipped over as she stumbled out, landing on the carpet with a muffled thump and a spray of dirt.

"Ah, perhaps it isn't fake," Constantine mused, and he clicked his lighter once more, casting a dim circle of flickering light around them.

Mira and Thompson had frozen in surprise when Bryony burst out of her hiding spot. Now Mira's face lit up. "There's Bry!"

"Yes," Thompson said, and he stared at Constantine. "I see that."

Bryony flung herself forward, grabbing Mira in a fierce hug. Some part of the plague mask Mira was wearing dug painfully into her collarbone, but she ignored it. Mira was safe.

The other girl squeezed her back. "Goodness, did you think we were dead?"

"I wasn't entirely sure." She pulled away, the tips of her ears burning. When she looked at Thompson, he was still staring at Constantine, his face suspicious.

"We can trust him," Bryony said to both of them, keeping her voice low. "I'm certain Lottie was lying about him. About a lot of things, probably."

Thompson shrugged and nodded, and Mira looked relieved.

Bryony turned back to see Constantine leaning over, handkerchief in hand. Fastidiously, he seized the stem of the plant, fingers shielded by the silk hanky as he tried to tug it into place.

"Oh, for heaven's sake, just leave it!"

Constantine snapped upright, pocketing his handkerchief with a huff. "It's so messy, though. This poor house is already tragic enough on the outside."

"We have to find the stairs." She flapped one hand at him. "And hurry! Ernest is looking for me."

"Ernest?" Thankfully, he began walking in the direction she'd been heading earlier. "What a dreadfully boring name. Who is this fellow?"

"Nobody important." There was no time to discuss what had happened, and besides, she wasn't keen on telling him how Lottie and Ernest had fooled her.

"The stairs where you melted the unfortunate Lady Abney are on the next floor. I thought they were rather artistic, actually. I shall recommend they keep them."

Bryony ground her teeth, hurrying down the hall after him. The man seemed to think this was an outing at the park or something. A door slammed shut somewhere in the distance behind them, and Thompson shot forward so fast he stepped on the backs of her heels.

"He's coming."

Constantine took an abrupt left as the long corridor finally split in two, and suddenly they were back in the kitchen Bryony had found herself in earlier. It looked nothing like it had before, since it was positively stuffed with people this time. The chaos of the party hadn't yet seeped in here. Servants in white aprons and neat white caps crowded along the counters, and the sound of chopping and the clattering of pots and pans mingled with the rush of water in the sink. They were all moving very fast and efficiently, but not many of them spoke as they worked.

Constantine paused at the stove, eyeballing a large pot of soup. "My, that smells heavenly."

Now he was going to stop for dinner? Bryony pushed her way through the kitchen and Mira and Thompson hurried behind her. If Constantine wanted to linger, then he could stay there, as far as she was concerned.

They were almost through the kitchen when he finally turned to follow, snatching a roll from a nearby tray as a servant went past, juggling it with a yelp of "Hot! Hot!"

The hall they were in was familiar now, which sent a rush of relief through her. Down the dark corridor and into the foyer they went, with Bryony leading the way up the staircase and onto the main floor, where she knew that to turn right would lead them to the parlor Lottie had locked her in the day before. She turned left.

"This way," she said eagerly. "It's up here."

The left passage still reeked of paint, as if the smell was trapped in this corner of the house. And there they were, the stairs leading up to the door she'd been foolish enough to open. She climbed them, biting at her thumbnail as she went, careful where she put her feet, though the paint was dry. She glanced back once, relieved that all three of her companions had followed. The painted monster was gone—it was under her feet as she climbed—but she couldn't help feeling nervous. Maybe there were more horrors behind the door. Something had to be guarding the painting now.

Finally she reached the top of the stairs and grasped the doorknob. There was no time to be afraid. Ernest might show up at any moment.

She slid her hand into her pocket and drew out the dart, which had been pricking her in the left hip for the majority of the night. It was nice to put the dratted thing to some use. Inserting it into the lock, she wiggled it slowly, tongue pressed between her teeth.

Nothing clicked into place. She kept digging.

Behind her, Constantine shifted. "Do hurry, darling."

"It's not working the way it should." She glanced back, annoyed to see that Constantine had managed to nab a cup and saucer during their dash through the kitchen, and was apparently enjoying tea right there in the stairwell.

"Good heavens! Do you think of anything but your bloody tea?" She turned back to the door just as a thin, pale arm reached past her. Mira grasped the doorknob over her shoulder and turned it. The door swung silently inward. It hadn't even been locked. The realization should have made her happy. Instead, her stomach sank. There had to be something really horrible in there if Lottie was willing to leave her prized possession unprotected. The door creaked slowly open, and Mira crowded up behind her, hand pressing into the middle of her back. "Do you see it?"

It took a minute for her eyes to adjust once she stepped in. Floorboards creaked underfoot. It was dark, and it smelled like old things, mildew and dust. A burnt-orange light from outside filtered through a lattice of boards over the windows.

Gradually shapes came into focus, boxes stacked just inside the door, old wooden chests with rusty locks. Junk piled up against every wall. Linen bedsheets had been draped over some of the furniture, creating a strange sort of white-sheeted aisle.

At the very end of this aisle was a large, rectangle-shaped white cloth, hovering in the air. No, not hovering—there were three wooden legs peeking out from the bottom. An easel.

Her blood rushed noisily in her ears, and she started forward.

"Wait, look!" Mira gave a cry of alarm and snatched at the sleeve of Bryony's dress, tugging her backward. At the same time, something behind the easel *moved*.

The attic went silent. The kind of silence reserved for graveyards and funeral homes.

Not a breath, not a whisper . . . as *someone* slunk out from behind the white cloth at the other end of the attic.

Only it wasn't just someone. Not another painted duke or shepherdess.

It was *her*. Bryony.

Or at least it looked like her. But taller, with graceful white limbs and a pale, delicate face. Smooth porcelain skin and red lips. Far older than the real Bryony. Certainly more sophisticated-looking.

This Bryony wore a long black dress, all silky and shiny and ruffled at the collar. When the creature moved her arms, Bryony could see that the sleeves were long and billowy. The other Bryony stepped forward, arms raised in a graceful gesture of welcome. As if she were the hostess at a particularly bizarre garden party.

It should have been impossible. There was no way Lottie would have been able to do this.

But as the painting crept forward, Bryony had the dull, sinking feeling of recognition. She knew what this was. She'd painted it in secret over a year ago, when she'd been fascinated with the art of self-portraits. She'd exaggerated things, of course, made herself prettier and older. Aunt Gertrude had found the portrait and confiscated it, saying it was a "disgusting display of vanity."

And now here it was.

The living portrait stepped closer, trailing both hands over the bedsheets on either side of her, gripping the fabric so that the sheets slid to the floor as she passed. Mirrors, the sheets had been covering mirrors, and now they reflected this terrible new Bryony a hundred times over.

"Bryony," Thompson said in a low, trembling voice. "That's not you. Not really."

She knew why he'd said it. Because she was going to have to kill her. Or rather . . . melt her as she had Lady Abney. She nodded, but she couldn't seem to move, or even think what to do next. All she could do was stare at the Bryony that was not her.

The painted Bryony took another step forward, skirts whispering over the floorboards. A smile curved its red lips, and its blue eyes danced. It looked straight at Bryony as it came slowly closer. It was stalking her, the same way the painted Lady Abney had. About to pounce.

If she could only stall it for a little while, she might be able to figure something out. "Wait," Bryony blurted. "I know what you want."

The painted Bryony pressed one hand to her chest, raising a single eyebrow in what was undeniably an expression of impatience.

Pledge your soul.

Eternal life. What Lottie had fought so hard for. What her father had sacrificed himself for.

And standing before her, a reflection of what she would look like if she gave up her soul. It was what the mirrors had been telling her all along. She would be young forever, and beautiful. A graceful, poised socialite, someone who would never be thought of as "disturbed" or called unstable.

She would never be hidden away again, never left alone.

When you looked like that, people would give you anything you desired.

An eternity of youth, forever able to explore the world, go where she pleased, paint whatever she liked.

Outlive everyone.

Watch Mira and Thompson and Constantine grow old in slow motion and crumble to dust before her eyes.

No. She didn't want that. She never had.

Slowly, firmly, she shook her head. "No."

The painted Bryony's smile seemed to freeze and then stretch, growing into a cruel, ugly smirk. Then its mouth flew open wide as it screamed and hurtled forward, feet pounding on the floorboards, pale arms outstretched.

Bryony whirled around and shot one hand out to Constantine. "Quick, your tea!"

He didn't move, just stood there slack-jawed and white-faced, watching the monstrous not-Bryony charging straight for them.

She growled and snatched the teacup out of his hands, and the saucer hit the ground and smashed at their feet. This seemed to wake him up.

"I say!" he sputtered. "What—"

Bryony turned and flung the teacup straight into the face of the oncoming painting.

Most of the tea preceded the cup by a few seconds, splashing across the monster's face with a hiss and sizzle, instantly melting her painted skin. The teacup followed, smashing the creature right between the eyes. The monster skidded, feet tangling in her skirts. She went down with a shriek and a gurgle, crashing to the floor.

Bryony grimaced, surprised to see the monster thrash, streams of white and black and pink flowing from her face as the painted features melted off.

"Ugh." Mira pressed her hand over her mouth. "How disgusting."

After a moment, the painted Bryony twitched and lay still, her face a featureless puddle of paint.

"Why did it work so well this time?" Bryony frowned at the empty teacup. "It didn't stop the Lady Abney monster."

Constantine stared down at the puddle on the floor-boards, looking decidedly put out. "Yes, well, the tea tasted rather orangey. More acidic, I should think."

She blew out a shaky breath. "Well, she doesn't look like a person anymore, so . . . so the curse can't work." She took a wobbly step forward and Thompson said, once again, so softly she almost didn't hear him, "That wasn't you."

"I know." She shuddered, trying not to look at the still form on the ground, starting instead toward the white sheet at the back of the attic. "Let's get this over with."

This time it was Constantine who reached out to snag her sleeve. "Just one moment, dear. How exactly are you planning on getting past those?" He gestured toward the mirrors, the ones the painted Bryony had uncovered. Lottie had lined them up like some kind of deadly walkway to the painting.

"Definitely not walking through that," Thompson whispered.

"It's quite clever, actually." Constantine said. His voice contained a definite tone of admiration, and Bryony scowled at him.

"Can we put the sheets back on?" she asked.

"Not without standing in front of them." Thompson indicated the junk piled up behind each mirror.

"She did it somehow, so there has to be a way to get past," Mira said reasonably. "I mean, what if she wants to move the painting?"

That was a fair point. Bryony craned her neck, trying to get a better look without stepping in sight of her reflection. To climb over the walls of junk that had been stacked up on both sides of the aisle seemed impossible. It was nearly to the ceiling. And most of it was heavy-looking steam cases and antique furniture. Moving it would take six or seven men.

"Spread out," Thompson suggested. "Look for another way through."

"We don't have time," Bryony said, but there were no other options, so that's what they did, fanning out across the dusty floor, poking into nooks and crannies. Every squeak from the floorboards made her heart gallop in her chest. Surely someone would hear them stomping around up here. And Ernest and Lottie would be heading straight for the attic, no doubt having guessed her plan by now.

"It's no use." Mira slumped against a tall set of drawers. "There's no way through unless you can climb like some sort of monkey."

Trying to picture Lottie doing that was ludicrous. It seemed unlikely she'd want to work too hard to get to her prize. If Bryony knew anything at all about her new sister, it was that she was spoiled. The only easy way was the direct way, straight past the mirrors. There had to be a trick to getting by them.

There was no way she could cover them all fast enough, even though that seemed to have worked before. But *why* had it worked? She took a deep breath and shut her eyes.

Artemisia Gentileschi painted herself painting. Rembrandt painted over forty self-portraits. Parmigianino painted his own distorted reflection in a mirror.

An idea had begun to bloom, raising the hairs on the back of her neck as things began to fall into place. "Mira," she said sharply, and Mira turned away from the chest of drawers, raising her dark brows.

"Hmm?"

"When you had the incident with the kettle, were you staring at it? Your reflection, I mean, did it catch your eye?"

"I . . . yes, it did. I couldn't look away. It was so spooky."

When she'd thrust the mirror at Uncle Bernard, he'd definitely looked at it. Like Mira had said, he didn't seem to be able to look away. And when she had first seen what the mirrors were doing, back at the house, she'd instinctively turned away. She'd known not to look. She had a theory now, and there was really only one way to test it.

"I think I can get past."

Chapter Twenty-Nine

"You're bonkers," Thompson protested, but there wasn't any heart in it. "What exactly are you planning?"

"I think the secret to getting past is not to look at them. Not even one glance. I think that's how they lure you in."

"And just how are you going to prove that?" Constantine leaned against the doorway, inspecting one of his silver cufflinks as if it were terribly interesting.

"Like this." She took two giant steps forward. It put her directly between the first two mirrors. Behind her, someone gasped, but she fixed her eyes on the white cloth ahead, on the easel, pretending she had blinders on. Heart thumping furiously, she told herself that she was fine. Still here. Nothing leapt out at her.

Don't look left. Don't look right. Focus on the easel.

"I think it's working." Mira's voice was hushed and full of excitement. "You're doing it!"

"Don't distract her," Thompson whispered. "Bryony, whatever you do, don't look to the sides."

Instantly, that was all she wanted to do. "Why? Is something happening?" Her voice cracked a little on the last word.

"Best you don't look," Constantine added. "But I'll tell you, they seem angry. We should take it as a good sign. Keep moving."

She took another step. Now she could sense movement out of the corner of her eye. Both eyes. Sheer instinct insisted she move to face the threat. Alarm bells went off in the back of her mind, but she ground her teeth together and forced herself to keep staring straight ahead.

"Walk faster." Constantine hissed. "Ouch, don't poke me, missy. It's only logical."

"He's right." Bryony forced herself to move more quickly, shoes clunking on the dusty wooden floor. It still seemed to take forever, but finally she was directly in front of the white sheet. She grabbed the edge of the cloth with trembling fingers and tugged. The sheet slid off with a soft shushing sound and crumpled to the floor, spreading over her shoes. The painting, unveiled at last.

She stared, open-mouthed. The most noticeable thing was that it had been ruined at some point. There was a wide, jagged slash right through the center, and the canvas surrounding the wound sagged limply around the edges. A man stood in the middle, posing with one hand tucked into the lapel of his dinner jacket. He was staring very intently at her, which made the skin on her arms crawl with goosebumps. In spite of that, the painting was so striking it made her breath catch.

Her father had been undeniably handsome. He had the same sparkling, porcelain skin that Bryony's self-portrait had had, and his cheeks were slightly flushed, the color of ripe peaches. His lips were red and perfectly shaped, a smile teasing the corner of his mouth. His expression might have been mischievous, but there was something hard about it, something hostile in the tilt of his head. The way his eyes glittered. Even though the curse had clearly malfunctioned, making the painting beautiful again, there was still something unspeakably hideous about him.

Someone whispered behind her. "What's she doing? I can't see properly."

"I don't know. Bryony?"

Mira's voice. Bryony blinked rapidly, shuddering. If she'd thought the mirrors had been hard to look away from, this was far worse. It was something about his smile, how it was somehow both beautiful and cruel, or perhaps the way he stared. Of course, he wasn't staring at *her*. But he must have been looking very intently at the person painting him. Unnervingly so.

This was her father. Her most definitely evil father. And here was absolute proof that he had sold his soul, that her uncle and aunt—as awful as they both were—had been right all along to only speak of him in hushed whispers or never at all. Here he was, the subject of her dreams for years, now a nightmare in the flesh. Here to shatter her delusions. Just one look at that face told her all she needed to know. That beauty wasn't always beautiful, not truly. That it could hide ugliness underneath.

The knowledge sucked her breath away and pulsed in her stomach like a heartbeat. She thought she might be sick.

"Grab the painting and let's go." Thompson's voice now, low and shaky.

She straightened her shoulders and took a deep breath. Moving was hard, as if her arm didn't want to obey her mind. Was that her father's curse at work? Another thought that made her freeze. This monstrous thing in the painting . . . would she end up like him? He had somehow become twisted and evil. Maybe something like that would happen to her too. She wasn't so different from him, was she? All she had wanted to do was paint beautiful things. She'd thought Mira was beautiful. At first, it had been the only reason she'd liked her at all. All she'd wanted to do was paint her.

Perhaps Bryony's own smile would become hard and sharp, and her eyes would glitter with a cruel light. Maybe one day she would look just like the painted version of herself that she'd melted only minutes ago.

"Bryony!" Someone was calling her name insistently. "Bryony, come on!"

"You've been standing there for ages." Constantine's voice now. "Bryony, listen to me, will you? I . . . I don't know how to say this. I tried to before." He cleared his throat. "I knew your father. Not well, I just met him once. He was a good man before the curse. But he wasn't like you."

The back of Bryony's neck was prickling, and she'd gone so still that her only movement was the rise and fall of her breath. Her eyes were still on her father's face, but she was listening intently, hoping Constantine would continue.

"He wasn't like you because he was alone. He didn't have family to help him. No Mira and Thompson . . . and no patron."

Bryony started, standing up straighter. She was still facing the painting, but she let her eyes focus on the wall behind it now, fully intent on Constantine's words. "What did you say?"

Constantine cleared his throat. "I tried to tell you earlier, but . . . I didn't try that hard. I confess I've been a bit ashamed. I was a terrible patron."

"The letter . . ." Her voice was barely a whisper.

"That was me. I tracked you down, tried to contact you. The letter and the grimoire were the only things that got through. I suppose your uncle told that horrible woman about me, because I saw a big shiny carriage at your house the last few times I went, and your uncle began to turn me away. He must have showed Lottie the letter, and she told him about the curse, because after that he conspired to block all my efforts. Of course, I had no idea who Lottie was at the time . . . just that as soon as she came into the picture, your uncle wanted nothing to do with me." He clenched the lighter in one fist. "It was maddening. It was Oscar's final wish that I take care of you . . . and I-I failed—" His voice choked off.

Bryony bit the inside of her cheek. "I . . . I burned the letter. I thought it was from her. She told me it was. She even quoted from it."

Constantine snorted. "I shouldn't be surprised. The cheek of that woman. As if she could string two sentences together that equaled even the worst of my prose."

Bryony swallowed. "I—why didn't you say anything earlier, back at the house? Why didn't you tell me?"

There was a beat of silence, and then Constantine sighed. "After I became a social recluse, people were rather cruel. High society loves to gossip, and I was sure you'd heard things about me. After Oscar died I had nothing left. I could not allow myself to hope. And I . . . I was rather afraid that if I told you, you'd reject me."

Bryony's mouth dropped open. He thought she'd reject *him*? "That's ridiculous."

Constantine laughed, sounding relieved. "Well, I'm glad you think so. And when we're finished with all of this, my home is open to you. But first, let's get this thing out of the way."

"He's right—you can do this," Mira chimed in, and Bryony once again focused on the painting. She'd been right after all, at least about one thing: she did have a patron. Even if it had never been her father.

But now she had to destroy the picture. The last bit of her father that was left.

"You're stronger than he was. You're better, and you have us." Mira's voice, fierce and low. It sent a jolt of determination through her.

They were right. It was time to finish this. She wasn't her father—she hadn't even known the man. He wasn't the family she'd dreamed of all along. This man was a stranger, a cruel, twisted one. Appreciating beauty was one thing, but being truly obsessed with it? That was different. And dangerous. She would never let herself be like that.

They were right: she, Bryony, was better than that. Smarter than that.

And now it was time to do what she'd come to do.

The feeling in her arms came flooding back and at last she could move again. Reaching down, she picked the sheet up carefully, settling it back over the painting, gripped the frame and picked it up off the stand. When she turned around, the hallway of mirrors was spread out before her. Oh yes. She'd forgotten about the way back.

Mira waved frantically. "Here, look at us! Just walk toward us. Look straight ahead."

She nodded, stomach fluttering. One step at a time. It was awkward holding the painting out in front of her; it made it harder to walk fast. But she fixed her eyes on her friends. First Constantine—her patron, at last—and then Thompson, who was so very brave, and then Mira. On the glitter in her blue eyes. Her impish smile. Her heart-shaped face. If they managed to break the curse, it would mean Bryony could paint her. And she *would* paint her, but not just her beauty. It wasn't just about that anymore. She would find a way to capture that spirit on the canvas. That was what made Mira beautiful.

As she reached the last pair of mirrors, a violent thump sounded from the stairs and the doorknob rattled violently. Her heart jammed up into her throat, and she nearly dropped the painting. Grasping the sheet tightly with numb fingertips, she froze.

"Go!" Constantine whirled around, planting himself in front of the door, turning the bolt to lock it. "For the love of silk and satin, do what you came to do, girl!"

Bryony ran, launching herself forward, thrusting the painting at Mira. The doorknob rattled, followed by a dull rasping sound. Someone on the other side was trying to shove a key into the lock. Mira caught hold of the painting, stumbling back as Bryony nearly crashed into her.

"Hold it!" Digging frantically into her inside pocket, her fingers closed around the little perfume bottle. Her hands were shaking so violently she was afraid the kerosene might spill as she uncorked the bottle. "Lay it down, quick!"

Mira threw the painting onto the floorboards, and Thompson ripped the sheet off. Just as she began to empty the bottle over the torn canvas, the paint warping beneath the splatters of kerosene, the door burst open. Lottie's voice, shrill and angry, filled the room. "Get away from it!"

Eyes watering from the fumes, Bryony jammed her hand into her pocket. Her fingers closed over empty space. No! Where was the matchbook? Ernest's voice drifted in from the stairs. "Do relax, lovey. She can't do much. That clumsy little oaf lost the matches."

Blast! Bryony's stomach dropped, and she bit her lip so hard it hurt. She must have lost the matches when she was shoving her way through the crowd.

Lottie took a step forward. Her face was flushed bright red, her blonde hair falling in messy curls around her face. The crown slipped down over her left eye and she hastily shoved it back up again. "Bryony, wait. Don't destroy the only thing left of our father. He wouldn't have wanted this. He'd want us to be together. Living forever, young and beautiful. I know you see it too. You're like me. We have the potential to turn this curse into something good."

Lottie pointed one trembling finger at the painting, and Bryony glanced down. Their father, eternally young and beautiful. His blue eyes were so like theirs; his smile too. But that mocking twist of the mouth . . . she'd seen that on Lottie more than once. The casual cruelty masked by beauty.

"I'm not the same as you," Bryony said, "and I intend to make sure I stay that way."

"Bryony!"

She turned to see a small shiny object flying through the air, straight at her face. The object struck the back of an antique armchair and bounced once before coming to rest on the cushioned seat. Constantine's gold-and-silver lighter. She dove for it. At the same time, there was a meaty-sounding thud from the doorway, and a muffled cry of pain. Her hand closed around the lighter and she straightened up. Something crashed into her, hard, knocking her arm. The lighter went skittering across the floor, and she staggered, her shoulder slamming into a set of drawers. "The lighter!"

Lottie darted forward and grabbed it, holding it aloft, smiling triumphantly. Then she stooped down and grasped something from one of the boxes that had tipped over during the fight. A cricket mallet with a broken handle. "I'd really rather it hadn't come to this. So lowbrow, but here we are."

Beside the door, Constantine was bent double, hands over his face as blood dripped from between his fingers. Ernest had an enraged Thompson pinned against the wall, an arm pressed against his throat. It was just her and Mira, about to face off with a madwoman with a mallet.

Mira glanced at her, and then over at the hallway of mirrors, hands moving quickly in their secret language.

Mirrors. Push her?

Now, Bryony signed back, and then they were both moving, launching themselves at Lottie. The woman's smile faltered, and she shrieked as they ran for her. She was in the midst of raising the mallet when they barreled into her.

Bryony's shoulder took the brunt of the impact, landing right in the middle of Lottie's corseted waist. Mira slammed into the woman's legs, coming in low to tackle her. The cricket mallet hit the floor with a dull clunk.

Their effort had launched all three of them halfway down the hall of mirrors, and when Bryony managed to untangle herself, she fixed her eyes on the golden lighter on the floor. It was just behind Lottie, who was struggling to wrench the crown off her head, since it seemed to have dropped down over both eyes in the fall. As soon as Lottie recovered herself she'd look for the lighter, and all she had to do was turn around. There was a beautifully black bruise spreading across the left side of Lottie's jaw. It was enough to give Bryony an idea. "Oh my, what an ugly gash on your face, Lottie dear. If you pledge your soul now, you'll have that forever."

"What?" The crown popped off and clattered to the floor. Lottie's head swiveled, and then her body jerked like a rabbit caught in a trap. Whatever she was seeing in the mirror must have transfixed her, because she remained perfectly still as Bryony leaned forward and snatched the lighter.

Lottie stayed frozen. After a second, she actually leaned closer to the mirror, her eyes wide and glassy. "No! You can't have my soul yet—"

A thick silver band shot out of the mirror and wrapped itself around Lottie's throat, and her scream dissolved into a strangled whimper.

Mira yelped and clapped a hand over her eyes. "Bry, hurry!"

Bryony ran, bolting back down the hall of mirrors, heart beating furiously. On the other side of the attic, Ernest released Thompson, pushing him roughly against the wall as he turned toward the painting.

Her lungs were bursting, blood rushing in her head, breath loud in her ears. There was no way she would make it. Three steps, and Ernest towered over the painting, reaching down for it. He smiled at her. A metallic clink as she flipped the lighter on and snatched at one of the nearest boxes, searching for something, anything . . . there! A frilly white doily with a tear in one side.

It would have to do.

She dragged the lace doily through the oil paint on the floor, the remains of the Bryony painting, and then held the lighter up to the cloth. It went up with a roar, and Bryony threw it. The doily flew through the air, a gentle, almost lazy arc, lace edges flapping gently, the flame flickering wildly. It landed on the canvas with a soft thunk.

The painting went up immediately, an inferno of flame, a blaze of red. A roar mixed with a pained shriek from

Ernest, who snatched his hands back so quickly he over-balanced and fell. Flames crawled over the curling black canvas, slowly hollowing out the frame.

Ernest didn't move to get up, curling into a ball with his scorched hands clutched to his chest, body shaking as he howled.

Transfixed, Bryony stood over the painting as the fire shriveled it. The painted man seemed to move as the painting blackened, writhing limbs blurring as if he were making one last desperate attempt at survival. In the last second before his body was consumed by flame, she seemed to catch a flash of something different. A terrifying image. Black, sunken eyes peering out of a pale, withered face.

Then it was gone, eaten away by the fire.

A shriek from behind her made Bryony whirl around, panic clutching her chest.

Lottie was sitting in front of the mirror still, but she looked different now. She had retrieved the crown and placed it back on her head, but it was dented and scratched, and a few of the jewels had gone missing. Lottie's skin was no longer smooth and creamy; it sagged around the neck and jowls. There were deep wrinkles around her eyes and mouth, and her lips had deflated into a thin, straight line. She looked worn out and very old. She kept shrieking, touching her face and then shrieking again. "It can't be. It can't be!"

Mira was still sitting beside her with one hand over her eyes.

With the painting little more than ashes now, Bryony thought it should be safe. The silver thing had retreated into the mirror without mummifying Lottie, so that was a good sign. Bryony crept into the hallway of mirrors, still holding her breath. The nearest mirror was full-length, and the Bryony reflected in its surface was certainly disheveled. Her golden hair had fallen out of its fancy updo, and one side of her face was smudged with paint. But she was reasonably sure it was her. Just to avoid any tricks, she tested the reflection, moving one arm and then the other, wiggling her nose and sticking out her tongue. The reflection did everything she did.

"Mira, you can open your eyes." She went over and took her arm. Wrapping her fingers around Mira's wrist, she tugged her hand down, but the other girl still had her eyes shut tight. "Are you sure they've gone back to normal?"

"I absolutely promise you they have. But if you like, we can get out of here before you open your eyes."

Mira nodded, so Bryony took her hand, locking her fingers through hers and slowly leading her back down the hallway of mirrors. Mira held on tightly, squeezing her fingers until they were all the way to the door.

"All right, we're well clear now," Bryony said. In the background, Lottie continued to wail about her face.

Slowly, very slowly, Mira opened her eyes. When she glanced down at the ashes of the painting on the floor—and at Ernest, who was still curled in a ball whimpering about his blistered fingers—a smile lit her face. "We did it!"

Bryony stepped back, startled, when Mira grabbed her in a fierce hug. Her short hair tickled, and smelled a little like strawberries, and her lips grazed Bryony's cheek, a butterfly's touch, before Mira pulled back.

Bryony's face went hot all over, and Mira ducked her head and stared at her clunky boots as if they were terribly fascinating.

"Stop moaning and hold still." Thompson was attempting to stem the flow of bright blood from Constantine's nose. But he was using the man's silk handkerchief, and Constantine kept trying to push it away. "You'll ruin it!"

In spite of the nosebleed and the fact that his bottom lip seemed to be split, Constantine caught Bryony's eye and smiled. She immediately had a dozen questions she wanted to ask him, but she settled on just one for now. "Do you really have a house in the countryside with white-on-gray trim?"

"I do indeed," Constantine said.

"I should like to see it soon," Bryony said, and flushed slightly at her own boldness, relieved when he nodded, looking every bit as pleased as she felt.

As they were turning for the door she remembered the lighter in her pocket, fishing it out. "Oh, here, I forgot. It certainly came in handy, didn't it?" To her surprise, Constantine pressed his hand over hers, curling her fingers around the lighter.

"You take it. It was your father's, after all."

Bryony stared at him in shock, and then down at the lighter on her palm, feeling more than a little light-headed. "He gave it to you? Will you tell me about it?"

"I'm afraid there's not much to tell, darling," he said, swatting Thompson's hand away again. "I asked for a light, and when I tried to give it back, Dorian said, 'You keep it, old chap,' and that was the extent of our exchange."

It may not have been much, but it was enough.

Bryony turned away, stroking her thumb over the smooth surface of the lighter, silver, with gold patterns etched into the center. It was enough to have something that had belonged to him. A connection between them that wasn't a curse.

Behind her, she could still hear Lottie moaning into the mirror. It might not be long before her sister came to her senses, so Bryony turned back to everyone—a little regretfully—and cleared her throat. "Let's go, shall we?"

They filed through the door and back down the stairs one by one, Constantine still muttering indignantly about his silk handkerchief.

"The curse is broken. Now what?" Mira asked. "The adventure's over. We saved London."

"Well," Thompson said slowly. "Mother and Father won't be home for ages. The traffic in London will be outrageous, so . . ." He glanced over at Bryony as they found their way into the front hallway, his brows raised. He was asking *her* what to do? He must have hit his head when Ernest pushed him.

"We have to make one stop here first," she said, and tried not to picture the beautiful easel and brushes still sitting in the ballroom. "I have to retrieve something of mine."

"What?" Thompson didn't look happy at the prospect of staying any longer. "What are we getting?"

"A very grumpy old man in the basement," Bryony said, and she turned and headed for the door.

Chapter Thirty

E ven though the curse was broken, the roads were still packed with carriages. Nobody knew what the four of them had done. Nobody knew that their paintings and mirrors were safe. Not yet. So now it was up to them to spread the word. Behind her, Uncle Bernard kept up a constant string of wheezing complaints. He didn't like being out at night and the crowds were terrible and the newfangled horseless carriages were so very hideous with their glaring headlamps, weren't they?

"Now what?" Mira said. "We'll never catch a hansom cab in this rush."

"We won't need to." Constantine removed the hand-kerchief from his face, looking down at it with dismay. "Ah, it's ruined." He sighed, and then turned back to them. "My house isn't far. This way."

It took days to get the police involved. Constantine had to explain the entire thing again, even after Bryony had explained it twice. It seemed it was more believable if an adult told them what Ernest and Lottie had done, how they had kidnapped her and locked her in their parlor and made her paint for them. Of course, they had to leave out all the most exciting bits, as the officers who came to visit would never have believed them. The official story the police were telling everyone about the quarantine was that a fast-spreading hysteria had hit, something in the water that had caused a strange plague as well as hallucinations. There was no way of actually disproving the lie, since the monstrous paintings had all disappeared the moment the curse was broken, dissolving into puddles of paint on the spot. So their story was much less exciting in the end. But kidnapping was kidnapping, and the police had agreed to investigate.

None of them had been allowed to come along on this investigation, so they spent a tense afternoon in Constantine's parlor, waiting to hear the results. Constantine insisted on serving them tea and cucumber sandwiches, saying something about tea easing the waiting process. Bryony only picked at her sandwich, not able to concentrate on eating. She had become rather good at ignoring Uncle Bernard's constant muttering, but right now she found herself irritated by it. The old man was hunched over in a corner armchair, playing with a pair of silver sugar tongs, clicking them together and chortling to himself. At least he seemed completely absorbed and happy. If the two of them were going to stay here until Bryony came of age and inherited her own house, at least they could be good house guests.

Mira was busy devouring the sandwiches at an alarming rate, looking a little like a chipmunk with both cheeks bulging.

"I say, do slow down or you'll choke." Thompson slid the sandwich platter away from her side of the table.

Mira gave him an exaggerated eye roll and spoke through a mouthful of bread. "What would Mother say?"

"You've no need to worry about what she'll say—not for another three days, according to their letter." He picked at one of the sandwiches delicately, his face stony.

Thompson and Mira's parents had extended their stay at the coroners' conference, even with all that was going on in London. Perhaps *because* of what was going on in London. Mira was delighted by this news, but Thompson positively radiated disapproval.

"I shall have firm words with them on the matter." He scowled down at his cucumber sandwich. "It isn't proper to gallivant in the middle of a disaster and leave one's children at home."

"I cannot *wait* to see you speak with Mother about it." Mira's face was rapturous at the mere idea. "You've never stood up to her a day in your life."

Thompson shrugged. "After facing a madwoman and being chased by murderous paintings, Mother doesn't seem particularly frightening. And we're going to be doing a lot of talking, in any case." He glanced down at the blue notebook on the table between them, full of Mira's scribbled notes. "It should be interesting."

A knock at the front door interrupted them, and Bryony flew to her feet, dashing down the hall. A somber-faced butler was already in the process of opening the door, and she nearly elbowed him out of the way in her haste. A surprised-looking policeman stood on the front step—two of them, actually. "Ah, Miss . . . ?" He raised his brows.

"Gray," she said firmly. "Bryony Gray."

His eyes went round. The wild rumors that had circulated during the so-called plague had died down, but now new ones had started up. It seemed the people who had escaped Lottie's party had been spreading the word that she'd attacked her own sister with some kind of monstrous man-lady hybrid painting. And, of course, while everyone knew that had been a hallucination, it still made her extremely interesting.

"Uh, well . . ." The policeman flicked his gaze up as Constantine appeared behind her, followed by Mira and Thompson. "We arrived at the residence to find Old Lady Plumberton is . . . ah . . . not quite all there. She just rocked back and forth and stared at a mirror. Wouldn't stop muttering about her face. She also seems to think she's the Queen. So, obviously a bit senile. We're thinking she may need Bedlam." The officer flushed. "Er, the Royal Hospital, I mean."

The asylum. The very same place Lottie had sent her grandfather. It was too ironic for words. "What about Ernest?"

The officer cleared his throat and tugged at the brim of his hat. "Well, we found a lot of things to back up your story, miss. But he denies it."

"Hogwash." Constantine placed one hand on the doorframe, glaring. "He's guilty as sin."

"We did find a room we believe someone was kept in, and we had a very hysterical Lady Abney storm the station yesterday afternoon. She confirmed your side of events."

He cleared his throat. "Though she seems to have a touch of hysteria herself. Anyway, we've taken him into custody. He'll face charges, all right."

Relief flooded through her, and she slumped against the doorway. Ernest was going to jail, and Lottie was no longer a threat.

"Oh, and we found your stolen things, Ms. Gray." The officer turned and waved toward the carriage.

Stolen things? Bryony stared at him blankly.

"Ah, splendid." Constantine said hurriedly. "We're so glad you recovered them."

The carriage doors opened and a third officer stepped out. He had a set of long wooden poles over his shoulder, and a dark-brown leather satchel in his hand.

The beautiful cherrywood easel she'd loved so much, and the box of oil paints in every color . . . now they were hers.

The policeman left it on the doorstep, and Constantine hauled the easel indoors. "I can set it up in the parlor for you," he said. "It will add even more color to the room. Really tie in the drapes, darling." He shuffled into the parlor with Mira on his heels, exclaiming over the pretty color of the wood. Bryony set the leather satchel down and flipped the top open, thrilled by the neat glass jars of paint all in a row.

And, she realized, there was something more. Tucked just behind the jars was a slender black-and-gold book. Frowning, she slid it out and examined the cover. There was a slip of paper tied to the front, words scribbled in spidery black scrawl: *For Miss Lottie Gray.* When she slipped the string off and pulled the note free, her heart skipped a beat.

The Picture of Dorian Gray, by Oscar Wilde.

This was it. Her father's book, somehow delivered straight into her hands. She could finally learn what had happened to him, what he'd been like. Both the bad side of him and the good.

She began to reach for the cover, fingers trembling, just as Mira appeared around the corner again.

"Coming, Bry?"

Bryony started, and then gave her a wide smile, flipping the top of the satchel closed. The weight of the bag in her hands was somehow both promising and a little terrifying. There were so many secrets to unravel about her past. About the truth.

But for now, there were more important things.

"Yes, I'm coming."

Mira held up one of the paintbrushes, something she'd probably found in the easel's tray. "Look, aren't they beautiful? And now you can finally paint without worrying." Mira smiled, her face flushed with pleasure.

"Yes." Bryony tucked the satchel under one arm and linked the other into Mira's, walking into the parlor with her. "And I know exactly what I'd like to paint first."

Acknowledgements

First I have to say thank you, again, to Shaun. Not only did you support me through years of writing, but you patiently endured the chaos that came with it. You never complained, not even when you ran out of socks and had to eat cereal out of Tupperware containers.

Huge thanks to my agent, Silvia Molteni, who had a vision for Bryony Gray from the start, and has been a tireless advocate. And thanks to the team at Penguin Random House Canada, who have been nothing but wonderful and welcoming, particularly Tara Walker and Lynne Missen, for getting as excited about the story as I was. Lynne, you truly took this book to the next level.

Also to all the people who read Bryony Gray in its earliest stages, my writing group: Meghan, Kellie, Kyra, you guys are awesome and you helped shape the story into what it is now. To the awesome beta readers: Elinor Sattler and Emily Marquart, thank you!

To the writer friends who have helped keep me sane: YA Word Nerds, our Sunday chats are so often the high-light of my week. I love you guys. The Wattpad4, you four are my writer soul mates, and I'm so glad I have had you with me every step of the way. To the 2014 Pitch Wars Group—I couldn't do this without the Table of Trust, particularly Kristen Hanson Reynolds and Peggy S. Jackson. And to Danny Cronk, who risked life and limb building several baking soda and vinegar bombs to test the "glass jar" theory. Thank you!

And to my family, for being excited and always asking what I'm writing. To mom especially, for never telling me to "be realistic" about this writing thing. And for reading endless stories to Meredith and me every night, because really, that's where all of this started.